Black Irises

by

John Delacourt

Black Irises
Copyright © 2016 John Delacourt
All rights reserved
Published by Blue Denim Press Inc.
First Edition
ISBN 978-1-927882-19-1

Cover Art—Alexia Lim
Cover Design—Joanna Joseph/Typeset in Calibri and Garamond

Library and Archives Canada Cataloguing in Publication

Delacourt, John, 1964, author
        Black Irises / John Delacourt.

Issued in print and electronic formats.
ISBN 978-1-927882-19-1 (paperback).--ISBN 978-1-927882-20-7(kindle).--ISBN 978-1-927882-21-4 (epub)

        I. Title.

PS8607.E482546B53 2016   C813'.6   C2016-905180-3
                                               C2016-905181-1

For the other JD – and for AS and my families

Other Work by John Delacourt:

Non-Fiction (Essays and Book Reviews)

"No Solace in the Dark," The Mark, September, 2011.
Review of Zadie Smith's *On Beauty*, Ottawa Citizen, October, 2005.
Review of *The Anchor Book of New American Short Stories*, Ottawa Citizen,
September, 2004.
Review of Ali Smith's *Hotel World*, Ottawa Citizen, June 2004.

Fiction

"Standardized, Patient," Black Heart Magazine (Austin, TX), March,
2015.
Ocular Proof (novel), Seraphim Editions, September, 2014.
"The Actuary's Alphabet," Empty Sink Magazine, (San Antonio, TX),
April, 2014.
"You Are My Music," Danforth Review: October, 2011.
"The Roman Alphabet," New Quarterly, Winter, 2005.
"Naked Girl Topology," New Quarterly, Fall-Winter, 2004-2005.
"Twelve Steps to Flight," New Quarterly, Summer, 2003.
"Alphabetical Inevitability," Queen Street Quarterly, Spring 2003.
"Mammoth," Pagitica, Issue no. 3, 2000.

"Politics in a literary work is a pistol shot in the middle of a concert—a rather coarse matter, but, on the other hand, something which one ignores at one's own peril."

– Marie-Henri Beyle (Stendhal), La Chartreuse de Parme ch xxiii (1839) in: Romans et nouvelles, vol. 2, p. 405 (Pléiade ed. 1968)(S.H. transl.)

1.

LAKE LESUEUR WAS six miles out of town, up along the ridge of the escarpment. It was gouged into the limestone bedrock as the glaciers retreated, a cut so straight and deep the waters did not mix and churn. There was just layer after layer of sediment along a bottom so far down, so cold and dark, that whatever floated to the bottom would never be recovered. Arrowheads, pistols, compasses encased in brass, wedding rings cast off by widows long since dead, it was all down there, a record of ages out of reach, far below the murky spectrum of emerald light. Lake LeSueur is where they found the floating body of Sydney Brewin.

It all happened because of the season's change this time of year, Peggy Vaughan said. "This is what happens every fall out in the country now, once they get back to school. Remember when we were kids it was motorcycles and boys? Now it's the girls and all the summer romances ending. That's all that's changed."

It did not need any further explanation for Peggy. She took one last sip of her second coffee of the morning then unpeeled a chalky blue stick of Dentyne. Super Mom, the coffee mug read, emblazoned with a caped blonde that could have been a stripper. Or Peggy thirty years ago. No sugar in the gum, three sugars in the coffee.

"Still they can't find the boy. Gallant says they've got a dog and handler up there. Probably going to get an OPP chopper to cover the area," said Guthrie.

"How does Bruce know?"

"He got here first this morning. Phelps, the Constable, he lives two doors down from him on Morton. Hadn't even had my coffee."

"Well, they'll find that boy soon enough."

"We'll see. All I know is Gallant's got me on this. Five hundred words for noon."

"He should do it himself if he was talking to the cops."

"Those days are over, Peggy." Guthrie grinned as he took in the smoked glass door of Bruce Gallant's new office.

"He's probably got nothing else to do, believe me."

Guthrie turned to grab his notebook from the mounds of newspapers, magazines and scraps of paper on his desk.

"Andrew Fisk … never heard of the Fisks." He had an arm through his jacket and was walking towards the double doors now, his gaze fixed on the scars in the floorboards as dark as cigarette burns. "Maybe from the new subdivision?"

"Not Fisk, Trask. Andrew Trask. He worked at the Hallmark with my niece Ashley. She said he painted his fingernails black."

"So, double suicide?"

Peggy nodded, solemn as church prayer. She turned over a page of the Toronto paper in front of her, licking two fingers with a sharp intake of breath. Scanning for the lottery numbers.

"I should be a couple hours at most. There's this, and I've got to file the council story for Gallant by six."

"Nice drive. All the colours now, the whole line of maples on Daly."

"I'll call in if I'm coming in later."

Guthrie took the long route up the escarpment. He drove slowly as he sipped his espresso. He could take his time; the council story was half done. The farmers fields rolled out in lines of broken stalks of corn. He flicked down his window and took in the morning air. The tilled soil was still dark and heavy with the smell of the rain last night. The sun was warm on the sleeve of his jacket.

There was a line of new campaign signs along the chain link fence of the quarry. What caught his eye first were the red and the orange ones with the names he couldn't quite place and would not remember. There were no blue signs save for one square on the corner by the traffic lights, easily the size of four of the others. This one had a photograph of the candidate under the big blue letters that announced what Gallant had called "the prodigal's return" in his column last week: vote Kent Wolseley.

Guthrie still hadn't really reflected upon Kent's return to town after more than two decades. Maybe it was inevitable; he should have understood thirty years ago, when Kent Wolseley had first become conscious of how his forelock looked, tousled so, and of how to jut his chin, that he was already creating a role for himself here. The soap star approach to handsome was still there in this photo on the sign, even if the jet-black hair was flecked with grey, the cheeks had become slightly puffier and the gaze into the camera was now strangely unfamiliar because of the crow's feet around the eyes. Kent Wolseley, Guthrie's first best friend was expected to win this by-election by a landslide.

And he could still remember Kent as he was at nineteen, extending his hand across the table at the Brunswick Tavern with theatrical courtliness, a gesture more than one of genuine reconciliation, because that night he and Guthrie had just cut short the argument that ended their friendship.

The police cruisers were parked along the shoulder of the side road, yellow caution tape hammocking in the breeze. Two officers were stretching out a new portion of the roll of tape to block off the road entirely. They must have called in reinforcements to begin a larger search for the boy.

Guthrie waved with his camera in hand as he walked from the car.

"Morning, Brian. Is that Ojal up there?" He could see her talking to Scottie Francis the coroner, just the faint outline of her slim silhouette under the shapeless blue coat, her long black hair tucked under the collar. Constable Phelps just nodded. "Think she could speak to me?"

"Think so. Don't know if she knows much more than you right now, Ian. But you're going to have to wait here, right?"

Guthrie smiled and raised his hands as if to show he wasn't bearing arms. "I'm not going anywhere."

Brian Phelps moved like his father the farmer, big strides, surveying the fields as if he was taking a read on the state of a crop. Once he got to where Ojal and Scottie were standing, you could tell everything about how Phelps felt about her from the distance he stood from the conversation, how rigid and formal he suddenly became. She nodded, acknowledged Guthrie with a thin smile and a nod and headed his way. Phelps and Scottie immediately relaxed as she left them, with Scottie rounding his shoulders, digging his hands deeply into the front pockets of his suit pants. A coroner dressed like a small town banker, that was Scottie. Guthrie could faintly hear the jingle of his car keys.

"Ian! How are you?"

"Still waking up. You been here for a while?"

"Uh huh ..." Ojal was eyeing a white pickup truck that had just pulled over. It had the Newton coat of arms on the door. Parks and Rec. Two men in workers' greens got out of the cab. "Just wait a sec. I should talk to these guys."

As she approached the two Parks and Rec guys looked Guthrie over, the older with the handlebar moustache recognizing something about him and deciding it didn't merit more of a greeting. It could have been a memory of what Guthrie was like as a young man or it could be a grievance formed when Guthrie's father arrested him for mischief or drunk driving decades before. No matter how many people had moved into the new houses around Newton over the last two decades, you could pick out the townies by the grudges they kept. Ojal murmured something to them and the townie shrugged, and they headed back to the truck.

"They didn't seem too upset about not getting into the lake, did they?"

"You just gave them an hour's break back at the shop, Ojal. You made their morning."

"Doesn't take much, I guess."

"Has Scottie provided the preliminary opinion on the body?"

"We were just discussing that. Death by drowning but he's thinking there might be drugs involved. Oxys in the glove compartment of that car. He'll know in the post mortem. He's just authorizing the removal."

"Uh huh. Any Toronto papers here?"

"Nobody I've seen. Just you. Come ... I want to see where the hell the dog guy went to."

Ojal nodded to Guthrie and he followed her towards the trail. They approached the curve of the path slowly, taking in the stillness, the muted voices ahead, the spindly poplars and maples glimpsed through the older pines, leaves like little tears of flame. They would all be falling in days.

Ojal shifted slightly at the sound of Guthrie's steps on the wood chip trail then she caught him in her periphery and turned to smile. So demure, there was just the briefest glimpse of fondness before her gaze went to the ground.

"There's no way of knowing what she was taking. But she was in the driver seat. It looks as if they were parked at the crest of the hill ... who knows for how long ... then she just released the brake, put the car in neutral and let it coast down into the water."

"Sydney Brewin ..."

"Seventeen. Her mother said she had her birthday two weeks ago. She seemed so happy. They bought her a winter coat. She loved it. So white, it still looked new after a night in that water."

"But the boy, this Trask kid."

"The door swung open on the passenger side when we hauled the car out. I've taken a baggie of what look like flecks of paint to me, right on the boardwalk where the car broke through. The door just had to be open before the car entered the water."

"He didn't drown. So maybe he leapt from the car."

Ojal shook her head, her gaze on the still surface of the lake. "If he did he's vanished. I've tracked every inch of that stretch this morning."

"It's a deep lake. Glacial. Maybe his body's snagged and held under the surface."

From a gap in the trees Guthrie had a view of the area in lockdown. As Ojal walked ahead, no sign of the search dog and its handler, Guthrie took out his camera and began to snap the shots he needed: the gap in the boardwalk fence where the car broke through, the tire tracks that led to the crest of the hill, the car itself, a black Chevrolet Malibu, spattered in algae and mud, hauled up on the back of one of Durante's new tow trucks that was the size of a tank. Then he took a photo of the surface of Lake LeSueur, so still, the waves like the soft lines the wind carved along a sand dune.

Ojal turned at the crest of the hill.

"I'm not chasing a dog this morning. I draw the line. Sorry I took you this far along the trail."

"Not at all. I think I got the shots I needed."

"Any shot of Drew Trask in the water?" She smiled "You really believe he'd be in there?"

"I would believe it more than a murder if that's what you're suggesting."

"I'm not suggesting anything more than I've got one girl dead of an apparent suicide and a boy missing, presumed dead."

"That's what you want me to write?"

She glanced down at the state of his engineer's boots. "When has it ever mattered what I wanted you to write?"

"I'd rather get it right for you than Gallant."

They began to walk back to the road together. She watched him as he held his camera up to his eye, thinking through another shot as the hill came into focus in the frame.

"You going to put out a provincial alert on the boy?"

"Probably. Why don't you call me after I wrap up with Scottie? I've got to go into town and meet Sydney's parents."

"Then the Trasks?"

"Just the boy's mother. His father lives in Vancouver. The mother says they haven't kept in touch for some time."

"If the kid's missing, he could be headed out there."

"Maybe. But Ian, please don't write that."

"Of course not." He forced out a laugh, as if to reassure her that he knew her mind, then he snapped the black plastic disc on the lens of his camera. "I've got enough to write a couple hundred words, I guess."

"You know I'll tell you more when I have it. That could be later today."

"Ojal, if I got the scoop on this boy before deadline today, before the Toronto papers even got a whiff of what went on, it would make my life a lot easier right now."

"I'll keep that in mind. After I have two mothers falling to pieces, I'll think of your deadline and you'll be the first one I call, how's that?"

"That came out wrong."

"Uh huh. Well. There's a lot that's not right about this morning. Don't trouble yourself over it." She gave him the briefest of smiles. He was surprised by how much it brightened him and wondered if it was too obvious to her. But she gave nothing more away if it was.

He made his way back to his car, feeling an odd sense of energy, as if he could break into a run. Hadn't felt like that in a while. Maybe it was just the espresso, Masciantonio's kid made it extra strong this morning. Better to put this feeling down to anything other than the realization that it now took a death in this town to make him feel alive again.

2.

BELLA FIRST SAW the cop car from her bedroom window. She had raised the blind to comb her hair in the reflection of the glass. She had to, the mirror was still steamed up in the crap little bathroom in this, her new home, and she was already an hour late for school. The cop car was idling, with a meaty forearm hanging out the window on the passenger side. She figured they were parked down there with a radar gun, catching folks speeding up to the highway.

When she was finally out the door, she came through the lobby and saw the headlights flash. The big forearm slowly waved her over, the outsized plastic watch glinting in the morning sun.

"Good morning, Isabella."

"It's Bella, just Bella, thank you."

"Okay, just-Bella. Why don't you have a seat there in the back for us, we need to ask you a few questions."

"I'm sorry?"

"Get in the car, Bella."

All right, maybe she was pushing back unnecessarily but she hadn't done anything. She was conscious of the cop's eyes on her from the driver's side, like a crocodile's. She got in the back seat, crossed her legs, glimpsed that predator look still on her in the rear view mirror.

"Am I allowed to ask what's going on?"

"Bella, this is Constable Phelps. I'm Constable Giannone. We could have gone into your building there, rung the buzzer, got your parents involved."

"It's just my Mom and she's gone to work."

"I'm saying you're not in trouble. We just need your help."

Giannone shifted in his seat, angled his bulk so he could look at her directly. He smelled of Drakkar Noir. How perv was that! There was a faint whistle as he breathed heavily from his nose.

"You heard from Andrew Trask?" Constable Phelps said, a bit too loudly, too irritated for the consoling tone Giannone was trying out. Phelps didn't turn to look at her, there were just those eyes in the rear view mirror. Good cop, bad cop, just like on TV. Cute.

"No. No, I haven't. Why would I hear from Drew?"

"Andrew Trask has gone missing. He was involved in an accident last night."

"An accident?"

"Your friend Sydney Brewin is dead, Bella."

Like a blue-black curtain, darker than night, she felt the sudden grief close in. She cupped her face in her hands. The weight of the word "dead" crushed her down. The tears. Could have been seconds or minutes that passed. She needed air.

Later, after the crying, after her chest stopped heaving and she could finally catch her breath, it would be the watery image of Sydney's face, too pale, her hair floating in a greenish murk, that Bella couldn't stop thinking about.

Giannone and Phelps just let her sob it out. They were silent. Finally, Giannone turned to face her.

"I'm sorry we had to be the ones who told you."

"Just tell me what happened."

"We don't really know yet. She drowned in Lake LeSueur. We believe Andrew Trask was with her. We came to you because we know they are your close friends."

Phelps finally turned in his seat. "We're going to give you our cards when you walk out of this car. You get so much as a text or a tweet or an I-don't-know-what-the-fuck from Andrew Trask, you call us, okay? Like immediately."

Bella nodded, staring down at her high-tops, feeling the next wave of tears starting to come on, her bottom lip start to quiver. What's worse, they seemed to be appraising her performance, these fuckers.

"I'm sorry we had to be the ones to tell you."

"Me too."

And it was true, she really was. She was sorry it was them rather than someone who just might understand what she was feeling. Yet who would ever understand, really? She took the little white business cards from the hand that had waved her over, then she muttered a thank you despite herself.

Once the cop car had pulled out of the parking lot and driven out of sight, she headed straight back for the condo building, to her room and to the safety of her tears. Sydney . . . gone. Nobody had ever had a friendship like theirs, such a deep connection. And nobody was ever going to understand what she was feeling now.

I just got broken.

3.

TANIS VAN DYKEN'S new place was in a condominium complex called The Coachworks. Guthrie's mother had worked there for three years when he was a boy and the building had been the head office for Ridley Auto Parts. While living in Toronto he would get back to Newton on holidays and pass this ruin on his nightly walks. It was like an office tower of the twenties that had been reduced to a squat four stories. The shipping and receiving area had been blackened by hobo fires and all the doors and windows were boarded up, then graffittied and hacked away at through a decade of winters. But now, walking up to the building, Guthrie could see that the limestone had been blasted, scrubbed and made vivid again. He could picture those Venetian blinds in the front windows that the sun had tinged to the colour of parchment. If you peered in, you could make out the women of accounts receivable, hunched behind electric typewriters as big as engine blocks. As he entered and walked towards the new elevators he recalled a Christmas party in that room on the right, now lit like a dance club and gleaming with chrome plated dumbbells and exercise machines. As he watched a pearl of light pass through the numbers above the elevator doors he realized he was suddenly and oddly happy in the moment, buoyed by the thought of seeing Tanis and of how this meeting might go.

She had called him just a day after Sydney Brewin's funeral. Her daughter Isabella—or Bella, as the girl had renamed herself last year—was close with Sydney. Tanis had read Guthrie's four paragraphs that had run on page three of the Monitor and couldn't help herself. There was so much more to this story, she said. They had to talk.

Well of course there was more to the story. There always is. Scottie Francis's report had now revealed that, aside from the predictable—Sydney drowned with enough oxycontin in her to kill a horse—there was the small matter of her having been close to three months pregnant. Yet what do you do with that? The simple truth was that until this boy Drew Trask was found, dead or alive, Guthrie could hardly march into Gallant's office, disturb the man's browsing for golf shirts on eBay, to say he had a new angle and should write a longer piece to expand upon the report he had filed. Yes, it was all very tragic and yes, a little puzzling, but kids do commit suicide while others vanish without a trace, unfortunately. If you're lucky you find the latter alive, but that could take months or even years. The last time he had mentioned the case, when he and Bruce had walked across the street for a Jamaican patty from Hong's Variety, all Bruce had said was "I like it, the way you're still digging on this one." It was all in the way Bruce said "still"—pausing, to wipe yellow pastry flakes from his lips—that told Guthrie Bruce Gallant couldn't give a damn.

Guthrie had met Karen Brewin, Sydney's mother, at the dental office where she worked. She had called him at the Monitor and offered to speak with him about her daughter's death. He hadn't spoken to Karen Brewin in twenty years at least, but he knew, by a story and photos of a bake sale that ran in the Monitor, that she had found faith and was in the congregation at Trinity Baptist up on the North Service Road. She still had the long, feathered blonde hair, a nineties version of the heavy metal Valkyrie look she had perfected when she was Danny Bergeron's girlfriend and allegedly modeled, topless, for a biker magazine. Now, in her white slacks and white moccasin flats, she had the detached, blissful air of a nurse who had been sneaking off with the Prozac. She walked with Guthrie to a table at the Coffee Time in the same strip mall where the dental office was and then provided him with the kind of terse, carefully formed answers that suggested she was acting on advice.

Q. I talked to Scottie Francis. He told me Sydney was pregnant. Did you know of this, Karen?

A. Uh huh. Course she told me. That's the kind of family we are, Ian.

Q. Karen, can I ask who was the father?

A. David Goring, okay? Who you should know is a fine boy. David's been a B+ student for four years. David, his mother Toni . . . Toni is a good friend of mine . . . do you remember Toni, Ian?

Q. Yes. Yes, I do.

A. There's Toni and David's father Dan. You know Dan. He's a Constable.

Q. I do.

A. They're part of our congregation at Trinity Evangelical Baptist church. We've got a fine pastor in Norris Arbic. David's a good boy. Dan's got twenty years at Argyle Regional. Remember he went to Haiti after that earthquake to build houses?

Q. Uh huh. Dan's a good man. Karen, a sensitive question here, I'm sorry. Was she going to have the child?

A: Yes. Yes, of course. Sydney . . .

(Sound of sniffling. Guthrie remembers handing her a napkin from the metal dispenser on the table, Karen looking up at him as if she just suddenly recognized him as the Ian Guthrie she knew in high school).

Thanks. Sydney understood the sanctity of life. She and David had plans to get married until she met those two.

Q. Those two?

A. Sydney just should have stayed away from Drew Trask and Isabella Lang. It's that boy. This is going to sound terrible, I know, but Ian, I'm sure that boy's a drug addict who hates himself. And he just . . .two possession convictions, he's got! He wanted to drag my daughter down . . . I guarantee you he fed her that oxycontin. I know that if they get him . . .

Dead air. Karen blew her nose into a paper napkin. On the tape Guthrie could hear a car pull in to a parking space just outside the window, sports radio blaring.

Q: Um ... another difficult question here ... I'm sorry, Karen ... have you considered this might be a suicide?

A: What?

Q: A suicide. I'm just wondering. Maybe ... I mean, with the baby ... maybe she felt she couldn't go through with it?

A: No, Ian. Not at all. Let me repeat for you: our Sydney was in love with David Goring. He was going to be her husband and the father of her child. She understood the sanctity of life and this young couple ... let me just tell you this young couple had everything to live for until Sydney starting listening to what Drew Trask and that Bella Lang had to tell her. I couldn't protect her. I tried. They've just got to find Drew Trask. And when they do, I'll tell you now ... I'll tell you now I have faith that the truth will come out. As Norris ... Pastor Arbic says, it always does. Thank you, that's all I have to say today.

He just needed one ear bud for this conversation as the elevator ascended to Tanis's floor. He'd played it over so many times, now, taken in the halting rhythms of Karen Brewin's quiet anger. Each time he heard himself say "difficult question ..." he felt the grim, gut-tightening confirmation that he had come to hate this job.

"Ian!" Tanis embraced him at the door and allowed herself that hoarse, quiet laugh that hadn't changed in twenty years. She pulled him close and gently pressed the small of his back until his leather jacket creaked. Her hair smelled faintly of rosemary. He mumbled his hello then followed her through the front hall into the living room of her condominium. Over the sleek purple velvet divan were a series of sepia toned photographs of desert landscapes. These last few years Guthrie had been in similar rooms with old friends. There was strong light from the requisite terrace where he would go to smoke, and drink good wine poured in small tumblers. These were the first homes after divorce.

Tanis had never looked so comfortable in herself when she was married, really. She would get her hair cut short and wear baggy shirts and blouses that draped below her waist—she explained it to him by saying she was self-conscious about her hips after she gave birth to Bella. But now she was growing her hair long again, the strands of grey had appeared in thick brush strokes and made her more attractive than she'd ever been to him. Just two short months earlier, when she and Guthrie had made the mistake (her words) of sleeping together, she told him "men have always just been diversions for me. Some genuine adventures with a couple of ordeals like Daniel. I just fooled myself into believing they could have been anything more."

Over the last two months the belief that he could fall in love with her had emerged into his waking life during still moments, late at night and in the early morning, as he moved from room to room in his empty house. And here he was.

As she went into the kitchenette to pour them both a glass of that dark and chalky Shiraz she loved, Guthrie tried to decide where to sit down between the divan and one of two squat leather club chairs that caught his eye.

"These are beautiful."

"You like them? That's a Finnish design from the sixties."

"You get them from your folks' place?"

She shook her head, smiled primly. "From Daniel. Before our marriage. He knew I loved them so he got them for that tiny apartment I had when I was in school. Who buys a young woman chairs like this? Of course I had to marry him."

She passed him his wine with such an offhand manner, affirming that he still qualified as a diversion. Now Guthrie was grateful they had chosen to sleep at his place back then and had avoided talking about how thoughtful her ex-husband was. Before Daniel slept with the architecture student interning at his office, of course. Guthrie looked at her hands cupping her glass of wine, the long ringless fingers, the tarnished and gently battered old silver bangle on her slender wrist. She was better than the soap opera plot this Daniel had put her through.

"Where's Bella?"

"She's working."

"Working?"

"At that horrible sports bar up by the truck stop. What is it, Shooters or something? She's bussing tables."

"You're okay with that?"

"She wants her own money. Given her mother's situation, that's understandable."

"You doing all right?"

"I'll be all right, Ian. But that's sweet, you asking."

For a moment he wondered if her call and all she had told him over the phone was just an elaborate approach to get him here and "play it out." But no, for all of her artiness, the paradox of Tanis was that impulsive acts did not seem to happen with her. It made perfect sense that, instead of the painter she once thought she was going to be, she had become an architectural drafter. There was a precise, unsentimental logic to every decision she made, clean lines and solid structural foundations.

"This place is great. Bigger than I thought."

"You like it? Not big enough, frankly, with Bella, but we chose it together." Her gaze went out towards the terrace. The shafts of early evening sunlight etched sharp lines just above her head. "She said it was funky. My daughter. This is what funky has come to, Ian."

"At least she can say that word and not sound completely ridiculous. As I would."

"And I think that's exactly how you like it."

"I think you're probably right. Cheers."

She raised her glass with his and laughed. "It's not you," she had said when she broke it off, "it's me and my issues with commitment." In a moment like this he could almost believe that.

"So listen. You probably think I'm just horrible. I mean after I called you."

"Not at all. Why would I think you were horrible?"

"Because of what I did. I mean with Bella, looking into what she knows. It's just that I saw your story in the paper and realized there's a lot more to this."

Guthrie smiled, pleased that he could suddenly look forgiving and maybe even wise.

"You know Sydney was like one of Bella's best friends."

"That's been going around, yeah." He leaned back in the chair now and held the glass of wine over his chest as if he was shielding himself. Why was he feeling protective? For some reason, he felt that Tanis wasn't supposed to be involved in anything like this. Sydney Brewin's death was a townie conversation. "Don't tell me she's got something on Drew Trask."

"No, not at all. Bella hates that boy now, in that way you hate when you're a teenager. I know she was jealous of the connection he had with Sydney. She felt he was taking her away from her."

"You probably heard … the longer this boy's missing, the more the talk seems to be that he's guilty of something. From criminal negligence all the way to manslaughter."

"Please." She shook her head and gazed into the wine in her glass. "I just can't believe everybody forgets what it was like to be that age. Want to hear my theory?"

"Of course." And he tilted his glass. "Here's to old friends."

"To old friends." And as she swallowed she closed her eyes as if she was willing a memory to be erased.

"You need to meet a woman and get married, Ian."

He laughed and stopped himself from correcting her with the word *re*-married. Why did it still feel important to remind the world he had stayed by Kate, right up to end, after the cancer had done its worst, transformed her into little more than a wraith under the heavy blankets on the bed? Like a badge of honour he still needed to pin on his chest after a decade? Best mourner, imperfect husband's division. But no—if this new state of middle age had not given him the gift of knowing what to say, it had at least given him some wisdom of knowing what not to. "You're probably right. Now tell me your theory."

"So this has come to me watching Bella grow up, and I doubt it is as profound as I'm trying to make it, but it's just ... I've seen it ... there are the same roles that different kids play that we played ... like there's some unchanging model of how we all grow up in places like this, what we're sorry for when we're young."

Guthrie smiled but would not look in her eyes, knowing it would make him seem bashful to her. "So you think there's a young girl and boy out there playing the roles you and I played?"

"All right, all right, I know it's not profound. Just let me put it this way: remember Darren Pemberton? From all Bella told me I know Andrew Trask is the kid Darren was. You think Darren would ever be capable of killing anyone?"

Guthrie slowly blinked and attempted a smile. He needed to wear a mask of serene reminiscence, concealing the sorrow he still felt about the memory of Darren Pemberton. The guilt. From time to time he had heard a little about Darren's life from high school people like Tanis. There was talk of Darren's time in theatre school, then of his move to New York. Guthrie had seen a photograph publicizing some play in Toronto where it looked like Darren had lost about fifty pounds and dyed his hair blonde. He was sneering for the camera. Then, years later, just before Guthrie had moved out of Toronto and back to Newton, he was walking out of a bar on King Street and Darren Pemberton emerged from the revolving doors of a boutique hotel, tanned and dressed like a teenaged millionaire in the bright colours of new money. He had looked right past Guthrie, as if he was no longer in Darren's thoughts as the one who betrayed a friendship, outed him and made his life a living hell in Newton. And that seemed as close to just as fate should get: the bullied and beaten boy a midlife success, the one who betrayed him a struggling hack.

"My father, Tanis, he knew a little about these things, he used to say we were all capable of murder, that was the problem."

"And you agreed with him?"

"No. But I rarely agreed with him about anything."

"Oh don't say now you're becoming him. Even if it's true." She laughed at her own words.

"So anyway. This Andrew Trask. If you don't believe he might have helped Sydney's suicide along . . ."

"I don't."

"Karen Brewin tells me he had two convictions for possession."

"Uh huh. Well, Karen Brewin. Jesus . . . " Tanis looked into the dark, shimmering red in her glass then gently swirled away her most uncharitable thoughts. "I want to be compassionate, the woman's grieving."

"But you think Trask had nothing to do with this."

"That's right, Ian, and I'll tell you why. Okay . . . I'm not proud of this."

"Not proud of what?"

She rose from the divan and gently tapped his fingers, as if she were reaching to take his hand and then thought better of the gesture. "Come."

She led him down the hall and into Bella's room. He took in the strong smell of too-rich perfume, the kind of scent a teenage girl wears because she's sure it smells like what a grown woman would choose. With the tangle of pink sheets on the bed, the crayon coloured clothes overflowing from the hamper, it looked like Bella was doing her very best to stray from her mother's fastidiousness and the dark, muted tones Tanis wore so well.

They approached the desk where Bella did her homework. Her laptop was playing a series of photographs, slowly fading from one to the next, which looked to be from a summer barbecue when her family was still together. There was Daniel, Bella's father, dark and handsome but definitely looking a decade older than Tanis, with his arms wrapped around his daughter. If Tanis felt anything at all as the picture appeared, she did not give it away.

"I just want to explain a little. When you go through what we went through, Bella and me, when you don't quite know how to read your daughter's silence and the fact she can hardly look you in the eye anymore, you get worried."

"You don't have to explain."

"Yes, I do. Ian, I've gone into her emails. I wasn't going to. I mean I didn't know her password. I never ever thought I would either, but I took a guess, typed some letters in and it worked."

"I'd probably do the same."

"No, actually I don't think you would but you're not a mother. Ian, I want to tell you the password."

"Why?"

"Ian, it's a, n, n, e, l, i, e."

"Oh."

"Exactly."

He closed his eyes and took a long sip of his wine, let it warm him as he swallowed deeply. He could see Annelie Danziger on a stretch of beach in Toronto, on one of the first warm nights of a June almost thirty years ago. Her chestnut brown hair, tinted copper at the ends of the curls, was still wet on her shoulders as she pulled on the grey sweatshirt she had so artfully torn. Annelie Danziger, the girl he loved and yet could tell no one. Annelie, who had tried and failed to kill herself at Lake LeSueur some weeks before she eventually succeeded, OD-ing on heroin in a room over the old Hi-Fi Lounge.

"So is this part of your theory? That your daughter or Sydney Brewin had become Annelie?"

She turned from him and typed in the letters in the password box. "It's a little more complicated than that. Annelie and I became pretty close near the end. She wrote letters to me during those weeks and months before she died. I was at Waterloo doing my architecture degree and she was downtown at the college of art."

Tanis gazed down at the blond wood floor, shaking her head. He could have reached over, held her hand and kissed her. Maybe he should have.

"As Bella started telling me about what she was doing in her drama elective, the friends she was making, a light went on. Which is so wrong. It's like I immediately felt proud my daughter was becoming a geek. Bella's always drawn well, but there were pages of sets and costume designs ... all for these plays and movies she and Sydney and Drew were dreaming up. I mean, you should see them, Ian. So imaginative. So good."

Guthrie could only smile. Flickering through his thoughts was an old Super 8 image of Tanis, transformed into a young Edie Sedgewick, kohl eyed, platinum coloured hair, running through an alley off Queen and Bathurst downtown. This was in one of Annelie Danziger's little movies she screened in her garage that summer so long ago, after Annelie`s relationship with Kent Wolseley had ended, and she was coming into her own..

"And I guess I just remembered how hard it was in this town, growing up, being in any way different and interested in art. I mean genuinely different, not you-know ..."

"I believe we called them poseurs. Pronounced like hosers."

"We did, yes." Tanis re-crossed her legs. There was a tilt to her gaze, the start of a smile.

"You remember Annelie had made those movies?"

"Of course I did. She gave one to me, some weeks before she died. Black Iris, she called it. She said she couldn't bear to look at it, all she could see were bad choices, she said. She knew I loved it, so ... bad choices ... you'd think I would have picked up on that."

"And you still have this movie."

"That, some photos and all those letters. One Sunday night Sydney and Bella were here, in this very room, when I heard them talking, I heard Bella mispronounce chiaroscuro, and maybe it was because Bella and I weren't talking much around that time ... it was only a month or two after we moved in here ... but I just felt this need to connect ... mothers, daughters, I don't know." Tanis walked to the laundry closet and produced a shoebox emblazoned with a geometric pattern in primary colours, sharp black lines. Le Chateau from the eighties. "This here. It's got all those old letters from eighty-three all the way to eighty-six when she died, the Polaroids of those nights we'd go down to Voodoo and the little movie too ... Black Iris."

"I think I remember that movie. I remember you and Annelie in it ... that garage at her folks' place where she'd project the movies. Remember her Dad, the little Swiss guy? 'Annelie vat is going on back zere ...'"

"Well, I gave this whole shoebox to the girls. I suppose I thought it would inspire them or something, give them a sense of what was possible. I mean ... the letters ... we were both learning so much, opening up to the world." As Tanis spoke she was sifting through the pages. She smiled at a paragraph on a page, brushed a few long strands of her hair away from her face as she handed it to Guthrie. *I swear I just hate it when Kent says surreal and he doesn't even know what it really means.*

"You know Kent's moved back here, eh? He's running in this by-election."

Tanis rolled her eyes and gestured as if she was brushing away a fly. "Please. I never really knew what she saw in him. I think it was only when she moved into the city back then that she realized how unbearable he was."

"We were all probably unbearable."

"Maybe. But you were different from him. Different in a way that made me think you might turn out interesting."

"Yeah, well. So much for that."

Tanis smiled. "You couldn't see it then. You can't see it now."

Guthrie laughed, but as he looked into her eyes, she looked away, back down at the photos and letter in the box.

"Anyway, I just handed over all of this to them without even thinking about how much Annelie's death so young might affect them. It's like I just totally airbrushed the central fucking tragedy of my life back then, the loss of my best friend."

"I don't think that's so wrong. You were thinking of them and not yourself. Why wouldn't they be inspired by her?"

"And they were. A kind of role model was all she was to Sydney at first."

Tanis exhaled sharply, stretched out her long fingers before the keyboard, then she clicked into an email. "There's this from Sydney. They were reading this play Annelie had written. These kids … they hardly text … even I text … for them it's like the nineteenth century, they wanted to write these long letters to each other."

I'm into act two now. Have you got there, Bel? Annelie Danziger was a freaking genius. Thank you, thank you and thank your amazing mother for finding this. Tonight I'm going to text you some of the lines I think are just awesome. Gotta go to work ☹

Guthrie stared into the words on the screen and at the little photographs above them. Bella had her mother's high cheekbones but the dark eyes and the crooked smile of her father. Sydney Brewin just seemed out of focus, like an image blurred by rippling waves. He suddenly felt tired and heavy, like an ache from an old memory had settled within him again. Tanis was right, she was on to something.

"Ian, I'm going to give you all this. I'm just going to print out these emails. With all of the old letters, you'll see what I'm talking about … what I never imagined …"

"Are you going to tell Bella you're doing this?"

She hugged herself even tighter. "I can't, Ian. Not right now. We've really just started on our own. She'd never trust me again, no matter how sorry I was. I can't lose her."

And without thinking Guthrie put his hand at the small of her back. Too late to pull it back and not to touch her. It felt as if a wire of tension along her spine just slackened as she sighed then quickly wiped away a tear.

"Just tell me what you want me to do."

Tanis gave him a sad smile and rose from her daughter's chair in one quick movement, leading him back into the living room. Guthrie switched the light off in the bedroom as if this was his home.

Back in the kitchen she was about to shut the lid tightly on the shoebox when she stopped and brought one of the pages to her nose. "I love that smell, don't you? Paper doesn't smell the same now."

"I don't think anything's much the same now."

"No, nothing except what happened with Sydney. Now sit down, have another drink while the e-mails print and tell me more about you."

***

On his way home Guthrie turned on the car radio and an old Bowie song was playing. He could not shake the memory it summoned up of being in the passenger seat of the Wolseley family car, heading into Toronto on a January night. He remembered having the window down to flick out the ashes and eventually the butt of his cigarette while he took sips of rye from the old nickel-plated flask Kent had. They were off to meet Annelie and Tanis and their friends at Club Voodoo and then over to the Hi Fi. *Everything will be all right … tonight.* And it was, for just those few weeks in summer, twenty-seven years before, it had really been all right.

4.

WHEN GUTHRIE RETURNED home he should have gone to bed, slept on all of this, put the shoebox with the letters and the photos away and approached the material in the morning with the clear-eyed detachment of any other news story. He had driven up his street, "last townie block before the tracks," and the lights were out in most of the squat, red brick bungalows save for a few flickering TV screens glimpsed through the curtains. Everybody got up early for the drive to work around here. Yet, when he brought the shoebox inside, and slumped down into the lumpy old sectional where the pale blue velour looked bruised in places , he couldn't help but pry open the box and look through the Polaroids, just to get a glimpse of who he was back then. So much confusion and pain and anger he had been feeling in those years, after watching the leukemia take his mother. Those months turned his father, so tough and cool and elegantly put together as a young cop, into a broken man drinking a bottle of Teacher's every couple of days, and Guthrie had no way to accept or understand such vulnerability in him. If he had known it was a dress rehearsal for what he would go through with Kate … they say the body reproduces every cell in seven years, which meant Guthrie had become a new man four times over now, but of course this wary, dark- eyed boy just barely in the frame of these photos, his hair as spiky and chaotically entangled as his thoughts, was still so deeply within him.

He lived there in the guilt he still felt over Darren Pemberton. Yes, Guthrie had truly found his calling as a hack the moment he had just casually mentioned in gym class, as the hockey boys began to ridicule him for his new haircut and his talk of strange music clubs in Toronto, who else he had seen at Club Voodoo, and who Darren

Pemberton had now called his friends. No truth teller—tale tattler; that was Guthrie. He soon enough bore witness to the brutality that followed, with Darren literally chased down through a shopping mall parking lot and humiliated, lipstick smeared on his bloodied and bruised face.

A hack's calling encapsulated Guthrie's contradictions: the townie and cop's kid with the striver who wanted to mix among the prepsters Kent introduced him to, all those heirs and heiresses apparent to the people who knew better. Newspaper reporting, half-muckracker's trade and half noble, priestly calling for the mandarinate of columnists and editors from the old-boy schools, was the perfect place to float through these latitudes—until it wasn't.

And then what happens to your life? What's the next act?

Enough: this talk just led to the familiar sleeplessness now. Flip to the other photos. There was Tanis and a couple of her dark eyed, anonymous boyfriends, one whose eyes shone red in the camera flash, then there was Vesna Drazic, Kent Wolseley and yes, even more beautiful than he remembered, there was Annelie Danziger. He walked into the kitchen with the flickering light over the breakfast table. It still looked like 1985 in here, with the peach coloured wallpaper and fake marble counter top. He reached into the third drawer, right under the knives where he put the bottle of Lagavulin three months ago, just because he couldn't throw scotch this fine away (thank God he still had some sense even sober). He poured a couple of fingers worth into a tumbler, just to read a few letters and compare them to all these emails Tanis had printed out.

Jan 8/2012: *You should hear my mom yammer on about her goddamn Reverend Arbic. "Don't you dare say a word about him, you don't know how hard it has been to put together a congregation in this town." Fucking hypocrites.*

Mar 16/84: *My mom says I should be ashamed of myself for the way I talk about my dad. "You don't know all the sacrifices he has made for you. You have no idea how hard it was for him when he first came to Canada and all he did to make sure we're all right." As if this has anything to do with what I am going through. All my life she has told me to think for myself. Now I'm supposed to forget what I know is right and just OBEY Prince Erich. What fucking hypocrites, both of them.*

Aug 19/2013: *I swear, Bel, I read what Annelie went through thirty years ago and it's like nothing's fucking changed. This town, these people want to crush everything real inside you.*

Tanis was right; there was something here. Correspondences, you could say. Like a vein into the past had been opened up, the blackened blood staining the present. Black blood . . . black iris. Guthrie swallowed deeply and just stared at the bottle. There wasn't even a shot left, might as well kill it. He raised the glass to his lips, felt that once-familiar deep consolation, the taste like smoke and silk, soothe his cigarette-ravaged throat. He'd probably be up all night now.

5.

THE ROTARY HALL on Borden Street in the old part of Newton hadn't changed in thirty years. It had the beige aluminum siding, scrubbed so clean of graffiti along the back wall that it looked like it had a tan line. But you could still see ghost words from a long gone time of teenage rebellion—ASSASSINATORS and NRK—in half-light. The pavement in the parking lot was rutted and pocked with wild thistle and chickweed, the reserved signs for the dentist's office were still legible even though Doctor Horner had retired at least a decade ago. If this hall was used for anything at all now it was for charity efforts with little hope of making enough at the door to pay for the rent—a high school concert for Haiti, advertised with lime green Bristol board signs, Guthrie could recall. It was a curious choice of venue for Kent Wolseley's town hall on crime, but the more you thought about it, given Kent's cultivated townie constituency, the more it all made sense.

What made less sense to Guthrie as he pulled into the parking lot was how packed it was. His was the fourth car in a little convoy that circled the lot in vain, only to come out and find the soft shoulders of Lawson Avenue and Sidmonton Street filling up with half tons and SUVs angling in with their parking lights pulsing, the half remembered faces of hockey coaches and hairdressers glimpsed behind the windshields. Old Newton was coming out for one of their own.

Except Kent wasn't really one of their own. He hadn't been for decades. Yes, he had come back and bought a home at the back of Newton pond with his new wife Veronica Provost-Wolseley over the last six months and yes, they had quickly established themselves, appearing at the Hospital Auxiliary ball and donating a Morrisseau painting that had been in Veronica's family for fifty years for the silent auction. Kent was proving to be a reliable fourth with his lawyer's pals on Sundays at Argyle Falls Golf and Country Club and Veronica, a junior partner at Futerman Gelber, was in a book club with the Mayor's wife where she had led some lively discussions on Joseph Boyden's latest, for she had worked with Indigenous communities for a couple of years before she joined Futerman. "A whip-smart power couple," Gallant wrote, in that "prodigal returns" profile piece. "Young, driven and on the fast track for greatness" apparently, but that track went right back up to Ottawa, where they had really spent the better part of their working lives.

And yet whatever greatness meant, it was a quality that had the power to splice out such inconsistencies from the flow of images that took a boy like Kent from early promise to a man with power, influence and national prominence. Guthrie could be honest to admit that really, no matter how many memories he had of Kent, they weren't as vivid as those of this candidate as he first knew him: as a kid so perfectly average looking his mother got him an agent for work in TV and movies shooting in Toronto, as the chubby teenager in tennis whites who'd battle for hours with him on the park courts, as the townie who managed an early escape from Newton District High school by suddenly, one September, just appearing to smile and wave from the passenger side of the Wolseleys' silver Lincoln, in the blazer and tie of St. Alban's school as stepfather and stepson headed off down the highway to Toronto. The little clip that ran in Guthrie's head now revealed the trajectory of the boy growing into the young man mysteriously chosen for the role he now played, and Guthrie wasn't the only one in town who realized it flowed with the power and simplicity of inevitability.

As he walked up to the entrance to the hall he could see the three technicolour logos of the Toronto TV stations emblazoned across the backs of trucks, the satellite dishes on each roof tilted towards the city. There were men who looked like old roadies and bouncers, vaguely familiar to Guthrie but for the grey in their beards and the size of their bellies, who were busy unspooling cable as thick as their wrists as they made their way around the back door of the hall. And on the porch-like entrance, and then again there, over under the street light, and there, in the parking lot, were the reporters, dressed for the occasion in muted, dark shades. All were poised for their first double ender of the night while the grizzled print journalists milled around the entrance, smoking, commiserating, punching away like puzzled old primates on their BlackBerrys. This was an occasion that merited national attention, and Guthrie was at a loss as to why this would be. The death of a girl? As Peggy Vaughan back at the Monitor said, it happened pretty much every year.

Row after row of those old wooden stacking chairs were filling up with the locals now. From the back of the hall almost all of the hair was grey, the figures leaning into each other conspiratorially or slumped in lonely, patient expectation of some moment of uplift and recognition. Would they be recognizing something of themselves in the Kent that would appear, or something once familiar and now transformed, made better in some way?

Guthrie craned his neck to see there, in the first row was this Veronica Provost-Wolseley, her blonde tresses swept back to reveal the long nape of her neck and a heaviness in her cheeks, the beginnings of a double chin. She sat beside Sarah Foran, the Mayor's wife, and his worship Glenn Foran himself, the reddish bristles of his freshly razored scalp catching the light. Veronica brought out the sorority girl in Sarah Foran, so the Mayor's wife said, and that seemed true, the way they were smiling and giggling to themselves.

The mayor was chortling to the man seated beside him. Guthrie could only glimpse him in profile but yes, of course, it was Pastor Norris Arbic from Trinity Baptist, Karen Brewin's congregation. Arbic's sculpted blonde beard and slender figure draped in a boxy suit gave him the look of a monk awkwardly descending into the fallen world again.

On the stage stood a banquet table, a pitcher of ice water, four tumblers and four microphones spaced out with an architectural precision, and four of the wooden chairs with their backrests wrapped in little felt skirts of the richest blue, the blue of Veronica's silk scarf and Mayor Foran's tie. "All about the details in campaigns," Senator MacDougall said, in response to why his party had deployed so many "resources" for this by-election. The Senator was there just two rows back from the mayor. Even Guthrie recognized that wispy grey beard and pock-marked ruin of a face that made him look like a wino dressed by a Bay Street tailor. Gallant had written that the Senator had become a mentor to Kent, a sure sign the party saw great things in him, given the Senator's history with the current Prime Minister, his cold steady hand at shutting down inquiries and burying scandals.

At precisely seven o'clock, two chubby boy-men in their church suits moved to wave the last of the journalists and stragglers into the hall as they shut the doors. The two rows of overhead lights suddenly brightened from dusky globes to shimmering balls of white, and from a side entrance the parents of Sydney Brewin shuffled in, followed by the candidate Kent Wolseley and yes, Staff Inspector Ojal Dhillon. The audience went silent. Kent turned, briefly flashed a smile for the audience and then gazed down at the floor with a solemnity fit for the occasion. He and these three other figures took their seats behind the table with a funereal grace that seemed older and darker than the occasion demanded.

Kent leaned into the microphone. He looked trimmer than he'd been in years, and the pale blue button-down and beige wide wale corduroys enhanced the impression of a man who hadn't changed from that better era in town, when the Ridley plant was still open and the quarry was running two shifts a day. "I'd like to thank you all for coming tonight. For those of you who may not know me and who have come because you care about the safety and the well-being of your kids and your friends and neighbours here in Newton, let me introduce myself. I'm Kent Wolseley, your Conservative candidate for the Argyle North federal by-election."

Sarah Foran whooped and began to clap, her dark hair shimmering as she glanced about, wearing her toothy campaign grin. Veronica's back tensed as she gave her friend a wide smile in return. The Mayor seemed oblivious to his wife as he stared into the screen of his device.

"This town hall on crime was going to be a very different conversation than the one we are unfortunately going to have tonight. There's a greater seriousness and a far greater sadness that we must acknowledge. An incalculable loss has brought us together. I would like to thank my honoured guests with me tonight, Finley and Karen Brewin, and I'd like to commend them for their incredible courage and strength in sharing their thoughts with us this evening. Karen, Finley . . . thank you."

Kent reached out with his right hand and gently squeezed Karen Brewin's. Finley Brewin reached for a tissue in the front pocket of his pressed khakis and brushed away a tear. He had yet to look up and acknowledge this audience, as if he wasn't quite ready to take in where he was and what he had agreed to do. Karen Brewin was not crying though. Her jaw clenched as she swallowed.

"I'd also like to thank Staff Inspector Ojal Dhillon for graciously consenting to come and for providing us with a perspective from the front lines on what's really going on out there on our streets we once thought were safe. As a few of you here may know, I grew up a couple blocks from this hall. Coming back and making Newton my home again, I've realized not everything has changed for the better. I know together we can and we must fix that, and this is our first step down that road."

Ojal looked to Kent and nodded with all the serenity and assurance she could muster. In her dress uniform and just the subtlest shades of lipstick and eye shadow she was safely disguised and unknowable, protected from the derision that Guthrie knew was the reflexive response from most in this hall when faced with an attractive young woman of colour in some position of authority.

She spoke of the need to look beyond statistics. Yes, violent crime in Newton was at its lowest rate of incidence in thirty years, thanks "in no small part to the guys on the front lines" who had done so much to make her feel welcome here and part of a team. Yet for the conversation tonight this audience had to look at whom was hurting who, where the rate of violent acts was increasing, and that was with "our young people, the future of this town." Along his row Guthrie could make out heads slowly nodding, even if the arms and legs of so many remained tightly crossed.

"We know we can do more for education and awareness in our schools, more to figure out some of the reasons behind the numbers," Ojal said, "and tonight is about listening to your ideas and your perspectives so we can all work together." She kept her eyes on the page in front of her, willing that small quaver out of her voice. Guthrie took in her finely shaped hands, the deep red polish of her nails that caught the light. He was glad he had remembered his little tape recorder; he really wasn't paying attention to what she was saying.

Kent thanked her as the tentative, scattered applause quickly faded, and then he paused to allow the room to be poised for the gravity of his introduction. "Just days ago Karen and Finley here lost their daughter Sydney. They lost her under mysterious circumstances, some say, but we all know there was a young man, yet to be found, who was with her right up to the moments before her death, one who had had a criminal record. If Drew Trask is ever caught and arrested, we all know he'll be protected and treated well. It will probably be months before he will provide his testimony in a court of law, if he is charged with a criminal offence. Meanwhile, both Karen and Finley will be left to wait patiently for justice, left to suffer in silence. That's how it all works. There are the rights of the criminal and there are the rights of the victims, and we all know what still matters most in this country, despite the efforts of our government to get things done for you up in Ottawa. I've got a few ideas about how we can improve the process, ideas that I'd like to take with me up there, should I be given the opportunity, but of course that's not what tonight is about. It's about hearing from you. And there is no perspective more important, more vital to this conversation, than Finley's and Karen's right now. Karen, I believe you'd like to say a few words."

As Kent made his introduction, Finley Brewin had finally looked up and taken in the crowd. Finley worked in baggage handling at the airport, along with a few of his former teammates on the Newton Blades, the Junior B team in town. He was one of those who had had a couple of years playing in the American league and then his knee injury and simply a reckoning with the limitations of his own talent had brought him back to Newton. He settled down quickly, married one of the pretty girls from high school. Finley had put on a few pounds but his farmer's shoulders and his broad chest allowed him to carry it well. He looked about twenty years older now that he had shaven off that grunge goatee and had stopped bleaching his hair. He put an end to all that peacocking when the RCMP questioned him about the drug trafficking ring uncovered up at the airport. No charges were ever laid and he had settled into the kind of stolid townie respectability that three generations of Brewins had eventually settled into. Still he hadn't quite got religion like his wife had; Finley's bewilderment at his loss had given him the gravitas of quiet suffering, but there was something in his eyes, a flicker of some wilder intelligence that told Guthrie he must talk to him before filing the story on the town hall tonight.

Karen Brewin pulled out two pieces of foolscap paper from the inner pocket of her suede blazer, brushed back the feathered strands of her bronzed hair as she put her reading glasses on. They were new and just like Sarah Palin's.

"I have come here tonight to tell you about my daughter, my little girl who grew up too fast, the child me and my husband loved with all our hearts even as it seemed we no longer knew her in the final months she was with us. I want to talk about what we believe are the reasons our Sydney became a stranger, and what we all might do to ensure such a painful loss does not happen to more of our sons and daughters here in Newton."

Finley Brewin nodded and touched his wife's hand. She did not pause or look his way. The Prozac fog in her manner had lifted for this occasion. She had found a videographer at the back of the hall that was her point of focus and she held it with an intensity that the measured calm in her voice could hardly conceal.

Every word on the page that she read had row after row of mothers and fathers and grandparents leaning forward intently, identifying with her forbearance, her unsentimental evocation of their own fears, their sense of something more than just a daughter lost..

"Many people have asked me how we are coping. Many of our friends and neighbours here have just been incredible, I want to tell you. The ironic thing about all this is that in the midst of such a tragedy, I doubt we have ever felt so much a part of our community and truly supported and loved. What has brought us together is, I believe, a collective wish for justice to be served. We all know this young man Drew Trask gave up his claim to the innocence of childhood when he took my little daughter's life." Guthrie heard a sniffle down his aisle a few seats away. Alice Wong, the grade school teacher, had pulled out a tissue from her little black quilted purse with the shiny gold snaps. "All we ask is that, if he is found, he be judged accordingly, so that all our rights, the rights of my family, the rights of our community, be respected and honoured as much as our courts respect and protect the rights of murderers."

In the silence that followed her last words, Karen Brewin slowly took off her reading glasses, carefully folded the pages in her hands and then just whispered a frail thank you into her microphone. Veronica Provost-Wolseley and Sarah Foran were the first people in the audience to stand and clap. Pastor Norris followed, his eyes welled up with tears. Guthrie knew that a man would risk the threat of violence if he did not rise with the rest of those in the room now too and clap along. "Thunderous," yes, he would type that word tonight, erase it and then type it again.

Then Kent looked up and, of all the people in the room, his gaze settled on just one person for that split second: Guthrie himself. Months later Guthrie would wonder if he really did see what happened next, because if anyone else did, he could not find them among the crowd, not even among the other journalists and videographers in the room who were recording every moment. Guthrie was sure Kent winked at him.

Perhaps it was just a sudden, spontaneous acknowledgement of their old friendship, the boys they once were. It could have been a way to connect with the deeper understanding of each other they both had. As much as Guthrie wanted to believe that this deeper part of him still existed, the wink was just as much evidence of a different facet of Kent Wolseley though, the part of the candidate that refused to take his adult identity seriously. For how could you? Indeed, not taking his own role as some local hack was necessary for Guthrie. A sense of the absurdity, of what finally came, in its meagre way, of their ambitions was all that was left of their better selves. And yet, any man truly worthy of admiration and public office would have never . . . Guthrie knew the gesture would haunt him in the weeks to come of this by-election.

Once all the questions were asked and the missing and presumed dead Andrew Trask had been convicted without court, trial or jury and given life imprisonment, the new president of the local riding association, Dean Vickers, came out on stage to announce that

Kent and Staff Inspector Dhillon would be staying for the coffee and the baked goods there on the back table, brought tonight by Vonda Graebel and her kids at the Lodestar school. Dean led the applause like the big, bearish camp counselor he was before he returned from Korea with his small angry wife and opened his travel agency up at the mall. Guthrie realized he would have to move quickly through the crowd to avoid Dean, who would be sure to ask him about the series of op eds he had written for the paper and submitted with a proposal letter where he suggested he be given a weekly column entitled "The Curious Canadian." Dean would give him that look where he stared too long into Guthrie's eyes in search of an honest response that clearly no one could ever provide for him, save perhaps for his wife in another language. His reedy, aggressive tone provoked the insincerity of politeness from everyone, an insincerity that no doubt kept him working away at the rants at his desk at the travel agency, with his thesaurus and Toastmasters book of sage quotations.

"I would just like to request your patience as Kent will be holding a brief media availability for our friends who have come tonight from out of town and then he'll be right back in here so you can jaw with him for a while. Now I would like to once again thank you all for coming, and if you'd like more information on joining the party and pledging your support, myself and Vonda will be staffing that table right there past the coffee urns. Less than six weeks to get out the darn vote!"

Guthrie saw Senator MacDougall bolting from his seat and moving with impressive speed to the side door entrance of the stage as Kent began walking off into the wings. An urgent conversation, it seemed.

Precisely three minutes later, the two flacks who had manned the doors were leading Kent through the crowd out on to the front steps of the Rotary Hall, where a pop-up banner emblazoned with the party's colours and a photo of the Prime Minister squinting in profile rippled in a gust of wind. The Prime Minister seemed to flinch in the cold. The flacks directed Kent to a spot in front of the banner that squarely framed him for the cameras. The scrum of reporters now circled in, blurting out their questions and jostling for position, and for the crusts of answers Kent was poised and ready to toss their way.

"Kent, did the Prime Minister tell you he'd be announcing his resignation today?"

"You've been a backroom guy for years, and now you're named as the outside leadership candidate given the two year run-up. Who's backing you, Kent?"

"Kent, are you already putting together a team for leadership?"

"Who's working with you Kent?"

Kent smiled, then he looked into the eyes of Graham Cousineau, sometime anchor for the national network, and he began with his prepared lines.

"No, not all Graham. And no, I have been focused solely on my efforts here In Argyle County for this by-election. Any talk of leadership is as much a surprise to me as it is to you."

The smallest ripple of laughter, coughed into shirt collars, went through the crowd. And with that, Guthrie watched Senator MacDougall, in his long, royal blue cashmere overcoat, turn from the scrum and begin to walk towards the parking lot. He stopped just once, hunching his shoulders, the lordly shape of his bulk and the flash of his gold signet ring under the streetlight signifying the mystery of these cabalistic codes of power and influence that always reduced Guthrie to a state of adolescent wonder. *What do these men know that I never learned?*

Yet as he walked to the parking lot, focused on getting in his car, lighting up, and driving for a bit while he started to write his piece in his head, he could see the interior light of a dusky grey sedan casting its glow over two figures. The hair caught the light and he realized it was Karen Brewin. It was not Finley in the driver's seat, though; it was Pastor Norris Arbic. The truck had not started yet, and the sudden click of a door shutting and the overhead light going out told Guthrie they were suddenly aware of people heading for their cars. The tensed way both of the silhouettes were now seated in this cab suggested they were having a very important conversation. In hushed tones, perhaps, but with a seriousness that took all their focus. That conversation with the Brewins, yeah, that could wait.

As he got into his car he knew he should just head home and begin to write this piece. Yet at the first intersection he turned towards Mill Road that led up to the escarpment. He felt like he just needed to drive with the music turned up, listening to each Mogwai track build and then implode into shattered fragments of wordless song through the fuzzed-out speakers of his car stereo. All he could think about was Annelie Danziger, her kohl eyed smile in an old Polaroid labeled "Film Shoot—Black Iris."

6.

FOR THE LANDSCAPE drawing exercise, Ms. Perham wrote on the board: "Do not fear mistakes. There are none."—Miles Davis. In the class, only Bella seemed to know who Miles Davis was, judging from the blank looks of everyone around her. She knew of him because her mother would play "Kind of Blue" and "In A Silent Way" in the kitchen now that she had decided she had time to take on the most difficult French recipes she could find. The Sunday night ritual included some kind of cocktail Tanis would pour for herself with that horrible Campari, kept in the cupboard above the refrigerator, and a lot of swearing, especially with the sauces. Still, Bella usually loved the end result, and she had come around to the Miles Davis as well. Yet she wasn't prepared to disclose this to anyone; she kept her hand down when Ms. Perham asked.

"Okay, doesn't matter who he is. I want you to remember this quote when you're out there. Just gift yourself with the confidence to draw blind at first, get the contours down on paper. Go for feel. I don't want perfection."

Gift yourself? Could you even say that? Maybe there actually are mistakes, Ms. Perham. Like, say hot pink streaks in your hair after forty. Still there was no need to be so critical; Ms. Perham was one of the good ones and she had just granted everybody fifty-one minutes outside the classroom. Bella could choose anywhere along the running trail behind the school to sketch, smoke, just be off alone by herself. Fucking awesome.

She hurried out of class and passed the cafeteria, so intent on getting some distance between the other kids with sketchbooks, all filing out into the courtyard in a general state of irritated befuddlement, that she did not get a glimpse of Carlene Dawson, Angie Brock and Brittany Lawrence. Bleacher girls: the ones who went to every Blades game, cheered on their boyfriends, like brothers to David Goring, the pack that once claimed Syd as one of their own. They were in the purple Sentra that Angie's dad had bought for her birthday, smoking, trying to come to a decision about taking the next period off and getting pumpkin spice lattes.

***

"Ladies … just look over there." Carlene pointed, with a stab of her DuMaurier Extra Light, at a figure moving quickly across the little screen of the window. "That's Bella."

"Shut. Up." Angie smiled, as if this moment had been, yes, gifted from the fates, uniting them in a sisterly bond. "Let's go."

They waited until Bella had walked through the parking lot and turned off behind the gym. Headed for the running trail, she had to be. If they hurried, they could get to the top of the ravine from the south exit of the school. They might even have to run but the exercise would be worth it. Might even be a warm-up for what could go down.

Angie was the first to crest the top of the ravine. With her volleyball player's height and broad shoulders, never mind the intense, dark eyed look she could throw you, she just naturally took on the role of the sentry, checking if the coast was clear and instructing any other kid who might be approaching this way after Bella that they could come no closer. If you were a boy and you objected, you risked the added threat of Angie's boyfriend, Dave Peller, hunting you down; Peller had over a hundred penalty minutes already and two game misconducts.

Carlene and Brittany calmly followed behind, their blonde hair tautly pulled back into ponytails, earrings and rings methodically taken off and stuffed in the front pockets of their spray-on jeans. They were ready for anything. It was all up to Bella as to how well or how badly this would go.

***

Bella had her ear buds in, blaring Against Me! and she had her gaze firmly set on the woodchip trail before her. It was just a honey blonde blur that appeared in the periphery first. Then it was Carlene's wide-eyed, angelic smile, her fingers delicately wrapped around the cord of Bella's ear buds. She yanked them out with one quick vicious pull.

"Hi, Isabella-bella. We're not disturbing you, are we?"

Brittany appeared on the trail just a couple of yards over Carlene's shoulder. Yet Bella could see, in how firmly Brittany planted herself on the trail, that she was ready to brawl if things went that way.

"What is it?"

"How come you've been so quiet since Sydney's funeral? It's like you're suddenly too good for everybody."

"Leave it alone, Carlene." Bella was doing her best to sound firm, confident, unafraid.

"It's like you've got a secret. A secret that you're only going to share with your fag friend Drew."

Carlene looked as if she was deeply and sincerely puzzled by Bella's behaviour. Then she paused and frowned, the disappointment in such an affront sinking in. She gave Bella a hard shove that sent her sprawling, her sketchbook sheets and pencils scattered in the mud. Brittany tittered and hurried to retrieve it all.

"Aw look, Carl. She drew Syd's gravestone."

"You fuck off, Brittany!" Bella sprung to her feet and lunged at Brittany, fist clenched and raised. Carlene calmly caught her wrist and shook her head. Bella could taste metal on the back of her tongue, feel her adrenalin coursing. And high up at the top of the ravine she could hear Angie Brock's "Do it now!"

"Here it is, girlfriend. We could so kick your ass but do you think we want to? It's just really simple. Out of respect for David ... for all that he's lost ... a child ... a future wife ... I need your solemn word you haven't been speaking to that faggot Drew, that you don't know where he is."

"Fuck you."

Carlene just gave Bella her feral glare, with the hint of a smile forming on her lips.

"You have been talking to him, haven't you? You've been keeping it a secret because you know David will fucking kill him. And my Brian, and Brittany's Ali and Angie's Dave will help. That's what's waiting for him. Why don't you tell him that?"

"Fucking kick the shit out of her, Carl. Let's get it done." Brittany lazily drawled from the edge of the trail, as if she was just suddenly bored by it all.

For a moment, Carlene seemed to be considering this. She tightened her grip on Bella's struggling wrist. And then she just smiled and laughed under her breath, releasing her. "No. Not going to give her an excuse to run to the cops. We know you lied to them but you better not lie to us. If you hear one word from that faggot, you tell us, right?"

Bella gently felt her wrist where Carlene had grabbed it. It felt hot to the touch, maybe a little bruised. It was all she could do, in complete humiliation, to nod in assent.

"So good then. That's all we need from you. For now."

Angie bent to pick up the sketchbook and pencils from where Brittany flung them. Like a ministering nurse she handed them to Bella. "There you go. Art therapy, girl."

Bella would not look up and acknowledge this as a moment of further ridicule. She just sat there, immobile until she heard their giggles fade, as they made their way up the ravine once more.

7.

THE COPS IN 52 Division downtown, where Ojal had earned her bars right out of police college, noticed how the streets had changed before everybody else. As Danny Fortune, the Detective Staff Sergeant who was still in so many ways her mentor had put it, "the interwebs has taken more trade off the streets than we ever could." Most of the prostitution and the drug deals—the messy transactional side of business as usual—now happened indoors. The wildlife on Jarvis and Sherbourne had been reduced to what Chief McVitie called a "core element." He had used this euphemism for the reporters in the room as he addressed Metro council, maybe to make it all sound manageable, but every cop who worked downtown had vivid images of what the core element was: the tweakers, the HIV infected, the paranoid-delusional. If you just looked at the stats, downtown had not been this safe in decades, but if you dealt with the humanity—say, the bare-chested crackhead screaming down Mutual on a morning when it was minus twenty , stats really didn't mean shit to you. The streets could be cold-hard vicious, and it seemed like nothing was going to make them better.

Which is why Ojal had feared for the worst when Danny Fortune called her to say "Hey, I think we found your kid Drew Trask this morning around Carlton and Parliament." If Drew did indeed have "substance issues," as his mother said in her interview with Ojal, two weeks in the company of the crackheads from that part of town would have taken its toll. In such a state the good people of Newton would have Drew convicted of manslaughter in their minds before the boy ever saw a courtroom.

So it was some relief to walk into the interview room downtown, paired up with the smiling Buddha himself, Staff Sergeant Freddie Aquino, and to find a calm, composed and frankly well put together Drew Trask on the other side of the table. Sure, Drew was a piece of work—diffident, full of himself, revealing nothing but a freshly inked tattoo on the inside of his wrist—but at least he would be able to put up a strong defense now that he was going to remain in custody on this criminal negligence charge. "That kid, he's a tricky fuck," Freddie had murmured to her, as they came out of their interview.

Bail is what Ojal had hoped for. She couldn't give a damn if she felt that racist vibe as Drew had given her the once-over, smirking disdainfully at her line of questioning, fixating on her running watch.

"Drew, why don't you tell me what you've been doing over the last few days here in the city?"

He bobbed his head to a song in his head, then warbled "Holiday" in falsetto.

You know we've got you on camera at the Stables. At the bus station buying a ticket. You don't think I looked at your record? You put yourself back in business, didn't you?

"I don't think I have to answer that."

The boy was at best an accessory; though it was now confirmed that Sydney OD-ed, Ojal's gut feeling was that it had made no difference at all whether the girl had gotten the oxys from Drew that night or from someone else weeks before. Sydney had been close to three months pregnant, pressured on all sides—from her boyfriend, from her parents—to do the wrong thing for herself. She had made up her mind that she was not coming back from the drive up to the lake.

Still Ojal would keep such thoughts to herself tonight as she sat across the table from Ian Guthrie. She owed Guthrie this meeting; she had promised that if Drew was found alive, she'd give him her first impressions, but solely on background. And yes, a drink with Guthrie was not the worst way to kill an hour on a Monday night. Out of all the journalists in town, the cops she worked with accorded him the most respect. His father had once been a Staff Inspector, and though the old man seemed to have ended his career in controversy, the "institutional memories" of him, as Constable Dan Goring put it, was that he was "a hard son of a bitch, a fucking legend." Guthrie had earned his own cred with those under her as well by writing a story a couple of years ago about a Staff Sergeant and reservist, Keith Lacey, who had come back from Afghanistan and been denied the benefits and treatment he deserved for his PTSD from the government. Guthrie was "on their side," and he had something of Danny Fortune's sly charm about him. There was a hard won wisdom in the look in his eyes. Yet in the awkward silences their conversations would sometimes descend into, she always feared he would ask her whether she was in a relationship or worse, he would ask her out.

They were to meet in the lounge of the Hampton Hotel— now called "The Games Room." Well past its good years, the Hampton was her choice because there was absolutely no possibility of any cops she worked with or anyone conscious of their image in town seeing them here. "Nobody squeals that you were in dive bars, it's alkie code of honour," was the way Danny Fortune put it to her, years ago; she liked to think she learned his lessons well. The anonymity was necessary because, regardless of the respect given Guthrie, the case against Drew Trask with Sydney's death was at a critical stage, and all she needed was to be seen as friendly with the local press for the beat cops who had it in for her, guys like Phelps, his pudgy little sidekick Anthony Giannone and even Dan Goring, to confirm for everyone at the station she could not be trusted.

When she came in through the back entrance, ten minutes late, it was some consolation that Guthrie was there in one of the back booths. He understood how careful she had to be. He already had a J and B in front of him and was reading a magazine, one that looked a little high toned for the Games Room.

"I hope I didn't keep you long."

"Just got here, no worries."

"What you reading?"

"This? Just ... an old friend's editing this magazine now. He's going to ask me what I think, so I better sound like I've read it."

She slid into the booth, her long, thin fingers making a quick, sweeping gesture across the table in front of her. She hated her hands; she feared they would end up like a crone's, just like her mother's. "Saw your piece on the Brewin case. Appreciate you keeping me out of the story, Ian."

"Of course. You called it on background."

"I wish I had more for you. Really. But thanks for not pushing on this with the families."

"Well ..."

"Well what?"

"I did talk to Karen Brewin. You know that, don't you? I mean I had to."

She blinked and nodded, her eyes firmly fixed on his. For a moment she seemed close to breaking into a grin but no, she wasn't going to give him that. "You've got to do your job. So there's nothing I can tell you about them, I guess."

"I didn't expect quite that much anger, did you?"

"You mean about Drew Trask."

"Karen Brewin hated that boy. It's like Sydney was just the sweetest, most innocent church going girl before she met him. I mean ... did you hear her at your town hall?"

"She's grieving. Looking for a reason anywhere she can find it."

"Well she's looking in the wrong place with Drew Trask, don't you think?"

Ojal smiled, looking squarely into Guthrie's eyes. As Lydia Chow, the frail old waitress glided past, Ojal waved her down. She ordered another J and B for Guthrie, and asked if it was possible to order a cranberry wine spritzer. That just made the old waitress crinkle up her nose. Ojal settled on a soda water and lemon, leaving Lydia to hobble away in her orthopaedic shoes, mumbling to herself. "What do you want me to tell you?"

"I guess just what you thought of him. You're the only one who's spoken to Drew since he was charged."

"I think he's a little shit, to be honest. He told me nothing."

"You pick up any sense he might have given Sydney those oxys and then walked away to let her die?"

"It's possible—and yes, that's criminal negligence. But I see no homicide motive there."

Guthrie nodded and looked to his periphery as if he was expecting someone to be approaching.

"I think you're absolutely right, Ojal. I believe they had both gone up to the lake, believing they would not return. Kid just lost his nerve, and jumped from the car before it dropped into the lake. And when he realized he couldn't save Sydney, he just ran."

"Uh huh. Well if he was feeling any anguish over it, he wasn't about to share it with anyone. Least of all me."

"I don't know. He was on his own, homeless in Toronto, was he not?"

Ojal smiled, play-acting serenity. She was watching Lydia Chow approach with the drinks on a tray. "I'll tell you what was interesting. He's got this new tattoo on the inside of his wrist. I suspect it's there to cover up the scar from his own suicide attempt."

"But you think it's some memento of Sydney?"

"I don't know. It's a black flower."

"A black iris?"

"Could be. I'm not a flower person. I've never been much of a girly girl. But I'd bet ..."

Guthrie leaned in over his drink and lowered his voice, as if he was revealing a secret. "Ojal, I think I've got something for you that might be of help in all this."

"What kind of help?"

"A friend of mine, Tanis Van Dyken, her daughter Bella had become very close with Sydney after she started turning from the church and that boyfriend of hers. She has given me emails where Sydney speaks of what she was thinking about her pregnancy and how difficult her life was before that night on the lake. Now, the interesting part . . . she also gave me a bundle of letters from her best friend from thirty years ago, Annelie Danziger. These are letters Tanis shared with Sydney and her daughter. Annelie Danziger killed herself. She OD-ed. She was pregnant at the time."

Ojal watched the way Guthrie was stirring his drink with the plastic straw. This all seemed to agitate him, as if he had some personal stake in the story.

"Uh huh. Why would your friend Tanis share all this with her daughter and Sydney?"

"You had to know Annelie Danziger. She was gifted. She had become interested in making movies, got herself a Super 8 camera and shot these incredible, arty little films. Sydney and Bella and Drew, they had all just bonded over all they were discovering in drama class, in listening to music. I mean you should read some of these emails. No texting for them—they're like letters from the nineteenth century."

"Of course they did. Drama queens. White kids in black clothes. Even I remember kids like that in high school."

"Ojal, I think there's something to all this." He reached down under the table and pulled out a black leather satchel that looked like it had been through a war. "I've been going through them all. There's a real connection. And I think it will make it very clear that Drew Trask had little, if anything, to do with what happened. Boy had his own suicidal thoughts."

Guthrie gently pushed the satchel across the table. Ojal's hand stopped it before it could cross the invisible border between Guthrie's past and her present.

"Ian, I can't take this."

"Ojal, I'm serious. Just read it all."

"Are you kidding? This is personal property. There's a Charter challenge all over this if I were to read even a few words."

"But you said yourself you don't think Drew's guilty of anything. I'm just giving you the kind of proof that allows you to push back ..."

"Push back? On what?"

"I was there at that crime town hall. It's clear they're putting a lot of pressure on you to ..."

"Pressure? No, Ian. There was no pressure. I was up there because I believed in every word I said. It's part of my job."

"To be politicized."

"You're telling me politics is not a part of my job? Hello? You think I'm oblivious as to why I got the job here when I left 52 downtown? Brown girl among the townie boys? Ian, please. Was politics not a part of your father's job?"

Guthrie leaned back. His brow knit, he was focused on the grain of the wood on the table. "I think he tried as much as possible to keep politics out of it."

"Your father got three guys above him dismissed, their names forever associated with a corruption scandal. If his goal was to keep politics out of his job, he failed miserably, my friend."

"I think he would have agreed with you, Ojal. I really do. He paid for it."

He was smiling and nodding, but she could tell she had wounded him. How does this happen? Every time it does, she knows she's going too far, and yet the words are already out of her mouth.

"Ian, look … I appreciate this. But you've got to understand … if I were to take what's in that bag, how much it would compromise me."

"I'm thinking it might help you, in the end. Ojal, this is me being helpful because if I help you, you help me. I mean, you get this, right? This is a transaction."

"I get this, yes. Ian, it's not a transaction I'm interested in, I'm sorry."

"I see. Me too." Guthrie nodded and pulled the satchel off the table. He hugged it closely to him in the booth, as if he had written all the pages himself.

"Ian, you know where all that belongs? It belongs in the office of Drew Trask's lawyer. I'm not suggesting it would be admissible, but …"

"Well … I've got to get to Drew first. The kid's not exactly available to the media."

"That may change. There's a bail hearing and from all I've heard, his father's got deep pockets and will be able to pay it."

Guthrie swallowed the last of his drink and swirled the two cubes in the glass like they were dice that had come up snake eyes. Guthrie was considering something, possibly the value of his wounded pride. He rolled up the magazine in his hands and tapped it on the table, as if he was signaling his exit.

"So like, soon?"

"Yup. Drew said he's flying in from Vancouver."

Guthrie reached into the front pocket of his jeans and pulled out a crumpled twenty, then slipped it like a love note under his empty glass.

"You think you could let me know?"

"I could, yes." She reached under the glass and slid the twenty back to Guthrie. It was almost a parody of the way he had slid his satchel across to her. "This one's on me, okay?"

"Oh no. I called you."

"And I'm going to call you, right? You can pay next time, after you get your interview and Drew tells you what really happened that night."

Guthrie rose from the table and gave her his weary smile. They were square once more. "If it were ever so easy, right?"

"Good night, Ian."

He nodded to her from the door with a little flourish that was almost charming, as he shrugged that old satchel up the slope of his shoulder. Maybe it was just the detective in her that caused her to wonder where he was off to now, what kind of home he went back to, a single man heading into middle age in this town. She waved down Lydia Chow for the bill as if she closed her eyes and willed away any further speculations about him.

8.

"I DIDN'T SAY anything about how the piece was written," Bruce Gallant finally stopped glancing over at whatever was on his computer screen and leaned forward. He was sitting in his new, ergonomically fitted office chair of molded plastic. It was quite possibly the ugliest piece of office furniture Guthrie had ever seen. "Did I give you that impression?"

"No, not at all."

"I thought it was competently done."

"Competently?"

"That's right."

"Thank you. That's something, I suppose."

"It's something but it wasn't enough for me to run it."

"And why was that?"

"Are you worried you're not going to get paid? Is that it?" Gallant was fumbling with the cufflinks in his shirt as he spoke. Two eight balls that shone like cat's eyes. There was something about this conversation that merited a rolling up of the sleeves for him. "You wrote the piece on deadline and I'm a man of my word."

Just the very thought of not being paid unsettled Guthrie but he was determined not to show it. On one sleepless Sunday night he had added up how much he could live on, calculating what was left from the six-figure settlement his father was awarded from his lawsuit against the force, Guthrie's own RRSPs, the sale of the house. If he made it to seventy-five or so, he might just avoid poverty. Still he needed at least a couple grand coming in each month Guthrie watched Gallant's eyes dart again over at the screen. What the hell was he looking at, porn?

"Bruce, I just want to know what the problem was."

Gallant sighed, ran one hand through his haircut. Vote-for-Quayle-in-'88. A good look for him. "The problem? The problem was the angle you took with the town hall, Ian."

"The angle? Those were direct quotes. I did not embellish here."

"Well, Toronto wouldn't like that tone."

"Is it the angle or the tone, then? Come on, Bruce. This can't be that hard."

"You have, in your own reading, taken a look at the new names on the masthead for the chain? You have recognized some names on that board, I'm thinking."

"What are you trying to tell me, Bruce? I'm working for these guys?"

"I believe you're not technically working for anybody. Your choice."

"No one but the readership out here."

"Such as it is." Gallant leaned back in the chair and for a moment his brow collapsed into contemplation. A memory of the chair giving him whiplash, perhaps. Then his moment of worry passed as the chair eased farther back.

"No one's ever pulled a piece of mine before."

"You've never written about the government with that tone, to my recollection."

"You realize what you're saying."

"I'm saying I'm not running the Socialist Worker, yeah."

Guthrie smiled, looking for a flicker of acknowledgment in Gallant's stare. "A little back story, Bruce. Kent Wolseley and I grew up together. He was my best friend until I was eighteen years old."

And now Gallant smiled. "Okay, then. You're jealous. I mean, I'm no psychologist but it reads like you're jealous of the success he's had."

"Jealous? I'm trying to tell you I went as easy as I could on Kent."

Gallant looked to the rafters, the exposed beams he'd requested with the reno job of the offices. "I'm going to say something here. Totally candid, okay?"

Guthrie nodded. His gaze went to the armrest of Gallant's chair, which had a distended loop of plastic affixed to it. A mug holder, it seemed. Bruce Gallant drank green tea. Perhaps Bruce was a much better husband and father now that he quit drinking.

"Look, I don't know the details of the settlement your old man got from the Crown. I'm just going from what I've heard."

"Really. Okay, Bruce. So what have you heard?"

"Don't get your back up, Ian. Your father was highly respected and you ... you know everybody thinks you can be a damn fine writer when you want to be. I'm saying nobody disrespects ..."

"Where are you going with all this?"

"Look ... you've seen how things have changed around here. I mean they've thrown more money at us with this reno job, got me on these useless conference calls twice a week about the digital strategy, but they've shut down four papers in the last year up north. Ad revenues are in the tank. I'm saying there's a lot that no one feels they have any control over right now so, you know ..."

"I don't know, actually. I'm serious, Bruce."

"So they micromanage. They start worrying about stuff they really shouldn't."

"Like what I'm writing."

"They don't need to piss off the government right now, Ian. Don't know if you know this but the Toronto media's not exactly on the Prime Minister's Christmas card list."

Guthrie leaned forward and put his hand on Gallant's desk. Gallant tensed up, roused from his orthopedically correct reclining position. "Bruce. It was a town hall, for Christ sakes. A town hall with some shit talker from Ottawa that nobody really cares about. And I say that and I know Kent. I'd say it to his face and he'd probably agree."

"I know, I know … my point is this. There's a lot of bullshit to my job, okay? But I've got a mortgage and a daughter who's going to Mac next year. You … from what I heard … with that settlement …"

"You're thinking I don't need this gig. I've got my dad's house, no family, cash in the bank …"

"I'm just saying it's a great thing to be proud. And you've got a lot to be proud about."

"You firing me? I mean technically you can't."

"No! No, all I'm saying is that …" Gallant looked down at white crescents under his finger nails. "I guess I'm just suggesting, as a colleague and friend, because I'd like to call you a friend … I guess I'd be asking myself, if I were you, if I really need this."

Guthrie smiled, looked down at his hands in his lap, and he realized how vulnerable he suddenly seemed. He could not be called a young man any more. After close to three decades of putting one word in front of the other, he could not respond convincingly. *Do you really need this?*

"Bruce, we've known each other, what, six years now?"

"Sounds about right."

"I think we both came in here and wondered what the hell we got ourselves into, wondered if we really wanted to spend the last ten or twenty years of our working lives out here, because there was no going back to the city."

Gallant picked up a pen on his desk and balanced it on the backs of his fingers. "Can't say I'm sure about that now. Jury's out."

"Bruce, I'm saying we both want to write well and to read something we'd read ourselves. Am I wrong? That's what I tried to do for that piece on the town hall."

Gallant rose and turned from Guthrie. It was true, you could tell more about how a man lived when he had his back to you. Gallant's starched, vanilla coloured shirt draped loosely to minimize the paunch, making it look as if he had new volume, cut a more substantial figure in middle age. He was trying to peer out from the blinds. He had to know he'd be looking out at the alley. His shoulders slumped as he exhaled. "What do you want me to tell you? You can write on anything you like, you just can't cover the by-election, all right?"

"That's what Toronto told you?"

"That's what I'm telling you." He turned and glanced over at his computer screen again, perhaps looking for his actor's lines there. "The piece you did on the Brewin murder …"

"No one's calling that a murder."

"No one but her parents and Kent Wolseley, right? That piece was very good. You should stay on that. I think a lot's going to happen in the next couple of weeks now that Trask has been found."

"You kept my desk."

"What?"

"With the reno job here. You kept my desk. You didn't have to do that. I wanted to thank you, Bruce."

"You're welcome. We should have a couple of interns in here after January so you may have to share it. But it's fine for now."

Guthrie rose from his chair and reached for his coat. Gallant had insisted he hang it on the new rack by his door. The rack gave the room "a little character," he said. "Just one thing, Bruce. Just for clarity. Did you actually flip my piece to anybody in Toronto before you decided to pull it?"

Gallant blinked but his expression remained unchanged, impassive. You could still see the freckled boy in him though his skin had aged from too much time in the sun. His golf pro years. When he reclined in that ugly chair and closed his eyes, did he see himself on courses he played? Everybody's got a landscape they go to in their mind, Tanis said.

"I did, yes. I don't send anything up the chain as a rule, but they asked."

"They asked."

"That's right."

"Who's they?"

"Don't get paranoid. It's not important."

"Uh huh. Well thanks for being straight with me."

Gallant just nodded, his gaze now directed at the door, like a finger pointing to where he needed Guthrie to be now. Guthrie obliged.

9.

DAVID GORING CAME into the police station with his father, Constable Dan Goring. Through the glass wall of her office window Ojal watched the two of them amble through the foyer entrance, the boy trailing two steps behind his father. Seeing how alike they were, Ojal thought of how attractive Dan Goring must have been in high school, forty pounds lighter, without the squarish military haircut, the thick neck and double chin he'd acquired from fifteen years of driving a cruiser around town. Dan solemnly nodded to everybody en route to the interview room as father and son made it through the hub—the maze of cubicles where the exercise yard once was in this old jailhouse building. The boy managed a smile, tight lipped and gracious, for all the words of condolence he received as they made their way from desk to desk. Ojal could see Bridget Norton, one of the dispatchers, rise from her seat and embrace the boy, her purple cardigan stretched tightly around her arms and hips as she pulled him close, her cheeks suddenly flushed and streaked with tears.

Ojal would be going in interview room #4 with the tape recorder and Constable Brian Phelps, who was the first one to receive the call from Karen Brewin that her daughter was missing. Phelps was no Freddie Aquino, that was clear; he didn't have his wit or his cagey, soft-spoken intelligence. No, Phelps was a tight-assed farm boy who had to let her know, in the first ten minutes of meeting her, he once qualified for the Olympic team for the ten thousand metres—perhaps because Ojal said she ran marathons when she spoke at the Kinsmen's club. Even in their morning meetings he was always squaring his shoulders and sucking in his paunch to summon up some of his preening old glory. As they spoke about the interview with David

Goring this morning he was giving her nothing. There would be these pregnant pauses followed by him playing dumb—"I don't see why we would ask him that, with all respect, Inspector." *With all respect*—try with all contempt. Phelps had known Dan Goring since the two of them were eight years old, he was going to make damn sure the report would say his buddy's kid was nothing but Sydney's wholesome, bright eyed boyfriend who was powerless to stop the girl's corruption from the decadent influences of Drew Trask and this Isabella Lang.

David Goring was sitting at the far end of the table, trying out an adult posture, with his hands folded in front of him, just a bit too neatly composed, as he spoke with Phelps. Far be it for the Constable to wait for her so they would enter together. No, Phelps had his ass on the table as if it was a hockey bench, which was appropriate, given the two of them were talking about how the Newton Blades were looking this year. As David glimpsed Ojal at the door he rose from the long conference table.

"Please ... don't get up, David."

"Staff Inspector ..."

"Let me say how I sorry I am. I know you and Sydney were very close."

She moved towards him as he frowned into his lap and pulled in his chair. With his tousled hair and slender frame he was the perfect teenage crush. Ojal understood why a girl like Sydney Brewin could suddenly find herself in love and expecting this boy's child.

"You know about how she was ... I mean that she was going to ..."

"You mean the pregnancy? Of course. I just couldn't understand how she turned away from all we had." He shook his head, gazing down at a fixed point on the floor. "I was ready. We were both ready for our life together. With the baby."

"David, it's okay," Phelps said.

"David, I spoke with Sydney's mother. She told me all about it. Nobody's blaming you for what was going on in her head, believe me." Ojal could feel Phelps's gaze on her, watching her closely for anything he could report back to Dan Goring.

David finally looked up at Ojal to detect if she was sincere. He squinted and grimaced, as if just the moment of connection was too much of a threat to his composure. Ojal reached out and gently touched his forearm before she could check the impulse.

"I loved her. It was her choice not to love me back anymore."

"David, I don't think you can know that she didn't love you anymore. She was very confused and overwhelmed …"

He rubbed his eyes with his thumb and index finger, let a sniffle escape and refocused on Ojal, with his arms folded, defiant. "You talked to Trask?"

"Andrew Trask? Yes, we did."

"And what did he say?"

"He's a little scared to talk about how this could have happened. You're friends?"

Dan looked over at Phelps and they both, for the briefest of moments, gave each other the same sly grin. "Friends? No, I don't think you'd be calling Drew Trask and I buddy pals."

"So you blame him for this. You think he …"

"Put it this way. Syd was as normal as you or me until she and Bella started …"

"Isabella Lang."

"She and Bella started hanging around that freak. You know he's dealing drugs. I told Dad and he says they couldn't put him away because he was a minor at the time. Even though he failed a grade because he can't read right. He's a year older than us, prac'lly able to drink in bars. Anyway … it's just … fucking freak …" He ran his thumb sharply now over the table's edge.

"David, I know you're angry about this. We're all sad and upset."

He looked up from the table and gazed into Ojal's eyes for the first time. And then something seemed to lock and harden within him. His lips began to move as if he was about to speak, then like a tremor the words passed back into silence. He just broke into a grin.

"You've talked to him, haven't you? You know he's going to lie to you. And Bella, she's going to lie to you. That's what they do. They just live in lies because they hate the truth about themselves."

"And Sydney. David, what do you think Sydney hated about the truth?"

"Syd liked to write stuff. Like all girls do, I guess. Her journal. She never showed me none of it. I never asked."

"But weren't you curious? I mean, she was probably writing about you, don't you think?"

"I guess I was curious, sure. I looked one afternoon, when she left her bag in my dad's car. Maybe I got the wrong book but there was just some kind of story in it, and sketches of girls that kind of looked like her ... only with bigger, darker eyes, longer hair. And an evil kind-of-Jesus looking guy. I couldn't make any sense of it."

"But you never asked her about it. I mean, it didn't seem weird?"

"No! Syd liked to draw. She liked to act. I mean, that's why she started hanging around with those two ... in the drama elective. Trask and Bella. Fucking Drac and Drella."

"And what did you think about that?"

"I told her it was fucked up. I told her people would start thinking she was a freak too."

Ojal bit her bottom lip and pulled her chair in closer. "David, I need to ask you this, and I know and respect that this is highly personal ... please understand, this is only for the case we're putting together."

"The case to put Trask away?"

"We can't know that yet. No one can," said Phelps. He nodded to Ojal, as if he had gallantly stepped in to offer some guidance.

"David, was there anything that happened between Sydney and you, after she discovered she was pregnant …"

"Anything that happened?"

"An argument … a violent argument. David, were you ever violent with Sydney?"

David smiled, then he slowly nodded to himself, staring at the small recording device on the table. "No. Never."

"Okay. Thanks. I just had to ask."

"Did fucking Bella tell you that?"

"No. It's simply a line of questioning. I've got to look for every motive here."

"Uh huh. I guess I wouldn't put it past her. Or Trask. Drac and Drella."

He shifted in his chair, his hands now flat on the desk. Big hands and thick wrists, the hands of the man he would be in a few years. Townie.

"Okay. Constable Phelps, unless you have any further questions, I believe that's all for today."

Phelps put a hand on David's shoulder and then the two shuffled out of the interview room. She could just make out Phelps mumbling something to David as they made their way down the hall.

She needed to talk to Danny Fortune tonight. They were out to get her from all sides out here in this fucking farm town, how was she supposed to perform? It's not as if Danny would have any answers, but he wouldn't offer any; he would just listen and understand.

Ojal watched father and son in the foyer by the doors as Phelps made his exit. Dan Goring clearly wasn't going to wait until the end of his shift to find out how it had gone; he met his son in the hub and walked him to the doors. He stood with his back to Ojal and the ladies in the hub, his hands at his hips, tugging on the thick black belt with his gun holster. The son nodded as he stared into the tiles. From where Ojal stood this looked like a moment drained of any consolation or affection, a directive flatly delivered to a diffident, younger version of the same self. The way both stood, they looked as if they had come to an uneasy truce.

Ojal felt as if she wanted to embrace the boy, protect him from whom he was becoming. She turned away, let the feeling dissolve within her, and walked back into the grey half-light of her office.

10.

I FIRST MET Kent Wolseley when we were both boys. It was at what could be considered a political event, appropriately enough. The Trudeau government had planned a journey of the National Dream train from coast to coast in summer, and it was scheduled to go right through our town one Saturday in July, just days after what we then called Dominion Day. In the centre of Newton, just a block up the Main Street from the Town Hall, a gazebo had been erected and Mayor Larry Coulter and our local Liberal MP Frank Laudermilch were going to give speeches on the importance of the train's journey in bringing together communities from across the country. It would be a summer of national pride and recognition "for our pioneering spirit and bold vision for a united Canada."

I suppose in most towns Kent and I would not have met and become friends. I was the only child of a cop and his bank teller wife, raised in a bungalow in a neighbourhood in Newton where the majority of fathers worked at the auto parts factory in town or at the truck plant down by the lakeshore. Kent was literally from the other side of the train tracks.

That split down the centre of Newton by social class was a relatively recent development then. The town had remained what we then called working class from its very beginnings, with a steady labour pool for the quarry and for Ridley Auto Parts coming from the farming communities and from the immigrants moving out of Toronto. The promise of affording your own home on union wages was real and fulfilled. Then in the early seventies a professional class started buying up the Victorian and Georgian style manors, row houses and cottages in the older part of town. There were young doctors, dentists and lawyers, as well as some of the high-earning bankers and senior managers who worked in Toronto and had realized Newton was still within an hour's drive of the city and the town's heritage properties were a steal. They took what were once derelict rooming houses and "hotels" and completely transformed the interiors, restoring the large rooms on the main floors to their original dimensions.

With the exteriors, they laid down sod, landscaped and gardened, petitioned for new sidewalks where the oaks that lined the streets had to be close to a century in the ground. But what was good for one side of the tracks was good for the other in those days before the parts factory closed its doors and the auto plant went down to one rather than three shifts a day; growing up you did not feel a divide between the well off and those barely making it. Everybody still had a reason to come down to the centre of town on a summer morning and wave their free Canadian flag, compliments of the Bank of Commerce, as the National Dream train stopped at the old station.

Some fifty yards up the tracks, where the route curved behind a tall row of Spruce pines, I had glimpsed a couple of boys I knew from school. I was bored—the arrival of the train was still an hour away—and curious as to what they were up to so I wandered off in their direction.

It was there I first saw Kent Wolseley. He was dressed in spotless tennis whites while we were in cut-off shorts and t-shirts. He had in his hands a row of firecrackers. He was instructing my friends on how to lay them along the rails so the fuses would ignite on impact. Glistening on both rails were lines of Centennial silver dollars that Kent told us would melt and bend beyond recognition under the wheels of the train. How did this boy know these things? And why had we just let him lead us into this mischief? You could say that Kent Wolseley had a sense of his destiny from an early age.

"That's how you'll start the piece?"

"After the general introduction, yeah."

"Hmm." Stephen Clarke let the steeple of his fingers collapse and folded his hands across his knee. The crease in his grey flannels was as sharply defined as the line of his salt and pepper beard along his chin. He leaned back from the table between them, his gaze taking in the framed photographs of Joyce and Yeats on the lemon yellow wall behind Guthrie and a brief, doleful moment of reflection dimmed the blue of his eyes. Age was toughening him, giving him the aura of an ascetic despite his best efforts to maintain that look of a dandified accountant he'd cultivated for years. "There's a lot of you in here. You know that's never been my cup of tea."

"I felt it was necessary. I mean, I'm declaring my biases in a way. Biases shaped over time."

"Do you remember back in … must have been ninety-six or so … Frawley had just settled in then … when he sent 'round that memo announcing Lara Barber would have a column in the Saturday paper?"

Guthrie buried his frown in the foam of his Guinness. This was what you had to expect when you took Stephen for drinks: the old bitterness. He had been out of the Standard for more than a decade now and had landed well with St. James media down the street. After toiling on the Business Report he had made his way back into solid respectability with his editor's job at the Torontonian. Sure, the magazine's best years were behind it, with its ads for retirement living and sensible travel clothing, but Stephen had kept it close to running in the black when everyone had predicted he would run it into the ground—and those were Stephen's words, allowing himself a rare turn of cliché. He could now afford to be a little generous about the provincialism and the errors in judgment of his peers. Still, it remained a precarious market in forgiveness here in the city, and Clarke was not about to dip in to his reserves at his age.

"Lara … what happened to Lara Barber?"

"The woman was barely out of university and Frawley imagined that readers would care about her diary entries. Why I was sulking at a party. Why I was sulking at an art opening."

"They did though, didn't they? I mean, people read her."

"Yes. And then they didn't, Ian. In fact the whole paper lost a little more of its staying power with a wager on the trivial. As is the way, it seems."

"You think I'm doing a Lara Barber here?"

Stephen squinted and glanced out the window by their table, as if he was struggling to recognize some memory through the grey sheet of rain. "She's a blogger now, isn't she? Writes about nappies and nursery schools."

"So this part about Kent and me as boys. It's trivial?"

Stephen cradled his glass and considered the colour. A little like honey, a little like Venice turpentine. As was his counsel.

"You've only got so many words, even in a magazine piece."

"I do, yes. But here's why it's important. I'm not just talking about Kent. I'm talking about the way my town has changed over the years, and how Kent's politics reflect that."

"As your politics do in kind, I'm guessing."

"I need to declare my biases."

Stephen crossed his legs and fidgeted with a coaster now, watching the letters T-E-N-N-E-N-T-S turn like spokes on a wheel. It always had to be this bar. In all their conversations over the years, Guthrie realized he and Stephen had never once talked about Stephen's childhood in Dublin. The past that Stephen shared began with London and his years at the Guardian and the New Statesman. Even what remained of his accent seemed safely anglicized. Yet he still insisted on coming here if they met, still ordered the Jameson's and kept his cards close to his chest like an old priest.

"This is new, isn't it? Your interest in politics. Is it living out there that's doing it to you?"

"I was always interested in politics."

"Then why did you spend so much time in the pansy patch? You could have done city desk. I would have put in a word."

"I was young and stupid. But I remember even you telling me that there are worse reasons to write than believing it might get women to notice you."

"I did not have a clue what you were going on about in those music reviews."

"The pretty women didn't either, if that's any consolation."

Stephen grinned, then he stroked his beard as if to conceal it. "Explain to me again why a five thousand word piece on an obscure politician is of interest."

"He's not obscure, Stephen. All the media and the money men know this guy and so do a great many who still read the Torontonian. It's TV. Remember that box in your house that you never turn on?"

"I'll have you know I have a flat screen."

"Whatever that might mean, right?"

"I'll tell you when I figure out how to turn it on."

"The point being he's been groomed for years. Ran an NGO out in Alberta, just like this Prime Minister of ours."

"What was he doing out there?" Stephen put his hands on the papers in front of him. "Or is that a stupid question."

"I would explain in the full piece. It's his father—his real father—who set him up there, introduced him to Dan Valgardson."

"Whom I should know."

"Oil guy. Was an MP for a few years back in the Reform days."

"You'd contextualize all this of course. I mean if I can't remember ..."

"Of course, of course."

"You'd work with Linda."

"Seligman? She at the Torontonian?"

"No, we can't afford her. She's been retired from the Standard but I'll be damned if I'd give a piece like this to one of these kids on the payroll. You'll need a real editor."

"So you'll give this a shot."

"Not quite so fast, Ian. I need to know you'll get full access."

"Of course I'll get full access. He's my oldest friend."

Stephen fixed his glare on Guthrie. "Except his people are already aware of you and shut one of your stories down, did they not?"

"Not exactly."

"No? Then what were we talking about on the way here? I mean, frankly I find it quite incredible but I've learned to suspend my disbelief in recent years." He downed the last of his whiskey and his eyes narrowed. "Ian, why do you want to do this piece? Really."

Guthrie had to look away from that gaze and choose his words as wisely as possible.

"All right. You want the honest truth? There's not just one answer. I mean, I knew you were going to ask me this. If I were to write a hatchet job, there will be those in Newton who have known both Kent and I since we were boys and who will assume it's my act of revenge on a rival, one who became far more successful than I ever could."

"Rival?"

"There was a girl when we were younger . . . it's not important . . ."

"And maybe I want to write it out of anger for what Newton's become, what Kent represents, but I like to think I'm smarter than that . . . a better journalist than that."

"If I thought that was your motive we wouldn't still be talking."

"Stephen, you don't have to say that to me. We've known each other too long.

But I realize no one really thinks of me as a legitimate journalist at all anymore. I'd be lying if I told you the idea of a guy like Bruce Gallant sitting in that editor's chair, telling me what I can't write didn't affect me."

"Now I remember where I heard of him. My God, yes . . . he was a summer student at the Standard. Mississauga Fats."

"Was he fat back then?"

"No, not really. There was some movie out that year with Tom Cruise as a pool shark. We called Bruce Gallant Mississauga Fats because he would bring a pool cue into work. Had this little leather case for it, like a flute."

"Yup. That sounds like the Gallant I know. He was the same with his golf."

"I don't know anything about his golf, but with the billiards he said he played in a league. We all suspected he just went off by himself each night in the hope that some young woman would find him interesting and mysterious."

"I'm going to call him Mississauga Fats."

"You won't."

"No, I wouldn't want him to think I gave him that much thought. But the truth is I do think I've never really written something to my full potential. I have no business thinking I am any better than Bruce Gallant." Guthrie watched Stephen's hand go to his beard as he tried to formulate a diplomatic argument in his defense. "It's true, you don't have to bullshit me, Stephen."

"You had opportunities."

"I know. And I fucked up. I underperformed."

"Don't come to me for approval or forgiveness or whatever sentimental notion you have in your head. I'm not interested. This is simple, Ian. If you think you can give me value for money and deliver a good piece in a month, I'm willing to pay you for it."

"That's exactly what I'm telling you. That's my real reason." Guthrie drained his glass and resisted the impulse to break into a grin. Stephen had given him an opening and he had played it well, but there was no reason to push it.

"When will this by-election be over?"

"Twenty-first of November."

"And you're sure he'll win."

"Without question."

"I'll need your piece that second week of November for Linda so we can run it for the December issue. The thirteenth is the Friday, appropriately enough. No later."

"That works, Stephen."

"Yes. It has to." Stephen uncrossed his legs and reached for his wallet, his eye on the waiter three tables away.

Ian, why do you want to write this piece? Really. As Guthrie drove up Yonge to head back to Newton, he couldn't stop himself from reviewing the answer he gave. Yes, it was really quite forthright in comparison to how he would have stumbled through such a question from Stephen years ago. Guthrie slipped through the traffic with a quick touch on the accelerator, pleased with himself that age and his time in exile out in Newton had provided him with candour and steadiness when the stakes were higher than he could ever admit. And yet, despite how articulate he had managed to be, the answer wasn't quite the full story, was it?

He reached down and grabbed his battered little BlackBerry. Now that the traffic had filled in and turned Yonge into a parking lot, he couldn't resist scrolling through his contacts. Evenson ... Farrell ... Francis. Scottie, my man. Scottie would be up for a drink this week. Ever since Guthrie had seen him walking with Ojal up at Lake LeSueur he'd been meaning to call him. Why not now?

11.

IT WAS ON her way out of the gurdwara, the smell of rice on the boil in the langar making her acutely aware of her hunger, when Ojal felt the old woman's hand on her wrist. In the delicacy of the touch and the soft lilt of the voice, she knew it had to be one of her mother's friends.

"Hello, auntie. How nice to see you here."

"Ojal, how are you, girl? And how is Rupinder with the diabetes?"

Manvir. Though that famous thick black hair of hers had gone grey and she looked like she had gained about thirty pounds, one look at the smile and those stunning green eyes of Manvir Kaur made Ojal feel like she was still a girl, back in Scarborough suffering through another village party.

"She's fine, auntie. Medication's helping."

"Ah good, good. Ojal, I want you to meet someone here. Come …"

And so Ojal let herself be towed along. It didn't matter how far you were from home, how old you were, how accomplished you had become, at the hands of the aunties you were always sixteen years old. That is, if you still were desirable but not yet married. She felt that same urge to scream build up in the back of her throat.

Manvir led Ojal into the vestibule where everyone was putting on their shoes. Yes, there was a man. Of course there was. But there was also a little girl in this man's arms, and now, as he turned to hand the child over, glimpsing Ojal approaching, there was also quite clearly his wife.

"Ojal, this is my nephew Jagdeep, his wife Amrit and this, hello little one! This is Jhoat."

"Sat Sri Akal … hello …"

"Ms. Dhillon. Very pleased to meet you …"

His hand was warm and strong in hers. Thick, broad shoulders in this beautifully tailored charcoal grey suit. Manvir's nephew Jagdeep … she never even mentioned him when it might have mattered.

"I saw you speak at the crime town hall. Amrit and I …"

"Hello … Sat Sri Akal…"

"Hello."

Amrit must have been quite beautiful before she got those glasses.

"Amrit and I, we were there. Really impressed by what you had to say."

"Well, thank you, I …"

"I wonder if we could talk. You see I'm running …"

"Jagdeep's running to be MP, Ojal," said Manvir, her eyebrows arching as if she was poised to announce this for the world. "He's going to win."

"I'd like to speak to you, and just get your thoughts on the crime prevention agenda here in town. It would be totally private, you wouldn't have to get involved with the campaign in any way. Would that be a conversation we could have?"

Her gaze went from his eyes to his chest as she nodded. She was so composed and professional, so completely the Staff Inspector in this moment. "I suppose that would be all right, yes." But what was she to do about the way her heart had begun to pound, the sweat she could feel in the palms of her hands?

12.

KENT WOLSELEY'S CAMPAIGN office occupied the last vacant lot in a strip mall just off the last highway exit into town. There was a Walmart, a Chapters and a new Canadian Tire and then nothing but tufted rows of balding sod and a scattering of maple saplings that marked the distance between the parking lots. A few had plastic bags stuck in their branches, fluttering like old flags in the wind. The autumn blasts had puckered and bent a line of Kent's campaign signs that marked the road back onto the highway.

There had been signs of the other parties' candidates out here at one time over the past two weeks, but they had disappeared just a day earlier, Gallant reported. He spoke of Jeannie Pincott, Kent's campaign manager, as strenuously denying any wrongdoing. "That's not how we play. If I ever heard of anyone on our team involved in that kind of mischief, they'd be gone." Gallant had edited out the expletives as well as Jeannie's proud declaration that she was from Truro, Nova Scotia where "ass kickings were free for that type thing."

The store lot where the campaign office was had weathered a few businesses over a decade; it was most recently a shop for bridal gowns called "Sposa Bella," run by Frank Tonelli's daughter Sophia. Frank owned the mall among his many properties out by the highway. Father and daughter shut it down with little more than a shrug after six months; it was a tax write-off for the Tonelli empire, and now Frank was happy to take the thousand dollar cheque he received for the rent from Kent's campaign and turn it right back into a donation. There was still a line of Corinthian pillars that led to the bathroom and panels of smoked glass along the back wall. An SP remained visible on the sign out front, jutting out from behind the flapping blue canvas of the Win

With Wolseley banner, stretched so tightly that it made Kent's smile look maniacal.

Now there were four rows of banquet tables, occupied by what looked like grad students who had slept in their chinos and button downs. They had laptops in front of them, murmuring on phones. Further back, loitering by the table near the boxes of Timbits and the urns marked "coffee" and "chai" with masking tape were the local constituents and volunteers: the grandmothers in hockey jackets and pearls, the middle-aged men with the telltale footwear of security guards between shifts. There was a map of the riding that took up twice the space of the Roman panorama that once graced the wall, then list after list of neighbourhoods to canvas, posted in fluttering rows like want ads on a bulletin board. There was an odd sense of quiet, considering how many people were milling around, as if everyone was poised for an announcement.

The "taxi guys" was the campaign euphemism for the bearded men in turbans who were now loading up the backs of three pick-up trucks with stacks of signs. Jeannie Pincott had the drivers in conference as she handed out lists and maps, rattling off directives like a hockey coach. Guthrie had heard from Gallant that Jeannie had a storied reputation from many campaigns as an enforcer who terrorized underlings, yet from here she looked all down home charm with her auburn curls, dressed in bonspiel cardigan and Mom jeans. She could have been a chubby captain of a curling team. The drivers towered over her, nodding solemnly, with quick, flitting glances at the two younger men heaving the last of the signs into each truck.

Guthrie waited until the group of drivers headed for their trucks before he approached Jeannie. She was already bustling along like a field marshal, gaze fixed on her BlackBerry that she had yanked from her cardigan pocket. Of course she had seen Guthrie, as she had reflexively turned her back to him when in conference with the drivers, but everything about her movements now told him he was not going to get a cordial greeting.

"Excuse me, are you Jeannie?"

"Yup. You're the reporter?"

"I am, yes. Ian Guthrie. I'm an old friend of Kent's ..."

"What happened to the other guy?"

"The other guy?"

"From the paper here. There was another guy."

"Bruce. You mean Bruce Gallant."

She finally looked up from the little screen in her hands and glanced at Guthrie with just the trace of a smirk. Despite her brusqueness, Guthrie could discern how carefully and expensively she was put together, with pearls and the flash of a platinum watch under the cuff of her cardigan.

"Sure. Whoever. He came and asked me about the signs. I'm not going to go through that again, am I?" She was moving fast, making a determined effort to have him struggle to keep up as she headed back inside the building. "Because if you'd think we're that dumb ..."

"I really didn't want to ask you about any campaign signs, Ms. Pincott."

"Then what are you here for?" She had stopped by the table and made a show of examining a small white box by the Timbits, still tied with string.

"I was hoping I could speak with Kent. We're old friends."

"Kent's got a lot of old friends. They're helping out on the campaign."

Guthrie watched her fingers work the knot in the string. Her nails were bitten down.

"I believe that would be a conflict of interest."

"Oh my God ... who brought the cannoli? Is this from Masciantonio's?"

A few of the volunteers at the banquet tables glanced back at Jeannie, unsure what or whether to answer.

"They are. Yeah, they're definitely Masciantonio's."

Jeannie was too enraptured by the first bite of the pastry to nod in acknowledgement. "Oh my Jesus, that's the real ricotta, kids."

"Ms. Pincott …"

"Jeannie."

"Jeannie, I'm going to ask Kent for a bit of his time. And if he says yes, I will be making a nuisance of myself around here."

She moved on from the table, cannoli in hand, as she looked over all the fluttering lists on the walls. She would still not meet his gaze.

"You can imagine how this really works, right? You gotta know anything you ask Kent, he's going to ask me, then I take it up the chain if I'm good with it."

"This is what I figured, yes. That's why I thought I'd come down here rather than meeting Kent on my own. Just so you know who I am."

"Good. Smart."

"Thank you." Guthrie grinned like he was one of her kids at the banquet tables. There was something about her disdain that he almost found charming. So much of it seemed a performance for the people in the office that he couldn't take it seriously.

"So what's your angle going to be?"

"It would be a profile for the Torontonian."

"For the Torontonian? This is Newton. This isn't Toronto."

"No. That's true. It's definitely not Toronto."

And at this she looked him over at last, from his scuffed boots to the width of the lapels on his blazer.

"Well, talk to Kent. See what he says first. If he can make a case for it, I can make a case for it."

"Would he be around?"

"What, you mean in the office?" She gestured across the tables, now speaking at a volume that all could hear. "Every minute that Kent's not out talking to voters is a minute this campaign never gets back."

"I understand he's busy."

She had already turned from him.

"I'm going to call Luch, see where they are."

She paced in front of the window mumbling into her collar while Guthrie stood in the middle of the office, an abandoned dance partner. He looked down at the little black notebook in his hands. What a pathetic affectation, an artifact from another time, it suddenly seemed. While Jeannie walked by the window she nibbled away at the cannoli. One bite, then another … by the time she was licking off the icing sugar on her fingers she was making for the door again.

"So they're doing Inglenook Boulevard over by Hadfield Middle School. I guess you know where that is."

"I do, yes."

"What's your name again?"

She gave a quick nod as he responded, her lips moving as if she was committing it to memory.

Hadfield Middle School was the new name for Bryce Street Public, where Kent and Guthrie had bonded after that summer day of firecrackers on train lines. He knew the houses on Inglenook from the days when he and Kent had walked by them on dark spring nights, coming back from soccer practice, cupping the lit ends of their cigarettes in the palms of their hands—Kent tired of the habit after a couple of weeks while Guthrie had never managed to kick them for more than a few days since. But then Kent was always better at not getting attached to anything.

As Guthrie pulled over at the end of Inglenook he could tell he had found Kent's black Mercedes SUV by the stack of signs in the back and the pulsing blue security light on the dashboard. Somewhere along this stretch of boulevard Kent was in somebody's house selling himself as the candidate, smiling, performing. The early night air smelled of fireplace smoke, dun coloured leaves swirled and scuttled along the sidewalk where Guthrie traced his old friend's steps.

After he had gone about a hundred yards from where his car was parked Guthrie could make out the warm, pale yellow glow of a door opening across the street, two figures emerging in long overcoats. There was a glimpse of blonde hair tied back in a ponytail, a camel coloured plaid scarf, the darker bulky figure beside the scarf chortling out that laugh that hadn't changed in thirty years. Guthrie broke into a run as he crossed the street to catch Kent and Veronica before they knocked on another door.

"Kent! Kent, it's Ian."

It was Veronica, Kent's wife, who had turned first. She had a tight, pinched look on her face. Kent put a calming hand on her forearm and she stiffened at his touch.

"Guthrie? Is that you?"

Guthrie slowed. He nodded as he gasped for air. "You had to figure sooner or later …"

Kent started to chortle and then let loose his belly laugh, his arms open for an embrace. Veronica shrunk and pulled away from him.

"I saw you! Saw you in that audience at the Rotary Hall! Why didn't you come grab me after, you bastard?"

Guthrie sailed into his open arms for the bear hug, laughing heartily enough that he could believe his own affection was real. "They had me working. The paper …"

"So you're still working for them. You know I would have predicted you would have been in the city in a couple of weeks back when you first started." Kent pulled him closer and directed his line of vision over to Veronica. "You've never met my wife. Honey, this is Ian Guthrie I told you about."

"That Ian, oh my God, of course!" Veronica held out a hand to shake. Perhaps it was just the way her hair was pulled back, but she looked like she had aged a decade since the town hall. When she smiled she had sharply pointed, slightly skewed teeth. For all her clear attentiveness to her appearance, this flaw made her more interesting. "You and I have to talk, my friend. I want to know everything."

"That's funny. Me too!" Guthrie clasped both hands around hers. He had never shaken anybody's hand like this before. "I mean … just about all this, of course."

"You still got the house? Last time we spoke—remember, at the funeral? You said you didn't know if you could live in it."

Guthrie had no recollection of such a conversation, but he knew enough about the adult Kent to realize this was his training; he memorized one snippet of information for each person he would come across again back in town.

"Still got the house, yeah."

Kent nodded, with a look on his face that Guthrie remembered as a drinking grin. There was tension in the wrinkles around his eyes, the tightness of his smile.

"I mean, if I'm living out here … I really can't live anywhere else in this town. It would only make things worse, wouldn't it?"

"I can see that, for sure."

Maybe it was just the presence of Veronica but both Guthrie and Kent had suddenly become self-conscious.

"We bought over on Grace Street but that's different, of course. My mother … thank the Lord she's still healthy."

"I didn't see her. At the town hall."

"No, I … my mother …"

"Bonnie's health isn't great right now," Veronica said. "I told her she should only come for the big ones."

As Kent nodded there was something in his eyes, just a moment when his gaze narrowed, that suggested he wasn't quite comfortable with the way Veronica said his mother's name.

"So did you come out to knock on some doors with me? Luch told us you were down at the campaign office."

"Did you meet Jeannie? Oh my Lord ..."

"I did, yes ..."

"She wasn't rude, was she? She can be absolutely graceless."

"I'm the enemy, I expect it."

"No, the Liberals and the Dippers are supposed to be the enemies, that's the point. That's her problem. If she gave you a hard time ..."

"It was fine. Completely fine."

"Interesting. Because I told her you were a dipper. Ha!" Kent began to take longer strides along the sidewalk now as they approached the next house. "You want to do a story on me, right?"

"I do, yeah, but it's not what you think."

"Think? I don't think anything. Dude, you're probably my oldest friend ..."

"It's a magazine piece. For the Torontonian."

"Oh I know Jack Radford at the Torontonian. He's lovely!" Veronica had reached out and petted the cuff of Guthrie's coat.

"You coming door knocking with us? This'll be good for the story."

"I'd hope to, yes. But maybe not tonight."

"The hell's Luch? Get you some door knockers."

"I told him to do the odd numbers."

"Kent, this is a longer piece, kind of an in-depth profile."

"You mean you'll need full access or something. Honey, he'll need full access."

Veronica's eyes widened with the word full.

Kent took in the stretch of boulevard, the faint hulking outlines of the houses in the dark. He watched his breath curl like smoke. "You know what I think? I think it's great you landed a piece like this, Ian. 'Bout fucking time. Well deserved."

In the distance they could see a figure emerge from a doorway, faded chinos shuffling along, then the doleful, saucer-eyed Luch fully emerged under a streetlight, his paunch bagged in a tight golf jacket of kelly green. He was fingering through the shiny blue "door knocker" brochure in his hands, K-K-K-Kent flashing like a cartoon animation.

"You done that side?"

Luch nodded.

"That was fast ..." Veronica said, with an eyebrow cocked for Kent. Luch seemed unconcerned, his fingers still moving through the door knockers, muttering numbers to himself.

"So listen, you know I've got no problem with it. I'm sure Jeannie told you, I gotta take it up the chain. It's different now, with that leadership story and all."

"Of course, of course. It's the only reason the Torontonian was interested."

Guthrie had meant to downplay his own success in landing such a magazine piece, but the quick flash of a scowl from Veronica told him everything he needed to know about the conversation as soon as he would bugger off again, leaving them to their neighbourhoods, the rehearsed memories of every little story Kent had for those he once knew on this boulevard.

"You don't want to do a few doors with us right now?"

"How'll be we wait 'til what your friend Jeannie says?"

"My friend Jeannie, yes." Kent had already begun to walk up the pathway of the next house to the door, with Veronica following close behind. He could tell by the stiffness in Veronica's shoulders what her conversation with her husband would be later. "You'd never think she had the PM's ear, would you? Whether I like it or not, she's all ours."

"It was great meeting you!" Veronica waved as if she was a child in the back of a car. It was all Guthrie could do to smile and wearily raise his hand in turn.

As he started his car and switched on his headlights, he could make out the blonde of Veronica's hair as they passed under a streetlight. Guthrie wondered if he would ever get Kent alone and actually talk to him in that blunt, disarmed and guileless way they once could as fourteen year-old boys.

It wouldn't be for this story. No, it would be for Annelie Danziger. And they both knew it.

13.

SCOTTIE FRANCIS, WELL muscled and packed tightly into his pressed jeans and black pullover, was stretching for the shot. The V-neck revealed a tuft of chest hair and a gold chain. Since his wife Mary left him, Scottie was struggling to look casual and self-assured. Now he pulled the rake from its place on the wall, steadied the cue and squinted down an opening on the table.

"Bank off the side and then the green."

"Good luck with that."

If you had told Guthrie at seventeen that he and Scottie would become good friends in middle age, he would have smirked and muttered his contempt for the Richie Cunninghams at Newton District High, how dead-boring the A students like Scottie were. No original thought, no questioning of what these mediocrities were filling their heads with in class. And there was nothing but prudish looks of scorn from Scottie for the music Guthrie made mixtapes of to blare in his Walkman. Guthrie had no idea, of course, of all the work that went into Scottie's button-downed conformity at the time, how he had to struggle, the only child of a single mother, to get his scholarships to university, then to get into med school and on through the years of building his practice. Scottie had succeeded through force of will, but at forty-five here he was, alone in his home town, mystified by how he had come so far and ended up right back where he started.

"Nicely done."

"Thanks. Here in the side again, then pink in the corner."

Guthrie winced and shook his head at the trajectory of Scottie's shot. "All you could do."

"Fucking A."

"All right, all right. If I get this then brown in the corner."

"You sink this, you're out of trouble. Not that there's any pressure."

"No, no pressure at all."

Guthrie leaned across the green baize and sharply poked his cue. He watched the red ball careen off the back of the table. Just missed. He muttered fuck like he was fifteen again.

"Scottie, remember Tanis?"

"Van Dyken?" Scottie leaned into the table to get further reach for a corner shot. Second last red ball on the table. "She still live here?"

"She does, yeah."

"What's she doing now?"

"She's working for some architect down by the lake on Hinchcliffe."

Guthrie watched Scottie's ball slow before it grazed the blue ball. "Nope. Not going to happen."

"Shit …" Scottie hung his head, play acting a man in quiet agony. "That Tanis, she still hot?"

"Listen, her daughter Bella, she was a good friend of that Brewin kid who offed herself up at the lake."

"Uh-okay then."

"You're not curious about that case? This one in the side then yellow, straight ahead."

"Should I be? Kid had enough oxys in her to kill a horse. No sign of any foul play otherwise. Case against that Trask kid's a crock. No, not curious. Though I am curious as to how you're going to make that, my friend."

Guthrie dipped his knees lower as he focused on the last red ball on the table. It was wedged in between the green and the blue.

"This is the thing … Tanis … she gave me a bunch of emails from her daughter and Sydney Brewin … along with old letters written by Annelie Danziger. Remember Annelie?"

They both solemnly watched the cue ball spin slower and slower and then ... yes ... drop into the side pocket.

"Hm. You're serious?"

"What do you mean?"

Scottie chalked his cue, puzzling out what was left to him on the table. "You remember Sy Heller? Doctor Sy Heller. He was Chief Coroner for Ontario a few years back. He taught me at U of T. Anyways, one of the first classes I had, he says, 'You from Newton?' I says yeah and he says 'Annelie Danziger, you remember that girl?' Just like you right now."

"Seriously."

"Seriously. Always remember that. Said he remembered her case from when he was Regional Supervising Coroner in the city. OD-ed on heroin, right?" Scottie sipped his Diet Coke from the cocktail straw. "Heller remembered it because some bartender guy got put away for that on a criminal negligence charge. That always stuck in his craw."

"Stuck in his craw. Why?"

"Because there were contusions, one on the side of her head by her temple, abrasions on her body, signs of a struggle and physical trauma. And pregnant, she was. Never even figured in the case when it got to court. He said he should have pushed on that one. Some funny business went on, he was sure of it. Should have been murder."

"Holy crap, Scottie."

"I shit you not. I mean, I couldn't tell him much. Annelie Danziger. She wasn't in my snack bracket back in the day." He raised his cue above his shoulders as he bore down on the cue ball. "I'm banking this. It's all I can do."

"I don't know, Scottie—those letters and notes of Annelie's. Tanis gave them to her daughter Bella and to Sydney Brewin. They were supposed to give them some inspiration ..."

"I remember. She was like a punk rocker, wasn't she? Could never figure out why she was dating your buddy in high school."

"Kent, you mean."

"He's back, eh? Isn't he running for Councillor or something?"

"Empee."

"Right. Think I read that. I always thought he was a shit talker."

"I was reading all these letters and stuff that Tanis gives me, and about a month before Annelie ODs, she's writing to Tanis about driving up to the lake for one last time. Which was strange. Because there she was, living in Toronto, studying art, doing what she loved. Had a new boyfriend that played in a band. And yet she had written that life had become unbearable."

"Hm."

"Nicely done."

Scottie was on a roll now. The yellow, the green . . . each potted with that sharp click of his cue you heard when he had found his game.

"Not sure what you're trying to find there, Ian."

"You think I'm pushing the connection?"

"I just don't see it. I mean Heller, yeah, he remembered the case, at least enough to call me Newton for the rest of the semester. But as far as he was concerned, he had wanted to see this bartender low-life go away for more than negligence."

"No question of suicide?"

"Didn't come out and say that. He just said it stuck in his craw."

"I'd love to talk to Heller."

"Me too sometimes. He was a great coroner. Died in oh-two. Shit, that's me scratched."

As Guthrie crouched into his shot he heard the ring tone of an old rotary phone. Yes, it was there, coming from the pocket of his coat thrown over the corner of the booth. Nobody ever called him on his BlackBerry.

"One sec, Scottie."

O DHILLON. Ojal, from her home phone. Guthrie grabbed the device and began walking for the door.

"Guthrie?"

"Inspector. This is a surprise."

"I just said I'd call you if I heard anything on that Brewin case. I'm a woman of my word."

"I got a call from 52 division about an hour ago. Drew Trask is out on bail. His father came through for him."

"Now that is something."

"There you go. Not sure if he'll talk to you but I guess it would be worth a try."

"And you know if he tells me anything of interest, I'll be calling you."

These were Guthrie's words of reassurance. Proof of his diligence, his detachment. No one would have ever known the impact Scottie made when he had told Guthrie that Annelie was pregnant when she died. No, there was just the slightest tremble in his hand on the baize steadying the cue. Hardly noticeable, would have taken a real detective to catch it. Or a better reporter than Guthrie was.

14.

DREW TRASK SET down the terms for his meeting with Guthrie in a terse email, one so clear and direct Guthrie had his suspicions about a guiding hand. They would not meet in Newton; it had to be in the city near where he was staying with a friend. They could speak for no longer than thirty minutes in a public, not a private place; he would send him the address and name of the coffee shop the morning of the meeting. Finally, Guthrie could not record any of the conversation. Everything Drew had to say was to "set the record straight"—such as it was. If he felt he could trust Guthrie "down the line," he promised that he would not speak to any other journalist in the weeks and months ahead. Guthrie set out for the city as soon as he got the email.

He probably should have told Gallant about this. If he was ten years younger, he would have relished how such a scoop would put Gallant on his heels, reluctantly impressed. Yet as he turned off on to the feeder lanes all he was thinking about was Tanis.

He suddenly realized it was important to him that Tanis believe he cared as much about their shared past as she did, that the years had not eroded the points of connection they had. Wasn't that really what the sex between them was about? He had first believed that she led him into her bedroom on a grey Saturday afternoon in April out of loneliness and that opened up possibilities beyond the moment. He could sense it that very afternoon, as she would not look into his eyes as she ground her hips into him, so taut and poised on his lap, and guided his hands to her breasts. Afterwards he tried to ask her about her life over the last two decades, perhaps as a way to figure out what she had come to love or fear. She responded with a kind of condescending vagueness, a smile that let him know she found such talk trite and sentimental. No, their intimacy, if it was about anything at all besides satisfying her curiosity, first had to be experienced like some rite of remembering. She demanded loyalty to the memories of their best selves, and now, when everything else between them seemed an open question, he found himself feeling obligated to prove he was up to the task.

He realized now that all those months ago, long before any of this, the shadow behind his attraction to Tanis was his memory of Annelie Danziger, and he was really not sure why she had such a hold on him. Sure, the girl was a talented artist and had that steely self-possession and ambition to take her writing—the plays and the short films she had begun to make—in a direction that showed sophistication beyond her years. But she was not quite the rare, delicate flower the girls made her out to be. Guthrie could recall the skinny kid who played flute in the middle school orchestra before she went off to Holy Cross, the Catholic high. She wore glasses with clunky plastic frames until the townie girls ridiculed her into wearing contact lenses that made her eyes water. He could remember getting a glimpse of her parents on a student-teacher night—Rudi and Gudrun, from Switzerland apparently, a compact and too formally dressed couple. Annelie was studious and quietly unexceptional then; she only really became attractive, elegant and mysterious in her last two years of high school. Yet how much elegance and mystery was there to her, really, when you realize she chose Kent, of all the possible boys on offer?

Maybe it was less Annelie's attractiveness than it was her ability to speak the truth and defend those who were bullied—those like Darren Pemberton all those years ago. This whole conversation Guthrie was about to have with Drew, no matter how objective he'd try to claim he was as a journalist, would inevitably be about trying to clear this boy's name, save him from that mob mentality Guthrie had begun to feel developing back in Newton, in the tone of the bar conversations and—closer to the bone—in the quaver he heard in Tanis's voice when she spoke of her fears about Bella's safety at school. *Comfort the afflicted and afflict the comfortable:* that was the reporter's code he took as his own all those years ago. At least he could get that half-right again with a story like this, if not find reconciliation with his own guilt from how he had caused a boy, just like Drew, to suffer at the hands of bullies back in town.

Now, as he braked along the long curve that sent each car speeding to the express lanes for the highway, he could recall that rush of excitement, if just for an instant, of being young enough to be seduced by the city, to measure his talents by its embrace of him. The women that he met and believed he might love over the years were merely stand-ins, provisional embodiments of such a seduction—even Kate.

Yes, all of the women but one, that is.

He got on to the lakeshore a couple of exits too soon, solely to indulge a memory. Around the time when he was first infatuated with Annelie he had taken this stretch with Kent and his new friends at St. Alban's, the private school Kent had transferred to for his last two years. They were heading to a party and there, out on the lake, didn't he see a huge wooden staircase, the size of a war monument, all in flames? All this talk of Annelie made him remember that staircase once more. Now he had to ask himself if that memory was even real or something he had once dreamed. That was something to ask Kent, perhaps.

This quick detour turned out to have its value too; Guthrie sped along the side streets that led through Parkdale, up across College and over to a tony stretch of Avenue Road with more than enough time to get his bearings, figure out where this café could possibly be. This was not the part of the city he had ever really spent some time in, especially when he was Drew Trask's age. Even the rich kids Kent had introduced him to considered it the neighbourhood where their parents went to shop and be seen. There was a second hand irony in a kid like

Drew choosing a place around here, which seemed entirely consistent with the tone of Sydney's and Bella's correspondence.

The café looked like it had once been some kind of studio, with its high ceiling and stark white walls. The weathered texture of the long wooden tables and the primary colours of the photographs that lined the room, blurry street scenes from what looked to be a corner of the world as remote from this little stretch of Toronto as possible, already rankled Guthrie. He glanced around to spot Drew Trask. Nowhere to be seen yet; there was just a young woman, swathed in black cashmere at one of the tables, peering into a laptop screen while she murmured Japanese into her white plastic phone. Yet as Guthrie glimpsed his blurry reflection in the gleam of the espresso machine, how pinched and beady eyed he looked in his old resentments of the monied, he realized he was simply relying on his old reflexes in a city that had changed beyond his understanding. It had been a decade now that he had been living back in Newton. Maybe all his better qualities were receding with age and what was left were hard edges, provincial attitudes and too much memory. A kid like Trask would think he was just a glum old man and he would probably be right.

He was halfway through his cappuccino, the best he had sipped in years, unfortunately, given how much he wanted to hate this place, when a young man bustled through the side door. His hair was now its natural blonde and not the jet black from the photographs. Indeed it was the bleached look of his eyebrows that made him almost unrecognizable. It was Drew's astrakhan coat that gave Guthrie the confidence to wave him down. Once he had, though, and he felt the woman's curious gaze on him, he realized he had become the man who would order Drew's services from the classifieds. This was middle-age; the inevitable few caricatures one projected for the young, and the absurdity in trying to dispel them.

Drew seemed winded as he approached, tugging at an artfully crumpled linen scarf the colour of parchment, his gaze fixed on the floorboards. "You must be Ian Guthrie." He held out his hand and shook firmly. He smelled of harsh cigarettes and a sweet, citrusy cologne.

"I'm glad that you got in touch with me."

"Yeah, well I kind of had to." Drew scraped a chair across the floor and folded himself into it, crossed legs, crossed arms, like sharp scissors tucked into a little drawer of circumspection. "I mean, it's a fucking witch hunt in that awful town. You heard about this town hall they had."

"I was there."

"You didn't report on it."

"I didn't see the point."

"Because what the Brewins said was total bullshit?"

"It felt like a stunt. And I can choose what I report on."

"So you chose to report on what happened to Sydney. Can I ask why?"

"Because I knew Annelie Danziger. I knew her well."

Drew's eyes widened for just a moment. His hand went to a pocket in his coat, fumbling for a cigarette he seemed to deny himself for now. "So you know about all that. Was it fucking Bella who told you?"

"I have not spoken to any Bella, no. Should I?"

"Eventually, I'm sure." He had now unfolded himself and sat before Guthrie as if he was waiting to be dealt his next hand of cards. "Isabella Lang's her full name. She calls herself—or called herself—Sydney's best friend. Which is total bullshit. Like almost everything she'll tell you."

"Uh huh." Guthrie sipped from his cup and nodded. One of the most valuable things he had learned from Stephen Clarke at the Standard was his advice to learn to use silence in interviews, let the subject fill it. The subject here—sorry, Tanis—was nothing like the Darren Pemberton they knew. He was older beyond his years for one, given his enterprising approach to exile from his home town, and yet he was also like a teenager in his huffing and fidgeting, as if he was trying on emotional responses like sweaters off the rack.

"You making out all right, here in the city?"

"I'm living with my boyfriend, if you must know. And Derek's got me training to manage his second location. Just over here on Scollard."

"Like a clothes shop."

"Why do you ask? You looking for a new wardrobe? It wouldn't be the worst decision you made."

"I don't think I could afford—"

"That's true."

Guthrie didn't want to laugh but the barb was so unexpected that he had to look away and just let a quick grin escape. "Still I might have to take you up on that."

"Be my pleasure."

"So Sydney, then. You going to tell me what happened?"

"I'll tell you what I know. That's a little different."

"And why is that?"

"Because I wasn't there when she drowned."

Guthrie smirked and pulled back from the table, the scrape of his chair on the floor causing the woman to glance their way. She looked mildly concerned as she continued to mutter into her phone. Was the chair that loud? "And you're going to tell me how that is possible."

"When I left her, she was barely conscious. I lay her down in the back seat and told her I was going to run for help."

"Why didn't you just drive?"

"She told me she threw the keys in the lake."

"What?"

"So help me God." Drew crossed himself with an unlit cigarette in his fingers. "I need this. You smoke?"

Guthrie nodded and motioned to the side door. When they rose together Guthrie winked at the woman. She looked momentarily dismayed and then busied herself with whatever was on her laptop screen.

When they were outside Drew seemed to have grown another couple of inches. He lit both their cigarettes with a dramatic flair. The sun shone directly on the wall behind him, bringing out new shades of red in the brick. "After we parked, we went for a walk to look at the moon. She said she wanted to be sure it was full. Anyway, it was when we were on that boardwalk by the lake when Sydney told me what she had taken. She said it was too late for me to help her. I swear, I practically dragged her back to that car. She just seemed so out of it I thought she was incapable of lying to me."

"Why would she lie to you about anything? I thought you were best friends."

"Maybe because she knew how I felt about all of it. I mean her pregnancy, all the weirdness with Bella. Their little cult of Annelie."

"It sounds like you've started your own cult of Sydney now with your new tattoo."

Drew took the force of his glare out on the passing cars. "So you talk to cops."

"Of course I talk to cops. I'm a reporter. It's what we do."

"Cops who have already made up their minds …"

"Look, I don't care about your tattoo and all that was about. I talk to cops because they give me the facts. Who. What. Where."

"But not why. And that's the most important thing about the story of Annelie, never mind Syd."

"Okay. I'll ask. Why would you say that?"

Drew looked away, his gaze focusing on a point on the old brickwork of a building behind Guthrie. His eyes seemed to cross and then he smiled to himself and shook his head. "You think with both of them it was just about getting knocked up or something?"

"Why don't you tell me why it was something else?"

Drew leaned back and folded his arms, slowly blinking, the start of a grin banished with a thought he wouldn't let himself tease out. He refocused on Guthrie. "Because I keep my promises. She kept hers to me."

"I see." Guthrie just nodded, took a long drag, played out the silence. "You don't have to keep any promise to Annelie Danziger, do you?"

Now Drew allowed that start of a grin to form into a smirk as he shook his head. "You know who Nicholas Poole is?"

There was something about the name that carried with it an old correspondence, like a rhyme from a song Guthrie had forgotten. He looked down at the sidewalk and the patch of soft earth. There were cigarette butts scattered like broken teeth from a brawl. "Should I?"

"Annelie Danziger was found in his room at the old Hi Fi."

"Nicky Poole. Of course. He was called Nicky then."

"He did two years in Kingston for that. Well, I met him."

"How?"

"It doesn't matter. Put it this way, I didn't hunt him down or anything. But what he told me I believe. He had nothing to do with Annelie Danziger's death. And from what she told him, she didn't have the nerve for suicide. She had decided she was going to have her kid. Thing is, she had written this note to Bella's mom where she had talked about what a prick her dad was because he was such a strict Catholic, forcing her to have the baby, how her mother didn't stick up for her, and how the decision was going to ruin her life ... because of what it meant."

"I know. I've read it. But I don't know what you mean when you say what it meant."

"Well ... sorry ...nothing sacred, nothing secret, eh?"

"Bella's mother, she's a friend of mine. She was worried about these parallels."

"Look, I don't care. My dad's lawyer said none of that is going to help me in court. If you read all of those old letters it should be obvious to you how Sydney felt reading them."

"Then why are you telling me it was not because she simply didn't want to have David Goring's kid?"

Silence. Drew fixed his gaze back on the brickwork behind Guthrie, as if he was watching a flickering silent movie there. Maybe one of Annelie Danziger's old Super 8s. "I don't know. Maybe it was just all that church and God talk her mother rammed down her throat. How about that?"

"Answer me this: you knew how Sydney was feeling, the state she was in. Yet you're up there with her, on the lake."

"You just answered your own question, Jack."

"And how is that?"

"She was my best friend, okay? You think I gave her the oxys? You think I even knew she took them until we were on that boardwalk? Look, we used to go up to the lake a lot, okay?"

"Even though you knew Annelie Danziger tried to kill herself up there just a few weeks before she succeeded ..."

"Yeah, well ... like I said, talk to Nicky Poole on that. Or talk to Gudrun Danziger."

"Gudrun, Annelie's mother?"

"Uh huh." Drew flicked his butt at the sidewalk, watched it roll onto the street in a gust of wind. "She's still around. Me, Bella and Sydney, when we first learned about Annelie, we went down to see her. But none of this matters. People are going to believe what they believe. The truth is we used to go up to the lake a lot because we liked it there at night. We could drink wine and just talk about all we were going to accomplish once we got out of that fucking town. Seems like a long time ago now."

"Before Sydney got pregnant."

"Look, I don't care what anybody believes, but if you want to write about what really happened, it's this simple—I knew what Sydney was thinking that night and I tried to change her mind. I just didn't know how far she'd gone before we even got to the lake."

"Uh huh. But you knew she was losing consciousness and you just left her there. You tried to disappear."

"I tried to get help. I was almost to the road when I heard the crash ... the car in the lake."

"Did you even try to save her?"

"Of course I tried! I fucking swam in there and did all I could to get to her. There was no fucking way." Drew shook his head, murmured to himself as he stared into the brick wall. "I spent six days in the Don Jail and I'm not going back there. And I'm not going back to that fucking town, either. You can put that in your paper."

"Have you spoken to Bella? Have you spoken to anyone in Newton aside from the-uh ..."

"Aside from the cops? No. I'm done with all of it. Once this is all over I'll never go back."

Guthrie moved for the side door, gesturing to Drew to go first. So much seemed to be roiling under the surface, but there was nothing about Drew that seemed malevolent. Like a hunted animal that had run to the fence line, if Drew lashed out it was only because he raged at being trapped. Of course Guthrie wouldn't write it like that, if he wrote it about this meeting at all. No, he wouldn't even describe it as such to Gallant. It wasn't worth the "suggestions" Bruce would offer for the piece. Maybe he should speak to Tanis about this meeting, surely she would have her opinion about Drew.

"I've just got one last question for you, Drew. Vancouver."

"What about it?"

"Ojal told me you were heading there ... at least they had camera footage of you buying a bus ticket."

"Who's Ojal?"

"Sorry ... Staff Inspector Dhillon."

"The brown chick whom I spoke to."

"The brown chick, yes."

"She's a piece of work, eh?"

"I don't know what you mean."

"Like I'm pretty tightly wound, I know, but she made me look like ... wow."

"You should have some respect. She talked to you because she doesn't want to see you go to prison for a crime you didn't commit. You should know who your friends are."

"My friends are dead or dead to me, old man. If you must know, I had bought the ticket to get to my father's place, okay? We're done here."

"I suppose that's true. Yes, we are."

Guthrie did not look back. He realized he really had little interest in dismantling all of the whirring parts of this suicide. Drew Trask would not go to prison. It was highly unlikely he would even face a trial, given the circumstances. After this trial he would undoubtedly careen from job to job and boyfriend to boyfriend for a few years and flutter like a moth around the dim lights of a few similar melodramas over the years. As if he needed to bury secrets from animal instinct, only to dig them up again like a whipped dog with old bones. It would end up being the most interesting thing about him, his ability to have bit parts in these tales well suited to after-dinner conversations in the safety of middle age. And whatever Tanis presumed—or perhaps hoped—would emerge through this investigation was probably best left in the past.

Guthrie began to drive downtown for his last real nod to work today, a quick meeting that Stephen Clarke had requested. He feared the worst; Stephen gave him virtually no details in the email, and that was not like him. He'd usually take every opportunity to bemoan the vaudeville act he had been forced to perform in with his job as editor. Whatever was going on, there was no news that Stephen felt inclined to share in these last few hours as he had returned to his daily business of putting the next magazine issue together. The buildings loomed larger, blocking out the sun as Guthrie moved farther along Bay Street, and he could discern just the faintest wisps of white smoke coming from the metal discs that marked the sewer lines and signified something of this new chill in the air. The city was not his home anymore, he realized, and would never be again.

As he trudged past each glass walled cubicle that marked the executive offices at the Torontonian, it was the waving gesture of Stephen's, a kind of Italian hello with an upturned palm, that caught Guthrie's attention and made him brighten. Stephen was on the phone and was nodding with a yogic serenity. Someone was no doubt furious with him, probably someone Stephen should care about within the upper echelons of whatever ailing media or telecom giant now owned the Torontonian, it was hard to keep up. Guthrie crept in, eased the door shut and folded himself into the chair on the other side of Stephen's desk.

A minute passed. Then two. Stephen was writing notes on a pad of foolscap paper. He finally seemed to remember that Guthrie was sitting there and mouthed "conference call." Guthrie could only smile and nod, easing himself into a look of serenity as he took in the few photographs on Stephen's desk. Stephen replaced the receiver.

"Bloody hell!"

"Is this Alicia?"

"She's twenty-five now. Over in London at the LSE."

"God, she was a kid when I last saw her."

"So were you."

"And yet you never were."

"That's correct. Never. Now listen. It's about this piece you're doing, against my better judgment."

"It's coming along, Stephen, I swear. Do you want to see what I've got so far?"

"Who the hell is Jeannie Pincott? Should I know of her?"

"Probably not. Why?"

"Who is she?"

"Didn't she tell you who she is? A campaign manager or something."

"She sends me this email, copies Doug Barber—"

"Who's Doug Barber?"

"He's the man who hired me. Who sat right there in scuffed loafers and no socks and told me everyone believed I could be useful except him."

"And what did you say?"

"I asked him to define useful."

"And ..."

"And he did." Stephen seemed to make his lips as thin as possible as he grinned. "So this little bitch Jeannie Pincott wants to lay down some rules."

"Rules."

"She has provided me with a list of people that you are authorized to speak with for your piece. She has also warned that if they hear that you are speaking to anyone else but these names, they will shut this down."

"And you told her to piss off."

Stephen leaned back in his chair and ran his crabbed fingers across his chin. "I did not, no."

"Why not?"

"Because I have indeed become useful, it seems." Stephen tried to laugh. The chuckle didn't quite make it out of his mouth. It just became a clearing of his throat.

"What do you mean?"

"Who the hell is this Kent Wolseley, anyway?"

"Aside from being somebody I knew at 18? So far I'd say just a shit talker who might become an MP. Spent twenty years inching up the greasy pole with that party, so I guess he deserves it."

"Mr. Barber has told me that every bloody piece on him at the Standard gets more click-throughs on a daily basis than anything else right now, all because he's been tapped as some possible successor to this bloody Prime Minister."

"I don't know what that means, Stephen."

Stephen placed his hand on a piece of paper on his desk and gently pushed it nearer to Guthrie.

"It means we're both going to be useful, Ian. That's the list. I ask you not to fuck this up."

Guthrie took it in his hands and began to fold it. Once. Twice. Three times.

"I understand."

"You understand. You didn't read one name there."

"I will. And I'll comply, Stephen."

In the silence they looked at each other and realized the distance between them was growing second by second. Stephen just nodded and looked at the matte black cover of the notebook on his desk. It was all he could do to draw this conversation to a close.

15.

A Mother Grieves

by Kerry-Anne Landy—November 2nd—4 comments

Karen Brewin never really liked photographs, not taking them or having them taken of her. "I don't know what it was. You know there's that saying about them, that they steal a little bit of your soul each time you hear that click." We are sitting in the kitchen of the Falmouth Crescent home she shares with husband Finley and son Troy, 19. Karen has just returned from the dental clinic where she has worked as a hygienist for twenty-two years and is still in her white smock and slacks. She has just brewed chamomile tea for us both and insists I try the ginger snaps; she baked them herself. The warmth and hospitality is only the more remarkable on this occasion, considering that in this house there is a presence missing now. Just four short weeks ago daughter Sydney Brewin drove the family car up to Lake LeSueur and never returned. "I really can't forgive myself now that I didn't take more pictures of my beautiful girl." What photographs Karen Brewin does have are in her hands—hands that tremble ever so slightly as she flips through them for me. There is Sydney as a two year-old girl, laughing on one of the swings on the set that used to be in the Brewins' back yard on Sumter Avenue. She is there again, a toddler in a bright red swimsuit, on the dock of the Muskoka cottage the family shared with Sydney's grandparents for six summers. The little girl's blonde hair *looks bleached by the sun. And what begins to emerge, in all of these photographs taken through the years, is a characteristic grin. It is of a child who seemed to enjoy keeping her own secrets, holding something back from the camera's gaze and indeed from all who loved her.*

More than a month after Sydney's body was found in Lake LeSueur, there is indeed very little that can be determined about the circumstances surrounding her death. Sydney's companion in the car at the time, eighteen-year-old Andrew Trask, charged with criminal negligence, has been released on bail but the police remain silent about any further evidence of wrongdoing; their investigation continues. It is this lack of resolution with this case that, Karen assures me, makes it all the more difficult to bear.

"All I know is there are two different Sydneys in my memory today. There is the Sydney who was my little girl and my bright, hopeful daughter, who had everything in the world to live for. That was the Sydney before she met that boy. The Sydney who she might have become afterwards, well … I just never really got a chance to know that girl. And I'll always wonder if she might still be here today if she had never met Andrew Trask. Him, with his criminal record."

She is unguarded and unrepentant about naming Mr. Trask, who was not a minor at the time of her daughter's drowning and was known to police.

It is expected that the Newton police will be announcing the results of their investigation into the death of Sydney Brewin sometime later this month. Until then, Karen Brewin has a few photographs, a wish for justice and ultimately some sense of closure in the case of her daughter's death. Both might not come easily.

"So what do you think?" Bruce Gallant smiled and leaned back as soon as Guthrie's eyes lifted from the words on the page in front of him. "I'd say she did a pretty damn good job for a kid of twenty-three, wouldn't you?"

"This is your intern?"

"This is Kerry-Anne, yes indeed. It was just going to be a blog post but I say what the hell, I'll do an edit and have it run in the weekend edition."

"If I was Drew Trask's lawyer, I might have some objections."

"Already put it through Legal, Ian."

"Drew could sue."

"That's not what Legal said, Ian."

"But he might still be charged with a more serious crime. This piece, it—"

"You met with Drew Trask. How come you didn't tell me about his criminal charges when he was a minor?"

"I met with him and we had a conversation on background."

"Ian. You can't spin an old reporter. What are you telling me?"

"I'm telling you that I keep my promises to my sources. That's what old reporters still do, Bruce."

"So he told you about his criminal charges or did you just never bother to ask? Or, you know, do a bit of digging ..."

"You tell me what you think, Bruce. I couldn't spin you if I tried, apparently. And yet you're perfectly happy with the way your intern Kerry-Lynne ..."

"Kerry-Anne ..."

"Your intern Kerry-Anne sits there and gets spun."

"Kerry-Anne was hungry enough to get the full fucking story."

"As told by Karen Brewin and the Conservative Party of Canada. You got this kid to write an unpaid ad for their tough on crime agenda in the middle of a fucking election. That's just an old reporter's take, I know ..."

Bruce leaned forward and put his hands on the spread of newspapers in front of him. The half moons under his roughly bitten fingernails became whiter. "Admit it, Ian. You had no idea about Trask's criminal record. Look, I know you would have told me, as any good reporter would. And you are a good reporter. Or, should I say, you were."

Gallant let out a sigh and whatever had kept him inflated at full air pressure—his delight in the blog post, the state of his blood sugar after one of Peggy Vaughan's bran muffins this morning—escaped from him with the deep breath. "I'm just asking you to give me a reason to give you my best stories, Ian. If a twenty-three year old out of J school can give me that in a morning's work . . ."

"I'd suggest that only a twenty-three year old would give you that in a morning's work. And that's without seeing the byline."

"Uh huh. But the thing is, Ian, you know how many clicks this got?"

"I've no idea."

"More than any piece in the last month. A blog post. We're in the middle of an election and this is what people are reading. I've got to explain that to my bosses because you know they're going to ask. They look at these numbers more than I do."

"What are you saying, Bruce?"

"I'm just saying, give me something. Give me some word of any developments with the case. You seem to get on fine with the brown girl."

"Pardon?"

"The cop. Bob Dylan's love child."

"You'd find Dhillon spelled differently if you read my copy."

"Give me a reason to read it, Ian. That's all I'm asking here."

"So you want a column with an angle that betrays my source."

"Just file something on this for next week's weekend edition. All I ask."

"I was actually hoping to do an election piece. There's the all-candidates coming up."

Gallant grinned as he shook his head, as if this was an old joke of Guthrie's that could still make him laugh. If he had to. "You know I can't say yes to you writing anything on Wolseley."

"Not on Wolseley, no."

"We already did the profile pieces on the other candidates. And I'm covering the two debates left."

"So this is essentially a no."

"Ian, if I let Kerry-Anne write one more piece on Sydney Brewin's death, maybe you want to work with her. She needs a kind of mentor and I just can't … with things on my desk …"

It was all Guthrie could do to nod as he rose from his chair. He wanted to remain civil, say nothing he would regret. "Please give Kerry-Anne my contact information. I'd be happy to talk to her."

"Thanks, Ian. You're a good man."

All Guthrie wanted now was to get out of the building, light a cigarette and slowly turn the thoughts of his own pettiness into smoke.

16.

WITH THE TINNY little sound of the bhangra ring tone, Ojal took her eyes off the page of this fat, sweeping multigenerational-multicultural-magic-realist-romance that was now the only sure-fire method to put her to sleep. 11:38. Who else could it be? Don't get up. Just let it ring. Just let him get used to you out of his life. She parted the curtain and there he was, the only car in the parking lot of the drug store, his headlights glowing with his pathetic need, his boy-man's persistence.

"What?"

"I lost tonight."

"Lost what?"

"The debate. I lost the debate. Kent Wolseley is going to win this."

"I'm sorry to hear that. I have to get up early."

"Can I not come up?"

"You know my answer."

"Why can't we talk about this?"

"Why can't you talk to your wife?"

"Please, Ojal. I lost tonight. Don't tell me I lose you too."

There was a deep, soothing music in his voice. She loved how he touched her. His strong hands, the musky, perfumed smell of his hair let down. Why couldn't the novel in her hands do something like that justice? In just these two short weeks Jagdeep had made her feel empty and cold sleeping alone.

"Just let me up for five minutes. A cup of chai. We can talk about this. We can make a plan."

"You don't need me to make a plan. You just have to be honest for once."

"I am honest right now. I need you."

She looked out through the crack in the curtain. She could just barely make out, under the streetlight, his silhouette in the front seat. Waiting. Pleading. She breathed out a heavy sigh.

"You're so much drama."

"Maybe. But I'm your drama. And you are mine."

"Five minutes."

She watched his headlights dim and go out, put the novel in the drawer of her side table by the bed. Let someone truly write how desire breaks your life open and how, once it does, the pieces never fit back the same. She heard the door buzzer ring and smiled for herself. She felt her heart pound as she let him in.

17.

KENT HAD PROPPED his elbows on the veneer tabletop and was staring into the little screen of his device. He was in his shirtsleeves, his rep tie askew, the large decaf, just black, was gradually going cold in front of him. "So they're doing this poll on who won the debate tonight. I can click for the numbers. Should I even look?"

Guthrie smirked and managed a croak of a laugh. It was just the two of them now in the Countrytime Donuts, Kent had dismissed his entourage and told them to drive Veronica home. This crew of sycophants—"the Team Wolseley troopers," all young men, awkward and graceless, always seemed to be with him. Now that they were gone Kent seemed liberated of his candidate persona; perhaps he no longer felt the burden of providing them with their role model. This was precisely when Guthrie knew he should be taping their conversation but it had been a few years since they had spoken like this.

"Are you actually worried about how you did?"

"I guess I'm just hoping we had a real, substantive conversation on the issues." Kent had deepened his voice and squared his shoulders as if he was in mid-close-up in the frame of the camera shot. It was his parody of a newscaster. With the start of a grin he collapsed out of the role all at once and slapped Guthrie on the shoulder. "Fuck that, I won! That's the point."

Guthrie nodded. It was a night of victory. Here in the donut shop, a few oldsters, vaguely recognizable parents of those whom Kent and Guthrie had known once, those who had long moved away, had come over and congratulated Kent. Gus Arnold, Vince's dad, his face gaunt and wattled, even went so far as to say Kent had "really stuck it to them, the goddamn phonies."

Yet now, in the sudden silence between Kent and Guthrie, as they both looked out on the long barren stretch of road that led to the highway exit, Guthrie was thinking about the less predictable incident that occurred during the debate. There was an email he received from the staffer for Patricia Rigo, the Liberal candidate, with the photos of Jagdeep Minhas leaving Ojal's condo, the time code on the shots confirming this visit occurred past midnight earlier in the week. There was no message apart from the photos, just two words in the subject line: "Booty Call?" The only reaction Guthrie would allow himself, seated there at the debate, was one raised eyebrow.

No wonder Ojal had seemed barely engaged about Sydney Brewin's death. She had this little romance going on. He allowed himself a smirk in the moment of realization he still had enough backbone that he wouldn't turn those photos into a story, that he was a different kind of person than these political people, who made careers out of stalking people, recording their every move.

He was just naturally taking the high road. Just two nights ago Guthrie had met Tanis for a drink and she had broken down crying, worried about her daughter; Bella had come home looking like she had been in a fight and claimed it was nothing, that it happened in basketball practice. He felt this surge of protectiveness for Tanis and her daughter, his over-active justice impulse that told him he was starting to care too much. And he knew what that meant.

Still, after he had gotten the email with the photos of Minhas from the staffer, Guthrie lost his concentration for a good part of the debate. He was glad he wasn't writing about the night, happy it was handed over to Kerry-Anne the intern, for he remembered little about what was actually said. All he really could recall were images and gestures, like the way Kent had moved his chair about a foot to the left of the other three candidates, breaking the symmetry so he was positioned perfectly in a kind of spotlight. This was a decision Kent seemed to make instinctively. Guthrie had scrawled "instinct" and "light" on the notebook page he was flipping through now, as Kent still tended to his blackberry. He turned the page and took in a couple of lines about Veronica's shoes—the blue of a robin's egg, spattered with drops of spilled coffee. Her plump feet were so tightly packed into them it looked as if the leather was about to tear and set her toes free after a few mincing steps. And the last note he had gotten down, there because he probably couldn't get over his anxiety about his work, was the way Bruce Gallant, in the role of moderator, was dressed, suited and tied in neutral shades that brought to mind the interiors of a bad roadside motel. What to do with all of this? It probably wouldn't even make the first draft of his magazine piece.

"So did you write how I smoked them all, even that dipper everybody was hoping would lay a glove on me?"

"I've got a few things down here, yeah."

"You think I went too hard on him about the money he comes from?"

"I guess I wondered whether it was relevant. I think a lot of people in the audience . . . "

"Ian, seriously. The guy's a dipper, a socialist, and his dad's one of the biggest developers in BC. Sent Jagdeep to dental school in California, for Christ sake. What does he know about the working man? It's relevant because he's putting himself out there as someone who knows what it's like to struggle making ends meet."

"It wasn't just him. It's the way you went after all of them. In just a couple of minutes of your opening speech you decided to go on about outstanding student loans, failed businesses, second mortgages. But no one on that stage got personal about you."

"That's not my problem!" Kent laughed a touch too loudly and leaned back in his chair. "You come to a debate, you do your homework, that's all I did."

"You don't think that, in going personal this way, you won a Pyrrhic victory at best?"

115

"Pyrrhic victory? The fuck is that, some bon mot from the poetaster's club? Jesus, Ian. Let me tell you what Lyndon Johnson once said. He said that the fact that a man is a newspaper reporter is evidence of some flaw of character. Johnson. Smart man. Well, smart despite being a Democrat, don't you think?"

Guthrie could not help but smile. Kent hadn't lost his sharpness.

"Look, it's just this going personal. I guess I just wonder if that's how you want to win. I mean, this is just my take on it, but at the end of the debate I didn't sense this surge of hope or uplift in the room."

"Yeah … well, I'll save the hope and uplift for another occasion. This is a contact sport, Ian. You think people were there tonight to hear me go on about the issues, or something? That's not what they vote for. They vote for who's real. I just made it clear who wasn't. There's only one way you can do that." Kent leaned in, as if he was about to whisper in Guthrie's ear. "You need the information, Ian. The information's everything."

It was all Guthrie could do to nod and smile in return. The information: it was precisely what he and Kent weren't sharing. At some point over their coffee, Guthrie just figured it would be inevitable that he would have mentioned the parallels he had discovered between Sydney Brewin's death and Annelie's. He would speak of the letters he had been reading where Annelie mentioned Kent, even sound him out about what he thought of her suicide all these years later. But there was something about that look in Kent's eye, the strangeness of his smile, that told him no, there was no point. No real *information* would be on offer. He'd have to get it himself. And he had a bad feeling about where that search was taking him.

"Tell you this, Ian, and you better not write this down. A man I like to call my mentor, an old MP named Dan Valgardson, Dan once gave me the best piece of advice of anyone. To be a great politician, it's simple: you've got to be honest." Kent leaned back once more, his grin widening, a masticated stir stick dangling from the side of his mouth. "And if you can fake that, you got it made."

18.

AFTER MORE THAN three decades Bonnie Wolseley still had her talent agency, Kids In Lights. Her website had a Toronto address but a quick search online revealed a vacant lot far west on King Street, where a billboard announced that the Mondrian—urban living at its finest—would be breaking ground. In 2009. A drive over to Kent's childhood home on a Monday morning, with two coffees and cinnamon buns from Ledwith's, the old grocery store on Main, confirmed that Kids In Lights was now "a little hobby" as Bonnie settled into her retirement years.

It had been at least five years since Guthrie had seen Bonnie, and even then it was only to chat briefly as she strolled along Main Street at the Farmers Market, weighed down with two cotton bags full of vegetables and the first batch of strawberries of the summer. She had been an attractive woman even then, dark eyed and slender, with just a few grey streaks in her hair around her temples—much like Kent's now. She looked dressed for tennis, though she had never played, as far as Guthrie could recall. And though she smiled and spoke of fond memories she took him in carefully, looking for signs of Guthrie's impending, decrepit bachelorhood in the wrinkles at the corners of his eyes, the state of his black T-shirt.

But this morning she greeted Guthrie like an old friend who had journeyed far and finally returned. Perhaps there was a bit more grey in her hair and she was a touch more slender but she looked to be ageing well. She embraced him at the door and there was the faintest scent of rosewater at the nape of her neck.

She led him through the main dining room. Every square inch of the oak table that could seat twelve was covered with stacks of newspapers and magazines, two tea sets and a laundry basket full of bleached and brittle towels. They both angled their way around an ironing board and then through the dim back rooms to the servants' quarters. The house smelled like a wet woolen sweater. Two large steel pots on the floor suggested that a leak in the roof had become a concern.

She made room, among the spread of papers ringed in coffee stains and headshots of child actors, some clearly adults by now with the look of their hairstyles and shirt collars, for the cinnamon buns and coffee cups. There was a low hum of an imminent crash coming from her computer.

"It's been years since you've been over, hasn't it?"

"Too long. Have you kept Jim's old stereo, with the big speakers?"

"I couldn't. Had to sell them and his cameras right after the funeral. It was too much."

"Kent and I, when you and Jim were out, we used to put those speakers in the dining room and play Jim's records as we made tacos and drank gin and tonics. I always wondered if your neighbours ever said anything about that."

"The Honeywells. I was at war with that family from the day we moved in here. It all started with the rose bushes. They're gone now. So are the rose bushes. The McKersies too. Gone. There's a lovely young family in their place. They brought their girl over, all dressed up in a little chinaman's suit a few months back. The Ings." Bonnie looked out the screen door as if she could see them coming through the back yard gate. "So how are you, Ian? You're still working at the paper, I see. Just a couple weeks back I saw your name."

"I've been keeping busy. You know I'm writing a piece on Kent for a magazine. The Torontonian."

"Kent never told me that! Well done, Ian! So you should. Are you still taking care of your Dad's place?"

"I am, yeah."

Bonnie peered into the paper bag. There was a wet, waxy stain from the cinnamon buns that seemed to have spread. She reached in, plucked a bun out of the bag and gestured with it to Guthrie. "I should get you a plate."

"Actually, I'm fine, Bonnie. You go ahead."

"Your father was a good man, Ian."

"Thank you, Bonnie."

"He didn't deserve what they did to him. I wanted to go to the funeral."

"You should have. It would have been good to see you."

"I never told you this, but when your mother died, you remember that week in Cape Hatteras, when you came down with Kent and Jim and I?"

Guthrie nodded. Cape Hatteras. He recalled being in a hotel room with turquoise walls, rented by two nursing students from Roanoke, Virginia. Mindy and Deb had come down to "par-tay" for spring break. While Jim and Bonnie golfed, Kent managed to get him and Guthrie invited back to the girls' room. He had spotted them heading into the liquor store, stopped them in the mini-mall parking lot and asked them to buy a bottle of Jack Daniels and then, as Kent said later, back in Toronto, regaling his pals Birozes and De Wylders, one thing led to another. Well, for Kent anyway. Guthrie was paired off with Mindy, who had an overbite, Twisted Sister hair and smelled of Charlie perfume. She had declared that she was not going to be unfaithful to her boyfriend Doug, who was in the navy in Maryland. "I got to tell you right off the bat," she had said, fidgeting with her locket. And besides she was Baptist. Guthrie was relieved as they sat together on the mustard coloured couch and smoked while a muffled, high pitched yelp came from the bedroom. He had never drunk Jack Daniels since.

"I called your father and told him that we had heard about your mother's death and that we wanted this trip to be our treat. We were thinking of the funeral costs, all of that, you know." Bonnie paused, and her gaze went to a framed print of a landscape painting of the English countryside, just over Guthrie's shoulder. "I never really knew your mother, Ian, but everyone said she was lovely. So petite. Like a porcelain doll."

"She was a good mother."

"Anyways your father wouldn't hear of it. He said my boy pays his way. I thought he was angry with me for offering."

"That was just how he was."

"That's right, that was just how he was."

In the silence Bonnie just stared out the window to the back yard. The frost had clouded and whitened the edges of each pane in the peeling, splintered grid. She tore at the edges of the cinnamon bun and chewed it slowly, savouring the sweetness.

"I remember when Kent first started doing commercials and movies. Do you still have his picture?"

"Oh somewhere . . ." She peered over the mounds of papers, momentarily vexed, and then breathed out a small sigh of frustration. It was as if all this had just accumulated like the puddles of rainwater in the pots, a force of nature she was powerless to resist. "He was talented. Born for show business. Just like Bob."

"Bob, his . . ."

"You can say it, Ian. Bob his father. That's an old taboo long broken in this house. Bob played piano in a rock and roll band. That's how I met him. The Rockingbirds. They played my high school dance. That was before he went out west and made all his money."

"He picked you out of the crowd."

"I was too young. I was still a girl. But everything happens for a reason. There was Kent."

"There he was." Guthrie grinned as if they could commiserate about what it was like to be pulled into all of Kent's energy, like a centrifugal force, as he was growing up. Pulled in and then expelled as it all spun faster.

"That grows you up fast, Ian."

"You didn't think about getting married."

"Married? You kidding? I was Bonnie Fleischer, a good Jewish girl who went to Lawrence Park Collegiate. Fleischers didn't marry Ketchums in those days, Ian. Not the Ketchums from Baby Point, my dear. There was no question."

"Did Bob at least help?"

"His family did. But Bob was a kid himself. He was expelled from St. Alban's. That's how he ended up out west."

"How did you make a go of it?"

"Well I suppose I didn't think about it. Nobody did. You just got on with things. I mean I got a job as a teller at the Canada Trust and then I met Jim. He was the best looking of the ones who would come in and flirt with me. And I was lucky. He turned out to be a gentleman."

"You never thought about raising Kent?"

"What, you mean Jewish? Now how do you know I didn't?"

"I just think of Jim."

"I'm teasing you, Ian. My mother and I didn't get on well. She would drag me to synagogue every week, had me reading Hebrew. I just couldn't live in her house after I had Kent. It was too much." Bonnie smiled weakly. Her eyes had watered, but she was determined not to cry. She gazed out the window. "You better not put any of this in your magazine, Ian."

Guthrie shook his head and smiled, feeling too pious for his own comfort. At moments like these he wanted to reach across, gently touch Bonnie's hand as if to stop her and say "This is a transaction, that's all we're doing."

"Oh no. We'll keep it to Kent, trust me."

"He's getting famous in his way, isn't he? That's always been important to him. It's probably my fault."

"And married. That must be a relief. I met Veronica."

"Oh you did!"

"She's quite an impressive lady."

"You know, Kent was almost married before. That was when he was first up in Ottawa. Lainie. Isn't that a lovely name? From St. John's. She had this music in her voice."

"He's never mentioned her to me."

"No, it didn't end well, I suppose. And I'm not sure why. Lovely family as well. We spent six Christmases together. The Dunsmores. I still send Lynn and Fred a Christmas card each year."

"But not Lainie."

"Kent asked me to have no contact and that was fine. You can't pry into all that, I know. It's not your life. He seems happy now."

"Seems like he's back here for a while too."

"I hardly see him. I told him I saw him more when he was living out west!"

"He's going to win this."

"The campaign? Well …"

"You don't think?"

"Oh it's not that, Ian. You know me. You know I went to Montreal for the funeral for Trudeau. Kent and I, we had the worst argument I think we've ever had about that."

Guthrie smiled. He could see in her the young woman in a bright red blazer, walking proudly through the fall fair midway among a small entourage of pale men in pressed golf shirts and shiny black shoes. The Minister of Agriculture was going to make a speech and announce the winners at the 4H dairy calf show. The big man was dawdling through the midway, shaking as many hands as he could, tipping his green cowboy hat to the ladies as he took in the scattered crowd around the Ferris wheel. The air smelled of beer nuts and warm sugary gusts of candy floss. Guthrie and Kent had come to the fair because there was word that Glenn Cox could get them in the beer tent.

But then as soon as Kent glimpsed the red blazer he turned to Guthrie, slapped the cigarette from his fingers and muttered that they had to turn and walk the other way. "That's my Mom!" His mother? She looked no older than the waitresses at the A and W.

"You don't talk politics anymore."

"No. I gave up on that a long time ago. Different times. Kent was always more like his father. I could see it in him even when he was a baby. It's amazing, how much of the character starts to show even in the early years." She looked down at her hands clasped in her lap, the large freckles and paler, shiny blotches. "Did you ever want kids, Ian? You were married there for a while, weren't you?"

"Married, yes. Then widowed. No kids."

"Ian, I'm so sorry. I didn't know."

"It's fine, Bonnie. Long time ago."

"You would have been a good father, I know. And Kent too, if he ever slows down. But this one, Veronica. I don't think she wants them. Too busy. She's in a hurry for somewhere all the time, just like him now."

"I haven't spoken with her yet. I mean, I have to. For the story."

"Uh huh." Bonnie tore another strip off the cinnamon bun then gave the keyboard of her computer a look of concern. "See if you can get her to sit still for two minutes."

Guthrie smiled as she shrugged and let the thought dissolve into the hum of her computer. "Veronica's on the list they gave me. Of people I'm allowed to speak to."

"Who gave you the list?"

"Kent's people. Or his party's people."

"They gave you a list?"

"Not me, personally, no. They made sure to go above my head."

"Am I on this list?"

"You're not . . . no."

Bonnie leaned back in her wicker chair and nodded, looking out the window as if she could suddenly discern a figure in the distance. "These people are different. You know, I never liked Valgardson, but—"

"Valgardson?"

"Dan Valgardson. That MP who gave Kent his first job in Ottawa. He was a Reformer. I didn't have any time for him and Kent knew that. But that Valgardson didn't talk down to you. Didn't treat me like the help."

"He's not on my list either."

"No, I suppose he wouldn't be. Ian, you talk to whoever you damn well please. What's wrong with these people?"

"Is that a real question? If it is, I couldn't tell you. I mean, I've always stayed away from politics. Except when politics became part of the story."

"I read your story on my friend Margaret's boy."

"You mean Keith Lacey?"

"That was very well done, Ian. How they treated him, and him fighting in Afghanistan. That was nothing but criminal. You should be proud. Your father would be proud."

"It wrote itself, unfortunately."

"Listen, do you want me to talk to Kent? He'll listen to me. I can tell him they've got to lay off you."

Guthrie rose from his chair and began to zip up his jacket, as if he could suddenly feel the chill of the winter coming on. "Please don't, Bonnie. That's not why I came here."

"It's not something you should have to deal with."

"I came here because I just felt it would be disrespectful to write a story about Kent's past and not tell you what I'm doing."

"You're a good man, Ian."

"You save that other cinnamon bun for dessert tonight. They're great cold. I should know, they've been my dinner more than a few times."

As he made his own way out he reached into his pocket and turned off his tiny tape recorder and winced at how loudly it clicked.

It was when Guthrie had gotten to the stop sign at the end of the street that he noticed, in his rear view mirror, a car pull out from its parking space. It was a white SUV, parked two cars farther up the street from his own. He noticed it upon leaving Bonnie's because he could have sworn he glimpsed someone at the wheel. The SUV made a U-turn in the street and sped off in the opposite direction and it was all the confirmation Guthrie needed. He had to hand it to Jeannie Pincott, she was thorough.

19.

UNDER THE HAZY glow of a streetlight, Ojal leaned against the oak tree by the pond. Glimpsed from a distance it looked as if she was trying to uproot it and push it into the ground. One of her legs was fully extended, the other tucked closer into torso, and then she paused, switched the weight on her toes and stretched her other leg to its full extension. So stiff and tight she felt, this was the third morning where she rose out of bed after hardly sleeping at all—the third morning since she let Jagdeep Minhas, a married man, share her bed again.

How did she become this kind of woman, one that was such a gora cliché out here in the suburbs? It wasn't just the physical attraction or her loneliness. No, she had felt her heart pound for other men, a couple she even worked with back in 52 Division, and she had resisted—even when they made advances. Devon Haines, with his linebacker's shoulders and his deep voice. "Let's not go there," she would say to him when he flirted with her, until Devon began teasing her by calling her Miss NeverWentThere. Well, she was Miss Finally-Been now and the truth was, of all the approaches that won her over, Jagdeep had figured out it wasn't by what he said, it was by how he listened and responded when he asked her about, of all things, her politics and her ideals.

How unsexy. How like a geeky high school student she got, stuttering, mispronouncing words, saying "nucular" for nuclear when talking of India, babbling on way over her head about the economy, her perspective based on nothing but talk radio and fragments of news stories in the back pages of the Toronto Standard. And yet, in the way Jagdeep listened, in the gentle look in his deep brown eyes, she'd let him follow her home, follow her into her bedroom. What a home wrecker this unsexy geek had become.

And she still knew no way to make this right. Jagdeep reassured her that he would tell Amrit, his pretty, and by all accounts, very bright wife ("she should be the one running," Manvir said) "at the right time" over the next few days, but Ojal knew that, if at first he was only lying to himself by saying this, it would soon enough become a lie to her as well. Still that promise was the only thing she clung to each night now so she could finally get to sleep.

Meanwhile her work suffered. She knew she had let important details with this Brewin case wash over her. She would print out the pages of the report and read them at her desk and it was as if the words were written in white. Of all people it was Guthrie, that shambling mess of some interesting former self, who had gently nudged her back into attentiveness with his calls and his concern for Bella.

Bella who was now approaching. The girl looked still half-asleep too, shivering out the chill in her thin black nylon jacket as she slowed her pace to a walk.

Ojal waved. The street was barren and silent even this close to dawn.

"Hey …"

"I was starting to think you weren't going to come."

"This is so fucking early."

"Best time of the day."

"Said no one ever."

Bella and Ojal began shuffling down the wood chip trail that circled the pond, their breaths turned to puffs of smoke in the morning chill. Bella, her eyelids still thick with black liner, sniffed and wiped her nose with her sleeve.

Yes, this was Ojal's idea, and it ran the risk of seeming manipulative and far too forward, maybe even creepy as a ploy for them to talk. Surely Bella would not trust her enough to text or email any responses to the questions she had. But it was no surprise to Ojal when Bella texted her to say that her mother encouraged her go to on this morning run, in the hope it might become a regular thing; "She says I could use better role models (gag)."

"So ask me. Don't be shy."

"Ask you?"

"About Sydney. It's totally fine. You don't have to bond with me. I've already got a therapist."

"I guess I just wanted to know what you think now, after you have had time …"

"You mean about Drew? Like whether he killed her?"

"I guess."

"I think he gave her the oxies. No question. You know he deals, right? Like that can't be news to anybody."

"I know his record …"

"He never stopped. He's always had connections. Rents himself out. I swear, he's got a whole other life."

"I got that feeling."

"But OD-ing? Like he did it on purpose to her? I don't see it. Drew'd prob'ly taken a few himself. That's why he freaked and couldn't go to the cops."

"This is what I was thinking."

"It wasn't the first time they went up to the lake. I know. I've been with them. And Sydney and me …"

As they came out of the path and on to a sidewalk a minivan sped past and caught them both in the glare of its headlights. Bella brought her hand up to her face and fell behind.

"Are you hiding behind me?"

"Sorry. It's a reflex."

"You'd think the cops were after you or something."

"Bleacher girls. They all become so brave in packs."

"Nothing changes."

Bella let a small grin begin to form at the corners of her mouth while she moved ahead. "I wish I could wake up and say the same thing."

"You were saying something ... about you and Sydney ..."

"Was I?"

"Something about Lake LeSueur ..."

"Right ..." Bella glanced around her as they approached the tree where Ojal had been stretching.

"So you'd go up there with Sydney. You guys would get high."

"Sometimes, sure. I mean it's kind of a spooky place, right? There's an Indian cemetery. People said they seen ghosts."

"Did you see a ghost?"

"We wanted to."

"Like who? Like Annelie Danziger?"

Bella smiled, then she let out a small cough of a laugh. "So you been talking to people."

"It's my job, Bella."

"Well if you're talking to Syd's parents, you know they hate me, right? They're going to blame everybody they can for this. Everybody but themselves."

"You think they're to blame for anything?"

"I'm not judging."

"It sounds like you are."

"It's not my place. Just don't trust everything you hear. S'all I'm saying."

Bella cast a quick look over her shoulder, with just the smallest smirk. "All due respect, that's why I could never do your job. Especially in this redneck town."

"Redneck?"

"You know all the cops you work with hate you, right?"

Ojal forced a smile. "And you know this because?"

"It's just out there."

"Uh huh. You pick these things up."

"They make it obvious."

"And you speak to them …"

"I kind of had no choice, didn't I?"

"What are you talking about?"

"The day of the memorial service. When those two fat fucks picked me up for the second time, walking home. You couldn't have waited like maybe a couple of days?"

"Bella, I swear. I never would have allowed that. Do you know who they were?"

"Philips or Phelps or something. He's the one who ordered me to get in the back seat. The other one, Giannone, with the creepy grin, stared at my tits."

"What did they say to you?"

"They called Drew my fag friend and asked me why I didn't like real boys. They told me the Toronto cops would slap the truth out of Drew."

"Fifty-two Division doesn't work that way, trust me. And what truth?"

"That I was jealous because Sydney loved that fucking David Goring way more than she would ever care about me. And that Drew and I were two queers who had fucked up a straight girl's life, all this redneck crap."

"This probably makes no difference to you now but I take this very seriously."

"And what does that mean?"

"It means if you're comfortable about going on the record, I could at least have them suspended."

"That's only going to make it worse. It gets around, trust me. My first day back at school, I go to my locker and some cunt has spray painted die dyke bitch in letters so big I could see it from way down the hall. I can't go to the washroom. I know what's waiting for me. I've got my mom picking me up every day, like I'm back at daycare. You think I'm going to be telling you anything on the record? Seriously?"

"Bella you should be protected if they're bullying you. All this time, I was worried about Drew."

"Of course. You think they want me to talk about Sydney or that fucking Reverend or Pastor ..."

"Norris Arbic?"

"You should talk to somebody about him, that's all I'm saying."

"Why don't we talk about him ... what you know ..."

Bella's arms started to pump faster as she edged ahead of Ojal. "Can't. Promise is a promise. For Syd. For Drew. Plus I know how Syd's mom ... ever since Syd stopped going to church ... that bitch hates me. Blames me now. Too many people need me to stay quiet."

"But what do you need to do?"

Bella ran for a few yards then stopped and turned. They were about halfway around the pond. The newly fallen maple leaves seemed that much more golden with the first rays of the sun breaking through the upper branches. The only sound was the ragged breathing of these two women, years and worlds apart.

"I just need to keep running. Far away from here."

She turned and bolted from the clearing, as if she were sprinting down a last lap. All Ojal could do was nod, murmur a yes to herself as she watched the slender figure, all in black, get smaller and smaller in the distance until she disappeared over the last barren hill.

20.

WHAT KENT AND I shared, and what I believe made us inseparable friends at a certain point in our lives, was an experience that caused us to question who we were more acutely than most kids in Newton struggling through their adolescence. On a ski lift in Banff, Alberta, the "uncle" sitting beside Kent, Calgary developer Bob Ketchum, told him that he was actually his father. This occurred just weeks before I had come home from school to find my father weeping at the kitchen table as he told me we had to pick up my mother from the hospital. She had inoperable liver cancer and had a few weeks to live. I suppose Kent and I both discovered that our connections to those we loved the most, and all the connections we would make with others through the rest of our lives, were far more complex and fragile than we had once believed. There are two ways you can take that information: you can turn inside yourself or you can push yourself out into the world. More than two decades later, the distance Kent and I have travelled on these different paths has undoubtedly made us two different men. Yet what interests me more are what similarities remain; how much more public I may have become than I ever imagined over the years, and how much more solitary Kent actually is, as he prepares for his inevitable stage entrance to begin a very public life.

Well, Stephen could do his worst to it; he could excise the whole paragraph if he liked. It didn't matter; Guthrie had to get it down clearly for himself.

And he had to get here and speak to Bob Ketchum in person. Yes, it meant going into the funds-that-shall-not-be-touched, and yes it was hard to explain, even to Tanis. But it was exactly what Kent said to him after the debate; it was about the information. You had to go deeper, look harder for the real story. And the real story was only told to you in person—not on the phone, not over email—and it was often with just the most unexpected slip of the tongue.

Now, as he sat in this booth at the Ranchman's Club with his black notebook open, that last paragraph, scrawled in the dim light of the Radisson hotel room this morning, loomed like a cloud of squiggles and knotted lines over a series of short dashes and scrawls that lined the length of two margins. These were the questions for Uncle Bob.

Bob, like Kent's mother, was of course not on the list of designated interviewees given to Guthrie. It was possible that Jeannie Pincott did not know he existed. Of those from Kent's time in Alberta whom Guthrie was officially allowed to speak with there was only Senator Bobbie Chan, whom Kent briefly worked for about a decade ago. Chan had already left a message for Guthrie from his Ottawa office; he sounded courteous and courtly and eager to give Guthrie twenty minutes of harmless banalities, which is what the Senator had probably been asked to do time and again for the last two decades. No, it was Bob Ketchum who would have the most complete version of events concerning Kent's time living out here. His stories would lead Guthrie to where the real answers were, as those around him worked to manufacture his destiny.

The server approached Guthrie's booth with a toothy smile and the poise and posture of an ex-dancer.

"You still okay with that soda water?"

"I think so, yes."

"He'll be here, don't worry." She tapped her fingers on the armrest of Guthrie's chair as if she were gently calming him down. Up close she was at least his age, the luster of her blonde hair a bit too bright, her smile the work of the surgeon's knife. "This is his booth. If he's not here in ten minutes I am supposed to get you a cocktail."

"So he called?"

"He doesn't have to, honey. Why don't you have a cocktail anyway?"

"What does Bob drink?"

"You want a double of Lagavulin?"

"That'll be fine."

She smiled and cooed.

Guthrie could sense that his presence was cause for conversation now. He shut his notebook and wrapped the black elastic band around it in a quick pantomime of self-importance, as if his seriousness might make him less of a figure of derision. He knew that very feeling was emanating from the two men lunching nearby, just by their glances in his direction, the snap appraisals of the state of his clothes and the cut of his hair. They seemed to need a diversion as they waited for their ribeyes, their house salads disdainfully picked over like unwrapped party gifts neither wanted. Their bulk was artfully draped in their grey suits, black cowboy boots polished to a military shine.

To think what Kent must have learned, just by trying to keep up with his father in those first days of his time out here. Perhaps that would be a perfect topic of conversation for Bob —as long as Bob felt comfortable enough to talk about all the wisdom he had to impart. The more Kent was peripheral in this conversation, the easier the interview would be.

Bob bounced into the dining area now, stuffing his money clip down the front pocket of his navy pinstripe suit. He carried his Camel filters and an old chrome plated Ronson lighter—one that Guthrie recalled as soon as he glimpsed it again—discreetly in his left hand. As he approached the booth his big eyes lit up at the sight of Guthrie. A few feet away he looked expensively primped and maintained, only the broken blood vessels on his nose and cheeks betrayed the years. With his smile they flushed from pink to brick red.

"It's Ski-in' Ian!"

"Bob!"

Bob's nickname for Guthrie was solely based on the one week they spent together with Kent. It was the last year of high school and, though Guthrie should have known better about these adventures after Cape Hatteras, he had saved up enough cash from working in Record

World to get a standby ticket with Kent to Calgary where, Kent promised, "after this you can say you've skied powder and got laid in the mountains."

"Good to see you back in the better part of the country!"

"Good to be here. It's hardly changed at all."

"That's why we love it here." Bob leaned back in the booth and then nodded to the oilmen. "Jer, Rolf, good to see you." They actually grinned, Jer revealing his very white teeth, and said their good afternoons.

"I figured if I was actually going to write this piece, I had to talk to you."

"It's great to see you're hanging in with that old trade. Got to be a tough living. My buddy Mervin's daughter, she went down to Columbia in the States there, got her journalism degree. Came back up here and after a couple of years went back to the U of A for law school. Good kid. She just figures the whole industry's on its last legs."

"She's probably right. I'm not sure what else I could do at this point, though."

"Get your real estate license. Look at me, you don't need to be talented at anything. Ha!"

"You've still got that old Ronson."

Bob forced a smile as he fingered the lighter in his hands. It brought to mind some complicated feelings for just a moment. "That's right. I would have had this when you first came out here. "My initials. Carrie gave me this just before I got her an engagement ring."

"How is she?"

"She passed away in o-six. Two heart attacks a week apart. She asked me to promise I'd quit these things. Seven years later I'm still trying."

"I'm sorry, Bob."

"My problem is that the most fun I've ever had, I always had a smoke in my hand, know what I mean?"

"I do."

"You smoke? Well come on, let's grab one outside."

There was a patio at the Ranchman's Club that was now, with the winter coming on, just a few tables tarped and chained along a redwood platform. It looked out into the courtyard of the hotel next door. From here the hotel rooms looked dim and forbidding with the curtains drawn on every window. There was a chill in the air that worsened with every swirl of the wind. Bob cupped his hand around the flame of the Ronson then handed it over to Ian.

"You still playing the piano, Bob?"

"You mean the gigs around town?" He shook his head as he blew out a smoke ring like a teenager. "Naw, I couldn't keep the other guys interested. They were all making too much money in their real lives. God, it was a good time, though."

"I remember, when you drove us from Calgary to Banff in that Caddie."

"I'm still driving one! Best car on the road."

"You had made it your mission to give Kent and I a musical education. Son House, Albert King . . . all the old Chicago blues guys."

"Ha! And J.B. Lenoir. Don't forget J.B. You kids were growing up with all that new wave crap. I remember you had your hair all chopped like you'd come out of the nut house. Had all your collars done up to the top button."

"I was a serious boy."

"You were a serious boy, yes. Had a pickle up your ass."

"Those guys, they were still playing. I remember going to see them at the Silver Dollar. I never would have known about them if it weren't for you."

"Oh, they used to come through Toronto all the time when I was a boy. Me and my band back there, the Rockingbirds, that was our education. The first 45 we recorded was a Son House tune . . . we could have made some great records."

"But you had to get out of town."

"That wasn't just because of Kent, no . . . my grandpa . . . well, pretty much the whole Ketchum family had some serious concerns about my future. But this was the thing, even then, when I was selling the Rockingbirds' records out of the back of my car and at every high school dance we played, I was making some serious money for a kid my age. Serious money!"

Guthrie did not know how to reply aside from nodding and smiling, which must have happened a lot with Bob. He hardly seemed to notice in the pause.

"Am I going to get to read this before it's published?" Bob asked.

"If you want to. I mean, you don't even have to be in it. This can all be on background."

"But Kent will know it's me, no matter what I say to you."

"Why's that?"

"Tell you something. I know you know the whole story of how we reunited."

"You don't have to worry. It's not going in the piece."

"I wouldn't care. The truth is I had had enough. You think it was my idea to be Uncle Bob to Kent for all those years? No, those were the rules set down by Bonnie's parents. The Fleischers. Iris . . . Jesus what a hardass that old dame was. I couldn't see him, couldn't even cut the check so Kent could go to St. Alban's if I didn't play ball. I didn't plan on telling Kent on a goddamned ski lift. It was just . . . there we were, talking like father and son, and the whole masquerade was just so fucking absurd." Bob glanced at his cigarette, already smoked down to its filter. He flicked it in a planter while he muttered to himself and then lit up another. "Anyway, Kent told me later on that night, while we were walking to dinner in Banff, that he always knew. He just never wanted to rock the boat. He wanted to be a good kid for everybody.

And this is my point. There is no background for me. There never is when it's your real father talking. Kent will know."

Guthrie just nodded. He wanted to tell him about how much Kent transformed when he came back from that trip. He had cut his hair so he would look "like a Kennedy," and suddenly had a wardrobe of button downs, tennis shirts and boating shoes that, in Newton, where the young alpha dogs rigidly imposed the townie uniform of Levis, tight shirts and Kodiak boots, was like an open declaration of the worst kind of rebellion. In comparison Guthrie's attempt at looking like one—any one— of the dour members of some noisy, pimply British band, best forgotten, just marked him as weird but harmless.

"And the truth is . . . I don't know if you know this, Ian, but . . . it hasn't been good between Kent and me for some years now."

"For how long?"

"If I think about it, I guess it actually began when he came out here. Maybe he figured it would be just like one long version of our vacations together. But you know I offered to take him on as he went through university, slowly give him a sense of what his old man does and how he made his money. I mean . . . I'm not bragging here, but I could take you across the Bow and just start pointing out all the Ketchum projects . . . I've helped build this town, my friend." Bob squinted as he blew out a stream of smoke, as if he had seen a figure moving behind a hotel curtain window. "Anyway then he meets fucking Dan Valgardson. And really, there was nothing I could tell him anymore."

"Valgardson?"

"He never told you about Dan? Oh Jesus. You see those two, back in the bar, Jer and Rolf? He's like King Hardass for those fuckers. Dan was an MP for the Tories then went Reform. That's when he took Kent under his wing. The worst of it is I introduced him! Took Kent to a fundraiser right here at the Ranchman's. You know, you hardly see your kid while he's growing up, so maybe, when you finally do get a

chance to spend some real time together, maybe you push too hard . . .
you forget there's a lot of things you still have to learn about each other
. . . come on, let's get some lunch." He put a hand on the small of
Guthrie's back and guided him back into the club.

"So when you say it hasn't been good between you for a while,
I mean, do you talk to Kent? Have you spoken to him about all this
hype around him . . ."

"Oh we're fine. I mean I was there at his wedding, gave my
speech. This Veronica . . . she seems a nice girl. I would have run
screaming from her kind in my day but . . . ha! . . . no, she's lovely in her
way. But what about you there, ski-in' Ian? You got a wife and any little
Guthries running around?"

Bob insisted, as the server came by, that there would be no
need for Guthrie to look at the menu. They were both having a couple
of "Bob FMs"—filet mignons—with "this goddamn Louisiana
remoulade you can't get anywhere else."

After dinner, he and Bob embraced and promised to see each
other before he left Calgary, a promise they both knew he wouldn't
keep, Guthrie walked through the downtown streets feeling saddened
and heavy.

And then he checked the irksome BlackBerry deep in his coat
pocket. Not one but three calls from the personal cell phone of O.
DHILLON. He ducked into the lobby of a grey office tower and dialed
her back.

"Ian I wanted to get to you as soon as I could. I just want to
stress it's not an emergency though. It is under control."

"What's under control?"

"Somebody broke into your house. Now I know you called
Eric here and told him you'd be out of town. I just want you to know
they have been vigilant."

"What did he take?"

"He. You think you know who it is?"

"No. I mean, I don't know. What did they take?"

"Ian, all we can be sure of is some kind of computer from an office. You better call your insurance. There's a photograph that fell from a bookshelf."

"That was an old laptop I gave my Dad. It's okay. There are not many things I can be sure of about him, but I do know there was nothing of significance on that except one file, an Excel sheet where he did his taxes one year."

"Ian, I'm so sorry."

"It's totally fine. I'll call my insurance and see if I can get a flight out tomorrow."

"It's your father's stuff."

Guthrie exhaled sharply as he tried to figure out why she was suddenly upsetting him. "You got any leads?"

"We've got a footprint by your garbage can. Possibly a tire track. No fingerprints."

"I'll try to get back tomorrow night."

"The guys here, they know it was your dad's ..."

"Ojal, can we not do this?"

"This what?"

"This talking about my father as if he was some fucking saint to all you cops. You know what, Ojal? You would have hated him. With reason. If he were on the force while you were there, he would have done everything he could to make it difficult for you because he was an old fucking bigot. And that's why all the cops under you still love him. But thank you for calling. And thank you for your thoughts. I'll take it from here. Call me when you catch the fucking guy."

Guthrie hung up. He hadn't hung up on anyone for as long as he could remember.

Later that night, as he emptied the third little rye bottle from his mini bar into a plastic glass, he called Ojal once and then clicked off before her line rang. And then again. He knew he needed to apologize but where to begin? How to explain it? The truth of it was he really didn't understand why he had said what he did. All he knew was that his intuitions about this story taking more out of him than he imagined were correct. And he probably should have taken a closer look at who was driving that white SUV that afternoon. It seemed so long ago now.

21.

@bellarella

hey

@drUtrask

Hey

@bellarella

where U at

@drUtrask

Toronto

@bellarella

R U OK

@drUtrask

I'm fine. Thank you for asking

@bellarella

what R U doing there

@drUtrask

Surviving. Staying positive. Living w/ Derek

@bellarella

Derek

@drUtrask

You don't know him. I don't know why you still try to know me

@bellarella

Y R U being such a prick right now

@drUtrask

Excuse me?

@bellarella

I'm reaching out and asking how you are

@bellarella

Here's the only place you haven't blocked me
@drUtrask
Should I be thanking you or something?
@bellarella
I could just H8 U like everyone else I guess
@drUtrask
Do what you like
@bellarella
is that what U said to Syd?
@drUtrask
You want this to end in fuck off, don't you?
@bellarella
actually no. I just knew that if I didn't reach out to U U wouldn't
@drUtrask
So why do you care?
@bellarella
were U never going to talk about this W me?
@drUtrask
Why would I?
@bellarella
because she was our best friend
@drUtrask
You gave her the ultimatum. She told me
@bellarella
ultimatum?
@drUtrask
You or me as her best friend
@bellarella
like you didn't talk about me
@drUtrask
Actually you didn't really come up much. Until you said that
@bellarella

dude. She was pregnant. You were giving her oxys

@drUtrask

Total BS

@bellarella

PLZ

@drUtrask

Not once

@bellarella

where did she get them then

@drUtrask

Like I'm the only person to ever have oxys

@bellarella

cops talking to me. LOTS

@drUtrask

So that's what this is about. You think I'm stupid?

@bellarella

U think Id rat U

@drUtrask

Nothing surprises me anymore. Why not txt me? Oh right because you save this

@bellarella

or maybe like I said because you blocked me ASS

@drUtrask

Sorry it's so long since I've checked who. So many

@bellarella

Im trying to help U

@drUtrask

Right. And how can you help me?

@bellarella

You know Goring's got his crew and

@bellarella

Syd's mom said she'd get them on you

@bellarella

For fucking Reverend Arbic

@drUtrask

I don't care what he tries to pin on me anymore. Far as I'm concerned he

@drUtrask

killed her right

@drUtrask

Tell that to your cop friends

@bellarella

You should talk to them too before they hunt U down

@drUtrask

No reason to hunt me down. I don't talk. I keep my promise

@drUtrask

To Syd. So should you

@bellarella

She wouldn't want this for you. Never mind me then

@bellarella

im saying is this shits real here and I wnt U to be safe

@bellarella

U may H8 me now but we wr once frnds

@drUtrask

That's true

@bellarella

just b safe you're innocent nothing fucking Arbic could say

@drUtrask

Not scared of him. Just keep my word. For Syd. A promise. RIGHT?

@bellarella

just b safe

@drUtrask

You too

22.

SLAPSHOTS, WITH ITS Thursday night special on pumpkin pie shooters and nothing but a Canucks game on the screens, was Ojal's choice tonight. Yet she had taken a stool at the stand-up bar and not a booth, ready to make a quick exit if she had to.

"Mr. Guthrie."

"Staff Inspector. Slapshots. This is novel."

"I thought you'd love this place. Local character and all that. And hockey."

"Never played. Listen, I wanted to apologize once again for that weirdness on the phone."

"No need …"

"There's no excuse. You were thoughtful and respectful as you always are, and I had found yet another way to be an asshole."

"You're building up a repertoire?"

"Something like that, I guess."

She jiggled the ice in her tumbler and brought the fizzy red drink to her lips. "The artistic temperament. That's what I hope you can help me with, Ian."

"What do you mean?"

"I followed your lead, talked to this kid Bella. And I hit a nerve when I mentioned this old case … Danziger."

"Annelie, yeah …"

Guthrie motioned to the bartender at the far end by the beer taps. The woman seemed sullen about the empty tables tonight, scratching her bare arms as if she was worrying off the salon tan. When she caught sight of Guthrie she nodded to his request and slipped a glass under the tap with a casual precision.

"I'm starting to get it now, if that's any consolation."

"Look, I just don't want to see this Trask kid go down for it, that's all. I wanted to give you an angle so you could push back on the lynch mob out here."

"Well ... as far as I'm concerned not even the criminal negligence charge is going to stick with Drew. And the real motive for Sydney Brewin's death ... I guess there really is something in this Danziger case."

Guthrie's gaze darted back to the bartender, the two townies three swivel chairs away. He took a breath, thinking through his words carefully. "Thing is, Sydney was better at suicide. When I read all these letters, I couldn't help thinking Annelie Danziger gave up on that kind of escape from her situation. Though I'll give you this, looking back on it all, the one part of the story that is similar is the criminal negligence charge—or should I say the lack of evidence for it to stick."

Ojal ran a hand through her hair as if she was gently letting these details seep from her fingernails into her thoughts. Yet the look on her face suggested she was still puzzling it all out.

"Explain."

"I remember at the time I followed the trial of this guy who was charged for criminal negligence. Nicky Poole, his name. Poole had a room on top of the Hi Fi Lounge where he worked as a bartender. That's where Annelie was found. OD-ed. They said Poole was dealing, they had him on a possession charge, but really, word was it was just a bad accident."

"An accident?"

"At the time heroin had made a comeback among the kids who hung around Queen Street. Before it became a mall." Guthrie shook his head and glanced up at the TV screen, wearing his mask of weary indignation, as if the commercial for a barbecue with a vaguely familiar actor was somehow related to his view on how the city had changed. "The stuff kids were smoking and shooting, it was dirty, though. Until somebody started dealing this higher grade heroin from Vancouver. And boom. Over the course of that fall not just Annelie but a few people OD-ed. Her death fell into a larger pattern that was emerging, a drug story for the media, the dangers of bohemian life in downtown Toronto."

"You believe that obscures some motive with her death?"

"I honestly don't know, Ojal. All I can tell you is I've been looking closer here, as I'm trying to figure out why this Sydney Brewin saw in Annelie some kind of role model."

"So you're still writing on this. I figured with Drew getting bail . . ."

"Trying to. The more I look back on the story, the more I think this Sydney was desperately projecting a connection … and emulating a solution to her own desperation about her pregnancy … the course her life was about to take … and that connection just wasn't there."

"Why not?"

"What do you mean why not?"

Ojal reached into her handbag and pulled out two pieces of lined stationery paper, folded in four. The writing on the pages, in fine black marker, was smudged in places. "I got this from Bella Lang two mornings ago. She pulled it out of a pocket of her jacket while we were running, just before she bolted away. I haven't heard from her since."

"It's a letter?"

"A letter from Annelie Danziger to this Tanis … Bella's mother. Look at the date."

Guthrie's lips moved as he took in the year, as if he had to murmur to himself to confirm this was real. "I thought Tanis gave me all of those."

"Well … not this one. It meant something to Bella, all right."

"I thought you weren't going to read any of these old letters … that they were inadmissible or something."

Ojal nodded and slowly blinked. She was tracing a wet ring from her drink on the table in front of her with one finger. "The girl is persuasive. I worry about her."

"And so you see a connection?"

"I see a parallel, all right. Both of these young women were pregnant, but not from any relationship with a young man they were with at the time."

"Pardon?"

"That's right. In this letter, this Annelie Danziger writes of a relationship she had with this musician. She calls him Tommy K, that some day Tanis had to meet him. Dark eyed . . . Greek family. Then she writes of how, when Kent Wolseley found out about this Tommy over the summer, he flew into a jealous rage. Violated her. That violation made her pregnant. She told him over the phone that she was going to have the child and . . . as she says here . . . he just lost it. Accused her of trying to ruin his life out of revenge."

"Let me see . . ." Guthrie brusquely scanned the pages. He had lost all pretense of calm detachment now.

"And here's the thing, with Sydney, Bella tells me she too was pregnant with the wrong guy's child. It wasn't David Goring's . . . no . . ."

"She told you that?"

"Uh huh." Ojal nodded, brushing two long strands of hair from her face. Her big dark eyelashes blinked away the intensity of their eye contact now.

"Then who was it?"

"That she won't say. She said she swore to Sydney she'd never tell. She's not going to betray her now."

"What difference does it make?"

"Because she's dead? Guthrie . . . you forget what it's like to be young. You forget the power of a secret."

"Oh I don't know about that. I had one of my own. I had a massive crush on Annelie Danziger and it enraged me she'd be with someone like the Kent Wolseley of almost thirty years ago. Which is not much different than the one now."

"Enraged you because she turned you down first."

"Kind of, I guess. I'd say she just sized me up and found me wanting. And I had outed a friend of hers, inadvertently made his life hell here in this town. I mean, look at this kid Drew. Not much has changed. But anyway, in my head I always thought her relationship with Kent was really for her parents. Fine upstanding Canadian boy. Bright future. And then she escaped to the city ..."

"Like you did, right?"

"Yeah, but I was in university, trying to become respectable. And she was in art school."

"And Kent didn't matter to her anymore. I guess that drove him crazy."

"That might have been. And maybe Sydney Brewin saw something of her own situation with David Goring in that."

"If that was so, Bella didn't see it. She said she just broke it off with David because she couldn't lie to him is all. About the baby ... saying it was his ..."

Guthrie shook his head and sipped his Stella. He made a church of his fingers and stared into them. "Thing is, Ojal. When I spoke to Karen Brewin, she told me she was going to make sure her daughter was going to have that child. And she was going to make sure Sydney married David Goring. Why would she say that if ..."

"She tell you her daughter left the congregation at Trinity Baptist? She tell you Sydney broke it off with David?"

Guthrie shook his head. Then he leaned back in his chair and took in the tables of heavyset men, oddly dandified for a night out here, dressed in expensive denim and fake flannel like celebrity chefs. He was doing his best to look unfazed. "And you trust this Bella?"

"I do, yeah. And it has become very clear to me when I talked to Bella that there is some sort of intimidation going on. Guys like Phelps, Giannone. I feel like they've been doing what they can to keep Bella quiet and to keep Dan Goring's kid out of this story."

"If that's what you think is going on, you've got some management challenges, as they say."

"Is it so hard to believe? I mean, from what you remember when your dad had my job ..."

Guthrie stared into what remained of his beer. "This town isn't quite what they told you, eh?"

On the screen above the bar a fight had broken out in the Canucks game. Two young bearded Vikings, helmets askew, were locked in an embrace as they flailed punches in wild directions, their mouths and noses smeared with blood.

"I want to talk to Karen Brewin again."

Guthrie nodded as one of the players readjusted all his armour in the penalty box, wiping the blood from his nose and lips.

"And I think I may have to talk to David Goring again. This kid was probably abusive and made Sydney's life hell when she broke it off with him."

"I don't know, Ojal. Maybe he was just broken hearted. But maybe he knows about who ... I mean maybe he's not going to keep any of Sydney's secrets anymore."

"Now that's a thought. Thank you, Mr. Guthrie. Not sure what I'd do without you."

She pulled on her coat that was cradled around her barstool. As the bartender had come with the cheque she took the bill Guthrie had left under the glass. It was the subtlest way she could tell him he did not have to walk her out to her car.

Guthrie walked out alone. The puddles of light on the slick black pavement rippled with another blast of winter wind. As the car warmed and the windows cleared he lit up what was only his third cigarette of the day. There was some promise in his renewed self-discipline. He tried to find some music from this decade on his little device. Any mannered three-chord commemoration of the bands he grew up with would do, just for its novelty. The car grumbled out of the parking lot. Nothing left of the evening, nothing to do but head back to his father's house to fall asleep with the television news on or write these notes that were better left out of his story for now.

23.

THE TURBOPROP SLOWLY cut through the clouds. Out his window Guthrie could see a patchwork of fields stitched together with silvery grey threads of country roads and Monopoly houses. Ottawa. None of this aligned with Guthrie's childhood memories of Gothic spires, a canal with small flourishes of tulips along the roadway that traced its path.

He had opened up his laptop and once again stared at the opening paragraph of his next Monitor story, hoping some words might come. He knew he had to get something down about Drew Trask's release; completing the piece while taking this "research trip" for the Torontonian was the deal he had struck with his conscience for justifying this expense. It had now been more than a week since he sat down with Drew and even with the Monitor's rather relaxed sense of deadlines Gallant had mused aloud about "maybe Kerry-Anne blogging something on that whole Brewin story" the last time Guthrie was in the offices. And yet every time he tried to write he just thought of Stephen.

"Don't worry about me, just write your goddamn story," Stephen had muttered, trying to sound as stern as he could from his hospital bed. The heart attack aged him a decade, the faded freckles on his forehead and his waxy looking hands were signs of a new frailty that, in truth, may have been apparent the last time they met in Stephen's office, but Guthrie just hadn't noticed. Yet it was also just like Stephen to be artful in how he presented himself, wingtips and grey flannels even through the paisley years, so the office story went. It was just like him to deflect all talk of his health and indeed much of his personal life, as if his forty years of marriage and the raising of an adopted child were the least interesting parts of him.

What they did not talk of in the hospital was whether Stephen would even return to his position at the Torontonian. Stephen would have brusquely dismissed any mention of whether that would matter with regard to Guthrie's profile being placed, yet Guthrie had been around long enough to know he was a virtual unknown among everyone else at the magazine. He would be considered just another one of Stephen's collection of louche old freelancers, the ones who had been among the first let go from any reputable publications when the old mastheads all started to fade into the inconsequential online.

It was not yet 5 p.m. when Guthrie got off the plane, through the airport and out to the taxi stand, but already the sky had darkened. The wispy grey streaks of cloud had taken on volume and a whole new range of colour, all the darker variations of blue pieced together with thin seams of pink and gold. Guthrie took his place in line and performed the role of the business class traveler, patient but eager for a quick conclusion to this moment of indignity.

He had a hotel room, a meeting with Lainie Dunsmore tomorrow that she deigned to confirm by email just two days ago, and he had an e-vite to a veterans' reception organized by Senator Bobby Chan where, as the Senator said, they could "chat and have a couple of scotchies." Any hope of speaking to Lainie's father who, judging by all Guthrie had read, seemed to have been some quietly powerful bag man during the Mulroney years, was dashed forthrightly enough when the old man picked up the phone at his law office, heard Guthrie out and then calmly, with that charming Newfoundland accent, told Guthrie that years ago he had decided, no offense, that the "journalistic profession was full of nothing but Liberal lickspittles and parasites" and he would never speak to any of them again. He was a man of his word, he said, but he wished Guthrie a wonderful stay in Ottawa all the same.

Tonight, he would once again review all he had written about Kent and this campaign—it had become a ritual—and try to figure out what to excise. He was breaking all the rules with himself, putting so much of his own story and the past in there in order to unearth some deeper themes, but what was emerging were images—like the burning staircase in the lake, a long forgotten clip of Annelie on the shore from one of her Super 8 films—that resisted any explanations he could come up with for their significance.

"The real stories only emerge in conversations," Stephen had said long ago. "You have to watch the truth, and the lies make their way through the body." Like reading trails of smoke with these effigies. He pried open the mini bar and fished out a small bottle of Chivas Regal, unscrewed the top and drank it down in one swallow.

***

"My father tells me you called him. He enjoyed that." Lainie Dunsmore leaned forward intently, beaming proudly. Her desk lamp cast a half moon of light across her features. Dark eyes, her colouring a shade away from olive skin. She was nothing like how Guthrie had imagined her, save for the air of privilege and the shine of keen intelligence in her eyes.

"I suppose I asked for it."

"And why do you say that?"

"I called him out of nowhere. Just like I called you."

"It was his mother Bonnie, wasn't it?"

Guthrie nodded deeply and bit his bottom lip. He wanted to speak of how Bonnie's tone lightened, how fond she still seemed to be about the woman who might have once been her daughter-in-law. Lainie's gaze went to the lapels of his blazer, as if she was measuring its width and deciding what kind of man he was: his politics, the remnants of his younger self.

"Well, Newton is close but I wouldn't quite call it nowhere."

"Bonnie seems very fond of you."

"Yes." Lainie allowed herself the briefest of smiles. "I was fond of her too."

"Past tense."

"All of that's long past tense. As it should be. You golf, Mr. Guthrie?"

"Never played, no."

She had caught his gaze fixed on the photograph behind her desk. Lainie was tanned, slimmer, holding a trophy with two paunchy men dressed in the country club active wear that signified a merry, prosperous surrender to middle age.

"That's our office team, two summers ago out in Chelsea. Client's tournament."

"You must play well."

"Runners-up. I don't much care for the game actually." She placed her palms flat on the desk like a croupier, poised for the turn of the next card. No rings on those fingers. "What did she tell you, Mr. Guthrie? I mean about me and Kent."

"She told me very little, really, aside from the fact that you were once engaged."

"Uh huh."

"She still seemed a little sad that it didn't work out."

"That's a lot of personal information to give to a . . ."

"Lickspittle, I believe your father called me."

"I'll say journalist."

"Thank you . . . but you can probably add friend of the family. Kent and I were good friends when we were teenagers."

She leaned back in her chair and slightly cocked her head, as if she was trying to place him from an old photograph.

"I don't think he ever mentioned you to me."

"No . . . I guess I could see that. Our friendship didn't end well."

"Things tend not to with Kent, yes."

"It has only been over the last . . . I think it's been seven years . . . that we've been speaking again. There were a couple of decades where we barely had any contact at all."

Guthrie could feel his blood pressure pulse behind his eyes. If he closed them it felt like he would see little Rothkos of red squares on black drift inside his eyelids. How appropriate he should be feeling this hung over and speaking of the still puzzling rapprochement. The call at the Standard, the cheery voice that sounded like he was still seventeen. "Just moved back to city!" Kent had declared, as if Guthrie would share in his excitement. "First time with a Toronto address in my whole life! Now how did that happen?" Guthrie had felt something like shame as he thanked him for his compliment about a review of his in the Standard, dutifully wrote down the address of the Harpo club where they were to meet for drinks with "some people you should get to know." There at the Harpo were two PR agency VPs dressed like Euro trash pimps, a brassy publicist, close to sixty, who seemed to cultivate the air of an old burlesque queen, and three beefy, thuggish lawyers—former Conservative flacks, apparently—with the same feral glare, stoked by their regular visits to the men's room together. After five painful hours of forced jollity and two hundred dollar bottles of Bordeaux, Guthrie, Kent and the publicist ended up at the gimcrack million dollar condo of one of the VPs, Troy, if memory served, where the lines of coke went around, cut neatly on the back cover of a Hello! Magazine. At around 3 a.m. the publicist declared she had been celibate for more than a year as she propped up one of her heels on Kent's knee. The freckled skin around her thick ankles wrinkled like a lizard's. It had seemed like the right time for Guthrie to make his exit. A day later, taking groceries home, it had occurred to him that he had served as a kind of prop for Kent, their reunion handled deftly as a device for all the guests to reminisce about whom they had been in the eighties. When he left Kent they both swore they would meet for drinks the following weekend and truly catch up on all the years. It never happened and they both knew why; all they had to show for the time between was a détente where they both tried to temper their cynicism and feign interest in each other's work.

"A couple decades. I think I might still need a couple more." She rose from her desk and moved to shut the door to her office. Guthrie turned in his chair but she murmured "it's all right, it's all right …" As she put her hand on the knob to close it she took a deep breath, glanced at her large black rubber watch, a token of some willed, sexless inelegance. "There are some people here in these offices who do a lot of work with this government. My clients are corporate."

"I don't entirely understand."

"I kept my mouth shut once for the party. I did it for my dad. But they're not his party anymore. I suppose they never were. They've shown that by the way they've treated him. I've never …" She was speaking in a new, even tone, extracting any possible emotion from each word, her gaze fixed on the corner of her desk.

"They … this party of yours …"

"Not mine. Not for a long time."

"They asked you not to talk about something … something about Kent?"

She nodded, letting out a deep breath. She would not lift her gaze from the grain of the wood.

"He became jealous … angry for no reason … and then he became violent. I want to say just once and that was the end of us but that's not true. And when he finally did what he did … I still think to myself I could have broken it off way before it got that bad." She finally looked up at Guthrie once again. "But I didn't."

"I'm sorry. This is important," Guthrie leaned in, his tone descending into his smoker's growl, "could you tell me what, exactly … I mean, what he did."

"Forcible entry. Sexual Assault. How much more specific do you want me to be?"

"Was he charged? Did you call the police?"

She leaned back and smiled, focusing on the door behind Guthrie. "I'm a pretty good lawyer. Clerked at the Supreme Court. You'd think I'd call the cops, wouldn't you?" She shook her head as her chin quivered, holding back her tears. "I just called my dad."

"And he ..."

"He picked me up and took me back to the house. Like I was sixteen again. I ended up staying in my old bedroom for three months. I couldn't go back to my apartment ... sleep in that bed ... I know my dad would have killed Kent if he had seen him. And I know he called Dan Valgardson that night and they talked for hours. I remember hearing his voice as I went in and out of sleep. I must have slept for sixteen hours."

"Dan Valgardson ..."

"You're going to write anything about Kent, you better know who the hell Dan is. Not that he would talk to you."

"And so Kent was never charged. There's nothing on record."

She slowly shook her head, placed her hands on her temples and ran her fingers through her hair, as if this could banish these memories from her head. "Whatever Dan managed to say to my father, Kent Wolsely owes his very life to him, not just his political career. The next morning my dad came into my room. He told me it would only be worse if it all went public. And it would inevitably go public. He told me it was taken care of, Kent would never see me again and that he would be leaving Ottawa very soon."

"They got him out of town."

"I suppose so. And kept him out. At least until this by-election of his is over, it seems."

"Do you fear his return? I mean he should be arrested ..."

Lainie smiled, savouring Guthrie's sudden, stuttering anger, the way the revelation had detonated, destroying a conception of Kent that had formed over decades in this stranger's mind. "No. I don't fear his return. I am not afraid of him in any way. I am not the person I was that night anymore. I haven't been for years."

"But he is still the man who did this to you."

"I don't know. You tell me. You're the one doing the story on him."

"You know I need to write about this. I mean, I can do everything I can to ensure your identity—"

"I don't care, Mr. Guthrie. Not anymore. I don't owe anything to these people. My father doesn't owe anything to these people. Do you think I would be sitting here otherwise? I would have told you what my father said to you when you called him."

"I understand." He turned off his tape recorder. "I may have to follow up with you on this. Just on some details as I put this story together for the Torontonian."

She nodded, reached into a silver box on her desk, pulled out a blue business card and gently slid it across to him. "My cell's on that one."

***

Senator Chan,

I'd like to thank you once again for the invitation to the event for the Veterans Cenotaph fund but I'm afraid I must return to Toronto earlier than I expected. I'm hoping we can still speak on the phone.

Guthrie could just barely hear the muffled announcement of his flight boarding as his thumbs tapped away on the keys of his device. He drained the last of his espresso as he watched the business travelers slouching nearby gather up their coats and glumly shut down their laptops. They all seemed to be relieved that they would be in the air imminently now, this city took a lot out of you. He made his way for the gate, watching a seagull float on a draft of air, just a few feet away on the other side of the glass. Must call Stephen, find out how he is.

Guthrie had been thinking once more of that night in Toronto when he and Kent had met at the Harpo Club. It was much later, after they had left the condominium and had caught a cab together that Kent had said something that took on a new meaning now. They were talking about the publicist, how aggressively flirtatious she had become with Kent, and Guthrie, simply trying to pay him a compliment (and yes, perhaps make the reconciliation as authentic as possible) had mentioned it had always been that way; of the two of them, the girls had always gone for Kent.

"You know why that was? Because I knew early on that girls really didn't want nice. Nice was bullshit. Nice was guys with acoustic guitars and opinions on Nicaragua. Nice was let me walk you home. Let me make you a mixtape, unh? I never told you but when I was fifteen I fucked Danny Graham's mother in the shed at the tennis club. She was the last bitch who called me a nice boy. And she didn't think I was very nice at all, believe me, and that's exactly how she wanted it."

Kent had just stared out at the foggy blue gloom of the early morning as the taxi sped past Queen's Park, the trees like broken hands gloved in black. Then he had laughed like Guthrie hadn't heard him in decades—a hoarse, squealing sound and then giggles that came out in a raspy torrent. Guthrie had put it down to all the coke.

When the taxi let him out first, he had given Kent a wave from the door of the apartment building. Kent had not waved back. Once he was finally in bed his last thought, before he had finally surrendered to sleep, was that he would probably never see Kent again.

24.

DREW WAS CELEBRATING. He looked up from the mahogany veneer of the table, blurred right past the crowd to focus on the ceiling. No we was not hallucinating the cherubs floating in a sky of pale blue and vanilla ice cream clouds. Sure, maybe he had indulged himself a little more than necessary given that Derek was in Montreal doing his buyers' meetings but how would he—how would anybody understand—how liberated he felt now? He had started after lunch when Melvin Kwan and Brock Wilson had suggested the new Claridge, the bar with all the wealthy brokers, bankers and corporate lawyers Derek so tiresomely cultivated as friends for them both. Now it was almost ten and he was still here with half a bottle of cognac and four lines of coke coursing through him.

It would be so easy for Drew to stay out, head over to Priape, truly make it a night to remember. But no, with this sense of liberation came responsibilities. Truth telling, despite the promise he had made to Syd, was necessary—and possible at last. So out the door and into the gust of cold autumn wind, dun coloured leaves scuttling into the dark corners of the street.

Maybe you could say everything happens for a reason. For instance why did he decide, among all the bars on Church, to go into Bang Tuesday night after work? Why, among all the tables, did he end up in that booth at the back with Todd and Vik? Sure, maybe it was just a matter of time before he would run into Jesse Drummond, now that the kid was moving downtown. This little strip of city was such a small town, just as gossipy as all the horrible little towns guys like him and Melvin and Brock had fled. But the fact is Jesse Drummond, little Jiminy Cricket in a pale blue button-down . . . what they both got up to was all that stood between finally going back to that cop Ojal Dhillon and telling her everything. Fucking Norris Arbic had no power over him anymore. God bless little Jesse Drummond and his soul damned to hell—by the good reverend himself no less now.

Taxi, taxi . . . take me back to my better self. But no, just a train of headlights zooming past, drivers looking away from his waving, tottering, wide eyed plea.

Shivering and ruminating, Drew had to hand it to the Reverend Norris, he had his powers of seduction. That first time he met Drew at the Country Time, he knew exactly how to get to him. He didn't try talking about faith—he knew Drew had left Holy Cross, he was a fallen Catholic boy who wasn't coming back to Jesus any time soon. No, the good Reverend just went on about his own "journey" first, spoke about how, back in the eighties, Drew might not believe it but Norris was "quite a bohemian" with his band called The Roman Candles (Google us!) but then hard drugs (he wouldn't say what) led to despair, to a relationship with a woman that took him to Mission, BC. Hippies, I guess you'd say, good people mainly. A failed attempt at goat farming, the woman leaving him to go to India. There was pathetic ponytailed Norris adrift, ending up in the worst side of Vancouver and then came his salvation one morning in a humble, former ashram near a place called White Rock (Google that too!). Thing is, said Norris, he could understand why Sydney Brewin would leave the church, he had his wandering years too, but Drew was her best friend now, could he not talk to her and bring her back into the fold?

Never should have met the Reverend again those couple weeks later, never should have spoken to him about his own feelings of despair and being cast out once he realized there was no hiding he was gay. But Drew saw in him a consoling voice, a person who cared. And so he just spoke too much.

Now from the taxi window, streaked in rain turned silvery in the dark, the wipers rhyming out the coke thumping rhythm of Drew's heartbeat, he looked out and realized they were already on Yonge now, already crawling through the traffic past Bloor and into his new neighbourhood. It would be hours before he could finally sleep, sure, an eternity to rewind the episodes that had led up to Syd's death, what he feared might be the central fucking tragedy of his life. But no, banish that fear, sorry Norris Arbic, you fucking pathetic old creep, you weren't going to have that power any more.

He came to understand Norris' M.O. in that third meeting—this time in the good Reverend's car, after he practically stalked Drew walking home from school. Now that Drew knew Syd was pregnant, now that she told him everything this snake had done to her, the fucking Reverend Arbic could go to hell, frankly.

But no. Because here was the deal, Norris said, he'd spoken to the boy Jesse Drummond in the congregation and found out how far Drew had taken his own seduction—when Jesse was just fourteen. If Drew imagined he was going to talk to anyone about why Syd really left the church, what happened with Norris and whose baby she was pregnant with, well … Jesse was prepared to tell the police everything about Drew because he'd come back to God at Trinity Baptist.

And Syd too … she swore Drew to secrecy. If their friendship meant anything … don't tell a soul. But who was to say where her soul was now, or what she would really want? No, he was liberated, thank you very much. Free to be a good person, to tell what he knew. Sweet, broken, heroic Syd, turning away from that jock boyfriend of hers, her mother … telling them nothing … Drew owed it to her now. Some justice at last.

As the taxi turned onto the street, Drew started to feel his heart thump with greater force. How was he ever going to give coke up? How he loved the pixelated, technicolour oblivion of a great rush. He knew where Derek kept more in the house too. Why the fuck not? Some porn and one final toot or two before he called the cop in the morning.

Number 72 was the last townhouse before the park. The porch light was on. Yes, that was his fault, not Derek's. The taxi driver stared dolefully out at the black wrought iron fence, glistening like a line of spears, while he ran Drew's credit card through the POS machine. He raised an eyebrow as the receipt came through. The driver was skeptical about either the generous tip or simply at the possibility of Drew actually knowing where he was.

And fuck . . . he had forgotten his key again. The spare, though (don't despair!), the spare was under the barbecue in the back yard. Drew followed the paved pathway as it curved around an ancient oak tree, the wrinkles in the bark fringed in crooked lines of moss. He could hear the wind stir the branches of the pines along the fence. The cold night air and the rain on his face felt so good, so pure.

It was the voice whispering his name that stopped him cold. Drew glimpsed the silvery flash of the blade. He got his arm up just in time to block the first thrust, to hear it tear the leather of his jacket. That tear was the last sound he heard.

25.

GODDAMN THIS ESPRESSO machine. It was just so Tanis: the cool elegant lines, matte metallic sheen to match the zinc of the counter, yet unpredictable and pointlessly mysterious in its workings. Guthrie had unscrewed the handle twice and tamped down the coffee further into its shallow metal bed yet all that came out of the two nozzles were a few dark, oily drops, and the burbling, rumbling groan had awoken Bella. He heard her shuffle down the hall in the direction of the kitchen.

"Mom?"

"Uh. No."

Bella appeared within his line of vision of the kitchenette, her hair shooting out left, right and skyward. She had a finger poked in one eye. Her fingernails were painted a new shiny black.

"Oh. Hi."

"Hi."

"Where's my mom?"

"She left about a half hour ago. Said she had a conference call in the office. You're Isabella."

"Bella, please."

"I'm Ian. Ian Guthrie."

"Hello, Ian Guthrie."

"Would you like one of these? I mean, if I can get this machine to work …"

Bella approached him. She looked younger as she pushed her hair away from her face. It was the pink in her cheeks, her eyelashes almost white in the morning rays shooting through the window.

"Here. I can do this. If you have a smoke."

"I do."

"Awesome."

She brushed past him and eyed the espresso machine as if it were not to be trusted. Guthrie liked her already. She jerked the arm that held the metal cap another thirty degrees to lock it in place and pushed the button by the little red light. The espresso flowed like water.

"I'm out of here once I drink this. Can I give you a lift to school?"

"Score. Just let me shower."

Guthrie tossed the pack of cigarettes her way and Bella caught it without looking up from the machine.

***

Before he unlocked the passenger side, Guthrie quickly snatched the Styrofoam takeout container and the two napkins on his seat and dropped them in the back of his car. Bella waited for the click of the door then swung her pink toddler's backpack, tattooed with names and phrases scrawled in black marker, just inches from Guthrie's head as she seated herself. Her wet hair smelled of strawberries.

"Your mom said she told you I was going to stay. I hope that wasn't a surprise."

"Like I'm going to care?"

"It's just . . . I know it was unexpected."

"Well, she's like that, my mother. Isn't she?"

He pulled the car out of the parking lot and was already regretting this trip. He wanted to show some empathy and warmth but he really wasn't feeling either.

Of course this shouldn't have happened. If both he and Tanis were in a better frame of mind, it wouldn't have. It had begun with the call from Shereen Trask in tears, asking if he was still covering the Sydney Brewin story because she had news for him: her son was in critical at Toronto East General and they weren't sure if he was going to make it. There was the moment when he almost crashed the car as he pulled over to the side of the road, the speed dialing of Ojal and voicemail . . . voicemail . . . why the hell didn't she tell him? He had one other cop number—Phelps. And Phelps told him yes, indeed, it was true but nobody really had any idea who did it. It occurred in a Toronto neighbourhood where all the Richie Riches live, somebody decided to knife a fag.

Was Ojal looking into it? Phelps just laughed to himself on the other end of the line. "Giannone seen her up at Slapshots having a drink with that Jagdeep Minhas guy. We all want to send him a thank you note. She's finally got laid. She won't be half the bitch she's been."

Phelps laughed a bit too loudly. Perhaps if Guthrie had felt he needed anything from the cops to write this story, he would have laughed along and then hated himself for it, at least for a few hours. But it was all too clear now that cops like Phelps had something invested in all this turning out a certain way. The knifing just had to be the Goring boy, he was probably going to leave Drew for dead. But Constable Dan Goring was one of their own, his family must be protected.

But put that aside for now . . . focus on the positive. Tanis had invited Guthrie in last night, and they spoke of what she had seen in Bella's emails, the possibility of him speaking to Bella on background. They talked of their own past and drank a bottle of a Bordeaux she had saved especially for him. She joined him for a few cigarettes on the balcony. She told him she had reflected upon why she resisted taking things more seriously before. It was too soon and it seemed too easy; he knew her so well, the years dissolved when they embraced, and that put her off-balance. But not anymore, it seemed; the sex was better than both expected after the emotional aridity of the last time they were together. Yes, she had dated since but the ritual seemed too forced. What was worse, she found herself imagining each one of those men as they had been as teenagers and none compared to how she remembered Guthrie. "You had something real about you then and now it's only stronger." This shouldn't have happened but here he was, actually happy and hopeful, perhaps it even might lead to love.

Now in the parking lot, he turned to Bella. "We might see more of each other, your mother and I."

"Which means we might see more of each other."

"This is my point."

"Well. I guess it could be worse."

Guthrie laughed before he could check himself. Bella just kept her eyes out the window to conceal her smile.

"I mean you don't look like a car salesman. Mom dated a car salesman, did she tell you that?"

"She didn't."

"He sold Audis and BMWs so this apparently made it okay. He smelled like a girl. A rich girl I'd probably hate."

"I don't smell like a girl."

"No. But your car smells like a Mexican restaurant."

"That would be last night's dinner."

"My mother's dating a dude who eats dinner in his car. You don't sleep here too, do you?"

"I don't, no."

"Just checking."

"So what do you do ... if you don't mind my asking."

"I write a little. I'm covering the local campaign."

Guthrie turned up Main Street. He could see two cruisers parked by the Three Star café. A young constable with a very pronounced Adam's apple was behind the wheel of one. He had a look as forlorn as a spaniel on a porch, eyeing Guthrie and Bella carefully as they drove by.

"Politics?"

"Sometimes. Sometimes other stuff too."

"I should read stuff like that, I guess."

"Why? I sure as hell didn't when I was your age."

"My mother and father did. Or so they say."

"Your mother?"

"Why does that make you laugh?"

"Because your mother and I knew each other when we were your age."

"You knew Annelie Danziger then."

"I did, yes ..." Guthrie could not help sounding wary and tentative. From all Tanis had told him, Bella was supposed to be very guarded about such a conversation, as if she would be violating a secret pact.

"Don't be so shy. Mom told me you were writing on Syd's death. The copycat thing, with Annelie Danziger."

"She did?"

"So what was she like?"

"What was she like?"

"Annelie Danziger. I'm curious because I've only heard about her from what my mother says. And what Annelie's mother—"

"Annelie's mother?"

"Yeah. So? What's so weird about that?"

"I guess I had forgotten about Annelie's parents."

"Her dad's dead. It's just her mother now. She lives out on her own in this condo near the lake, out near Prince Edward county. Carbury. Syd hunted her down. Soon after she got her license we drove out to see her. Me, Drew Trask and Syd. She's like eighty. She paints. Practically got a shrine to her daughter."

"She believe her daughter committed suicide?"

Bella just looked out beyond the mown lawns and the squat bungalows of this neighbourhood, weighing up how much she was going to divulge.

"I really don't know, but all I can say is that it's a shame you can't talk to Drew right now. You know about what happened?"

"I heard, yes. I think what happened to him might be connected to Sydney."

"Of course it's connected. Jesus . . ."

"And yet he was in Toronto, found bleeding in an alley after a bad hookup."

"Uh huh. You believe that?"

"What, you think you know who did it?"

"It was no bad hookup. It was David fucking Goring, Syd's ex. I guarantee it. David Goring and those fucking hockey boys, they hate Drew. And they hate me. They troll my Facebook page, text me messages, say don't go to the girls washroom, they have some bleacher girls waiting for me. Again."

"Bella, this is serious. You should talk to the cops if this is happening."

"Yeah . . ."

"I'm serious."

"As if the cops are any better in this town. Anyways, he's going to get better."

"I'm not so sure."

"I am. And when he does, Goring'll be busted."

"It's major, what happened to him, they say. He lost a great deal of blood."

"I can't believe that. Somebody's got to tell the truth with all this."

"And you think Drew—"

"I know, believe me. Drew can set you straight on Syd too. More than I can. He talked to Nicky Poole, the guy who knows the real story with Annelie Danziger."

"The real story."

"So he said. You talked to him, didn't you?"

"He may have mentioned Nicky Poole but—"

"From what I know, that old guy really had the dirt on everybody involved."

"From what you know ... Drew didn't tell you?"

"I said I didn't want to know the details. You got to understand, with Drew, after a while, it was like he felt he was in this competition with me for who would be Sydney's best girlfriend. I was like fuck that."

"What happened?"

"I kind of just walked away from them both. In my mind it was a way for me to tell Sydney that she had to choose—Drew or me. And ..."

"Sounds like it was complicated."

"Yeah, it was complicated."

"She felt something for you?"

"I didn't think she knew what she felt. She was dealing with something major. Something that cast her off from everyone she once trusted ... you wouldn't understand, Ian Guthrie."

"No ... that's probably true."

Guthrie eased his foot off the accelerator pedal as they approached the school. It had been years since he had driven this way. The line of oak trees had thickened, darkened the shade along the sidewalk. Drew had mentioned Nicky Poole when they met and what had he done about it? Precisely nothing.

As Guthrie pulled over to the curb along the side of the school, he turned to Bella. She was eyeing him cautiously, as if he were capable of darker motives. Her small, delicately formed fingers tightened along the shoulder strap of her backpack.

"You going to be okay there today?"

"I'm going to be fine, Ian Guthrie."

"You have to tell somebody all you know about Syd. Especially now, with Drew ..."

"Right. But I don't really want to get attacked by the bleacher girls again, thanks."

"That won't happen."

"Really? And who can make sure of it? The cops? Maybe Constable Goring? Thanks for the ride there, Speedy Gonzalez." She allowed herself just the smallest laugh for him as she opened the car door. There was so much of Tanis in the way it sounded.

"Just be careful."

"I will. Thanks!"

He checked in his rear view mirror as he eased back onto the road and there, a few car lengths away, was a white SUV. But no, this one was a different model. Had to be. And he was sure a kid came out of the passenger side. And then he was less sure as the SUV moved back onto the road at the same time and began to follow him closely.

For the next three blocks he was determined to treat this lightly. He forced a laugh out but it just felt odd and self-conscious, as if he had begun to talk to himself. As his car slowed to the red light on Gardam Avenue, the SUV accelerated, closing in on his bumper, flashing its lights.

So this was enough. He drove on for a few hundred yards, until there was a stretch of field with a billboard featuring a sketch of the new medical centre. As he slowed on to the soft shoulder the SUV still followed. His breath was ragged and he felt a little weak as his pulse raced from the surge of adrenalin.

He stopped, got out of the car and turned to walk towards the SUV, with his shoulders pinned back. He was thirteen again, in the boy's locker room, ready to take a swing at David Feldcamp.

He heard the tires of the SUV grip, then spin and roar with sudden acceleration. It was but for a moment that the grill of the car seemed headed straight for him, the momentum ensuring certain death.

Through the corner of his eye he could see the long grass and twig sedges that lined the ditch. As he moved to leap in its direction he heard the wheels of the SUV grip and sharply turn. It passed him and just missed his bumper.

It was just a few seconds later, as he caught his breath and watched its tail lights flash at the next intersection, that he acknowledged that yes, he could make out a grinning, chubby boy-man's face, vaguely familiar, that was behind the wheel. And yes, there was a moment, as the car headed towards him, that one hand behind the wheel cocked an imaginary pistol and fired.

26.

THE RALLY FOR Kent Wolseley, with the Prime Minister in attendance, was up at the new Punjab Banquet Hall on the Fourth Side Road. It was just three lots north of the industrial park with the U Haul office and the shady employment centre that advertised an online paralegal course and EMS training. The parking lot for the Punjab used to be a canola field. The green and gold in late summer never failed to astonish Guthrie, the colours were as vivid as an acid flashback. The concrete pillars at the entranceway of the Punjab rose more than two stories before they propped up a section of corrugated aluminum that extended from the roof, glistening in the early moonlight.

    With the lot looking full, the party faithful were beginning to angle their cars along the soft shoulder of the side road. Guthrie hadn't seen anything like it since the Blades had made it to the semis for the Sutherland Cup. There were more mini vans and pickups with personalized license plates the closer he got to the banquet hall. "BALLR" … "KHALSA1" … "BYUTEE." He surveyed the pine tree air fresheners, saint's medallions and dream catchers hanging from the rear view mirrors, trying to distinguish what might be the signs and symbols of this tribe that seemed so dormant most of the year, until the Prime Minister or one of his MPs did some sort of funding announcement at the hockey arena or agricultural fair, poster sized cheque in hand.

    The main lobby area smelled of carpet glue and men's cologne. The hall's board of directors, stout and suited, with greying beards and bright blue turbans, milled around near the doors, proud to be the welcoming committee. They were hugging the younger men they knew, reaching for the ankles of the older men with quick, elegant touches, and stiffly shaking hands with the whole families of white folks who all looked dressed for church rather than a rally as they made their way into the hall. All the way up the curve of the wrought iron railing there were teenagers with Kent Wolseley teeshirts and odd, avid grins, posed like a chorus line. They brandished inflated thundersticks in each hand. "Living On A Prayer" was blaring from deep inside the hall, the song's chorus soaring over the voices of a room that looked already full to fire code, with at least an hour before the Prime Minister's motorcade was scheduled to pull in.

Guthrie wandered over to a raised platform where the video cameras were setting up and jacking in, looking for those few broadcast guys he still might know, when he glimpsed Veronica Provost-Wolseley, nodding and smiling as Vonda Graebel from the Lodestar school was pressing her point with a raised finger. Vonda had once been a track star at school and went on to the provincials at one hundred and two hundred metres. Now her chinos were pulled tight across her broad backside, her long black curls tied back, revealing a greying at the roots. All the anxiety of fearing she would not escape this conversation for some time was in Veronica's darting looks out to the crowd around them. There! Yes! A lifeline. Guthrie approached and could see the tension in Veronica's tight grin dissolve.

"Ah! Ian Guthrie. Good to see you, sir!"

"Good to see you, Ms. Provost-Wolseley."

"Did you just get here? You want to see Kent, don't you?"

"I ... hadn't expected ... but yes ..."

"I've got him in the kitchen. We're working on his speech. Well, fine tuning, really. Vonda, can you scan the letter from the Ministry and email it to me?"

"I can do that, yes, and actually ..."

"Thanks, Vonda. So Mr. Guthrie, come with me."

Veronica took Guthrie by the elbow as if she were leading him out onto the floor to dance. She moved gracefully, her small feet sharply clicking in five hundred dollar heels. She was probably a superb dancer, but in the ballroom steps of another era.

"Thank you sir for that rescue. Jesus motherfucking Christ."

"Vonda Graebel."

"Vonda goddamn Graebel. Tell me, does she give you a dyke vibe? She gives me that dyke vibe. I'm mean I'm used to eyes on my boobies every time I stop to say a word out here, but not from the ladies."

Guthrie laughed, but it was less from imagining Vonda Graebel as a lesbian than from the jolt of sudden intimacy in Veronica's profanity. They had only spoken, what, a handful of times?

"How has it been out there knocking on the doors?"

"To be honest, Ian, hard to tell. I know the polling says we've got a big lead but I'm not seeing it in the neighbourhoods. Lots of orange signs on lawns."

"Maybe it's just the neighbourhoods you're going to."

"It's Minhas. Talk all you like about the taxi guys, and Harpreet who runs this barn, I think we're losing the brown vote to him. And it's bigger than you think out here by the highway. These folks only moved to town over the last two years. Kent as some townie growing up in the old part of Argyle, that angle doesn't mean anything to them." She strained to keep the smile on her face, doing all she could to make their conversation look light and merry for the eyes on them as they moved to the kitchen doors. "That's why we're spending so much time on this speech. He's got to connect tonight."

"I didn't know you helped write his speeches."

"At first Jeannie wasn't going to let me. They've been trying to keep me away from the day to day. I get that, it's campaign one oh one. Don't let the wife try to run things."

"You get along with Jeannie?"

"I think we understand each other now. We get along enough. I mean, I'm sorry, they just don't know Kent like I know him, and that's going to matter as we get down to the wire."

As she pushed open the swinging doors there Kent was, sleeves rolled up and rep tie askew, his suit jacket slung over a banquet chair as he recited the lines on the few wilted pages in his hands. He was pacing between Senator MacDougall and two paunchy old flacks in pinstripes leaned up against a meat locker, arms folded, heads bowed like monks in prayer. It looked like MacDougall had the same pages as Kent in his hands. With his mimsy drugstore reading glasses slipped down to the tip of his nose he was the song master, his laptop open on the long butcher's table behind him, ready to type in his changes from paragraph to paragraph. In profile Kent looked like he had put on about twenty pounds.

"Honey, Ian Guthrie's here."

Kent looked up from his pages with a weary campaign grin. "Ian ... good to see you back with us. Picked a good night, buddy."

Buddy? Guthrie could feel the pretense of an old friendship dissolve in that single word. He said his hello and nodded to MacDougall and the flacks. MacDougall glared and then retracted into his more peaceable pose, dealing with how these phrases scanned on the pages.

"When we get the final draft done here, I thought we could flip it to Ian," Veronica said. She seemed to be addressing the old flacks rather than the Senator. "There's some good stuff here for the magazine story."

"Still some ways to go," the Senator growled like an angry old hound. "You might want to show him around the banquet hall."

"No, no, it's fine," Kent waved his pages in the air. "Where you been? I mean I figured you would have been at the doors with us a lot more, Ian. Seems like you been talking to everybody but me and the team. Or maybe anybody else, more like it."

"It was background. I needed background." Guthrie was trying not to care about the hostility to his presence from MacDougall. The Senator huffed then turned his back and mumbled to his sidekicks about where a printer was in the banquet hall, his eyes would not meet Guthrie's.

"Seriously? I mean, Jesus, Ian. We've known each other for close to thirty years. Background's the last thing I figure you'd need. That was going to be one of the great things about having you on the trail, buddy."

"The magazine wants an in-depth profile. The editor sent me a bunch of questions I had no answers for. There were a lot of missing years, you got to admit."

"Ha. Your missing years, not mine. I wish I could make a few years go missing. I wouldn't be looking like such an old fat fuck." He grabbed the flash around his waistline. "Look at this! That's too much time in Tim's each morning, right, honey?"

Veronica managed a thin-lipped smile, just the faintest nod. "Are you close? Those last three paragraphs were a mess."

"They're fine! I will make it work. A lot of it's going to be decided in the rear of the room, honey."

"Don't say things like that. It makes me nervous."

"Makes us all bloody nervous," said the Senator, poking at the keys on the laptop with his two thick index fingers.

"Makes you nervous because you all know I'm right, and you hate it when that happens. Nobody's going to give a good goddamn anyway. They're all here for the Prime Minister, not me."

"Uh huh. And who's the Prime Minister here for? Am I not right, Ian?"

Guthrie nodded to Veronica with his fulsome grin. He felt like a court eunuch, turned gutless because of his own hypocrisy.

"He needs to see you're serious and ready for prime time, honey. Now everybody else has done their jobs tonight. We've got a full house, got all the networks and two double-enders happening at nine from the floor. The Prime Minister's going to scrum and you're going to be standing there right beside him."

"The potted plant."

"The new MP for Newton - Argyle North."

Kent nodded slowly and bowed his head. "Yes, dear." The flacks tittered to themselves.

"I'll let you get back to it."

"Good to see you back, buddy. Let's figure out coffee over the next couple of days."

"That would be great." As Guthrie smiled for Veronica he could feel the Senator glowering at him. "I'll phone the campaign office."

When he opened the kitchen door the hall there was now a solid wall of broad shoulders and squarish backs in front of him, Win with Wolseley signs and thundersticks jutting and bobbing overhead. Yet Guthrie couldn't really recognize many of these churchgoing—and gurdwara going—faces, aside from Phelps and Giannone over there by the cameras posed in the same wide leg stance in their roomy cut jeans and plaid shirts, drinking Diet Coke in cans like beer at a barbecue. They were surveying the crowd as if they were savouring the memories of the moving violations, the impaired and the assault charges they had written up, discretely nodding to themselves when they recognized the perpetrators of the minor offences, now forgiven and absorbed back into the throng of the hard working, good people, pumped and patriotic tonight.

He didn't see Jeannie Pincott moving through the crowd until she had caught up with him and given his elbow a nudge. There was something a little different about her, something that seemed too shiny and photo shopped, though there was no trace of make-up on her face.

"Ian Guthrie. How are you."

"Hello … It's Jeannie, right?"

"Ian, I think we're going to have to pull the plug."

"Pull the plug? Pull the plug on what?"

It was her hair. She had dyed it and now the curls had a stronger, reddish sheen, as if she had shampooed with nail polish.

"I don't think we can have a story on Kent in a national magazine. We're just not sure how it's going to go out here."

"Just not sure? You kidding? It's a lock! Look at this barn."

"This? We do this for every event. Cripes, I don't think I'm talking out of school when I say we bus these folks in from the lists we've got from three other ridings. On the ground, truth is we're all a little worried."

"But this story's bigger than this campaign. I don't have to tell you …"

"No. No, you don't. I'm sorry. The centre just doesn't like the idea of this going ahead."

Guthrie smiled to himself as he gazed down at his brogues. He was not going to show anger. He was not even going to attempt a little condescension, although he didn't mind the thought of Jeannie Pincott considering him to be a prick.

"Stephen Clarke at the Torontonian. That's who you want to talk to. He's the man that wants this draft before E day."

"You're welcome to stay for the rally of course, but I can't get you any time with Kent or the Prime Minister, you understand."

"Talk to Stephen Clarke. And you should get yourself some kid … what do they call them … a click clack, a girl to be Kent's press thingie. That way you don't have to talk to guys like me."

"Kent's good and staffed, thanks." Jeannie smiled. "This was my choice. I needed to know you got the message."

"I got your message."

"Great. Thanks so much." She gently touched his forearm as she turned back and headed for the kitchen. "Nice talking with you."

Guthrie knew his smile looked fake as he stared straight ahead at the empty stage. He could feel the eyes of those who had witnessed this tense little conversation stay on him, reading him as an outsider, an interloper, dressed like a failed new wave nostalgia act in his thrift store blazer and black jeans. *You sit around getting older … there's a joke here somewhere and it's on me.* Stephen would have his back.

And there just a few feet from the exit was Ojal, in a red silk salwar kameez, her hair worn loosely at her shoulders, laughing with a couple of other women Guthrie did not recognize. Her eyes widened when she saw him.

"Ian! Just a moment … excuse me, auntie, I'll be right back." She made a couple of half-bows for the older ladies and moved to meet him at the doors.

"Staff Inspector. You're looking festive."

"Oh shut up. I had to come. You know how many of my team are here tonight? Like maybe all of them."

"Show of support."

"Show of politics as usual. They all figure I'm a dipper or something. They talk out here. And it's the men, not the women. They're worse than the aunties."

"Are they on you about Minhas?"

"What?"

"Minhas. The night Drew Trask was assaulted—"

"So you know. That's why I wanted to grab you before you went."

"The night he was assaulted I tried you."

"I saw that."

"Phelps had you scoped at Slapshots with the guy. I just thought wow, they really are on you. Like goddamn surveillance."

"They said I was with Jagdeep Minhas?" She shook her head as she gazed out into the crowd, smiling as she tried to let her bitterness dissolve. "You know why I was out with him?"

"I couldn't care—"

"I'll tell you why I was out with him. He asked me to endorse him at the gurdwara. And I told him what I told Kent. It's not my job to play politics."

"And here you are."

"And I'll probably show up at Jagdeep's rally too, but I don't endorse anybody. I can't believe they watch me so closely. Unbelievable . . ."

"You got any leads with what happened to Drew Trask?"

"I talked to Metro. A couple guys from 52. Good detectives. They figure it was a bad date. Boys in his line of work, these attacks happen. And more than you think, believe me. They've got a couple leads. He was out the night before at a couple of bars on Church, acting a little aggressively. Drew liked his coke."

"You don't think it could be anybody out here? Bella Lang—"

"I've talked to Bella."

"You should talk to her again. She's got a couple ideas. She mentioned Goring's kid."

"Of course she would. Ian, it's not like the days when your dad was running things, as hard as that might be to believe. I need something more than the hunch of a girl—"

"A girl who's being bullied now. And stalked and threatened online. But you probably know that. You talked to her."

Ojal walked him closer to the doors, with her eyes fixed on the narrow opening between the bodies still filing in. Once she had got them to the top of the staircase she whirled and faced him, glaring.

"Guthrie, why are you being such an asshole?"

"Drew Trask is probably not going to make it, Ojal. That's a homicide. And it will probably go unsolved because you're too goddamned worried about the knives out for you with these thugs than you are about doing your job. You're right. It really is different from my dad's days. God knows I can be hard on him but I'll tell you what, he knew when politics was getting in the way of his job. And he had the guts to say fuck it, I'm going to do the right thing."

"It might be wise for you to step back, Ian. Step back and think to yourself, maybe she *is* investigating this. Maybe she's doing this in her own way so the case doesn't fall apart like it did so many times in, oh, I don't know, Danny Guthrie's day. And maybe she isn't always telling me everything for reasons of her own."

Guthrie realized he was standing with his hands on his hips, glowering. Great, now he was channeling the old prick, the way he used to pose after he had he lost his temper with Guthrie's mother.

"I have no doubt there are many things you don't tell me. I understand our conversations are transactional."

"Transactional, yes. Ian, I'm sorry I might not be able to give you a story yet. A story that might just really give you something worthwhile to write for once. But there it is."

She turned from him, and he just watched the flow of her dress at her ankles, as she moved across the ornate little squares that made up the carpet pattern. With the gold earrings she was wearing and just that lightest touch of eyeshadow, she really was more beautiful than he had ever seen her.

With no possibility of an interview tonight, Ojal had at least done him the service of giving him a less humiliating exit from the hall. He nodded and smiled at the Win With Wolseley thunderstick kids as he descended the stairs. He passed Norris Arbic and smiled for the good Reverend—Arbic solemnly nodding in return. Yet just as he went through the glass double doors, he could see the black motorcade of three SUVs slowing along the side road, blinkers flashing to turn into the parking lot. He could hear the rumbling of a crowd filling the banquet hall entrance, the shouts and cheers of those assigned to provide the rousing welcome, hoping it was victory that was about to arrive.

27.

THERE WAS AN "About" tab on the website for Diamonds In The Trash, the consignment boutique in the east end of the city that had to be written by Nicky Poole himself:

Nicky Stiletto is a rock and roll survivor with the scars to prove it. From his earliest days of the punk explosion in Toronto, fronting the legendary Modan Garus and making a name for himself as the bartender / house raconteur at the fabled Hi-Fi Lounge, Nicky's seen it, done it and lived it down. His muse has taken him to Montreal, Manhattan and Los Angeles where he wrote songs for a number of chart topping pop and country acts and opened Galerie (Fast Eddy) Falcone, a bar, gallery and performance space showcasing the work of such punk legends as Martin Rust and Donny Mason a.k.a. Stickboy. Yet no matter what adventure has beckoned, the one constant for this rock and roll chameleon has been his inimitable sense of style.

It was while working back in Toronto as a script consultant and wardrobe assistant on Bryce McDonagh's Genie Award winning film "Three Chord Largo" that he had, as he calls it, one of those "hard core epiphanies where you see the road ahead forking, and you just know where you've got to crank the wheel." And so began the journey that led to Diamonds In The Trash, the boutique, museum and pre-owned vinyl emporium that has become, as the Torontonian's Marsha Blum phrased it in her feature column, "a new wave nostalgia lover's cabinet of wonders in the heart of hip and happening Leslieville."

All hard core epiphanies and purple prose aside, Guthrie knew he would inevitably try to get hold of Nicky's book if and when it was ever published, if only to read about Annelie's death and Poole's time in prison. Yet judging from the terse, dismissive way Nicky dealt with Guthrie's questions on the phone, perhaps he had erased that whole chapter from the gritty memoir from the very beginning, the selective memory of a rock and roll chameleon being an acquired trait.

"He had this girlfriend, Annelie Danziger," Guthrie opened when he finally got a hold of Poole.

"Uh huh."

"She died at the old Hi Fi Lounge, in one of the rooms upstairs."

"Yes, sweetie. My room. And yes I did my time for it."

"Are you comfortable speaking about it?"

"I don't want to be quoted, understand? And no tape recorders."

"I understand. Could we at least meet for a coffee?"

There was a pause. Guthrie could hear Nicky Poole take a long drag of his cigarette and then exhale as if he was expelling his last reservations about this conversation.

"Store's open from twelve to six most days. I only drink espresso I make myself. You come in, I'll give you fifteen minutes."

Diamonds In The Trash was on a block between a pawn shop that repaired and sold second hand bicycles, all rusted and stacked and chained up to every post and parking meter, the pale green blinds drawn down in the windows, with the silkscreened red swallow and Chinese characters on each faded to pink. Nicky's store looked dark from the street as well but the door pushed open and there was the smell of Tibetan incense, and garishly painted portraits of what looked to be old punks, drag queens and an ill advised series of old women with lapdogs. Each was signed Stiletto in the right hand corner and hung in an ornate frame, spray-painted gold. Past the racks of creased leather car coats and brightly patterned polyester shirts and dresses was the long glass case that once displayed the mummified man; it was now cluttered with rows of bangles, buttons and sunglasses. And there, behind the cash register, his small, closely shaven head topped with a black silk skullcap, was Nicky. He was drawling into an old phone. He raised a finger and mouthed "just one sec" as Guthrie nodded his hello.

Guthrie busied himself at a corner table full of cameras. He found a Super 8 projector, one that looked like it still might work, when Nicky finally hung up with a parting "must go, sweet man ... toodle-oo" then sighed in exasperation.

"Sorry about that. You're Ian Guthrie, aren't you?"

"I am, yes."

Nicky breezed past him, marching with a boyish, intense stride, up to the front door. He stepped out into the street briefly, put his hands on his slender hips, and sighed in quiet defeat about the afternoon desolation. His cowboy belt with its turquoise stones glistened in the sun. In silhouette he had the ropey arms of a rehab regular. He flipped the sign to "closed," pulled the door shut and turned the lock.

"I'll try not to take too much of your time."

"Oh, it's fine. It's not like they're beating down the door today, is it?" Nicky perched himself back on his wooden stool, legs crossed, as he reached for a Sobranie and his nickel plated lighter from the counter. "You smoke? I'd offer you one but these are my financial ruin and I can't spare any. Here." He kicked another rickety stool and moved it about a foot along the other side of the glass case. "Make yourself comfortable."

"I read about you on your site."

As Guthrie seated himself Nicky took in his notebook with an arched eyebrow. His black eyes and the silvery sheen of his stubble caught the light. He had a monkey's grin that put Guthrie off balance and had him already fidgeting with his pen.

"Did you? Good. This should take no time at all then. I doubt I can tell you anything new. But this article on Kent Wolseley. What's ... he a politician now?"

"He is, yeah. Running as an MP out in Newton."

"Tell me he's not going to win."

"Looks like he is."

"Do you know who Artaud was?"

"I don't, no."

"It doesn't matter. Just trust me, he was a genius. My favourite line: people . . . are . . . stupid." Nicky expelled a hoarse little laugh. He had small grey teeth that looked like they were made of porcelain. "The Garus, we were going to call our second album Theatre of Cruelty. That's from Artaud. We should have."

"I guess that will be in your book."

"It'll all be in the book, honey, if it's ever released. I've got to get a new publisher. Mine just went tits up and I've got four chapters to go. This is the luck of Nicky Stiletto. Born under the sign of Saturn."

"Drew Trask told me about you. You remember Drew?"

"The kid who came to me about Annelie Danziger. Drew, yes. The boy was cute."

"He's in critical. He's been unconscious for more than a week now. They're not sure if he's going to make it."

Nicky gently placed a hand on his chest as his eyes widened. "What the hell happened?"

"Knifed in the alley behind his house."

Nicky peered down at his feet and seemed to wince. "Well, I just hope the kid makes it and recovers. He seemed sweet."

"No suspect identified yet."

"Not hard to believe. Though in our day it was the cops themselves, so I guess we should all be grateful. You ever hear of the Cherry Beach Express?"

"Only heard, but I just figured it was an urban legend."

"That's where the cops took me after they picked me up after Annelie Danziger died. But they had to make sure it looked like a Don Jail beating."

"Why would they need to? I read they found her in your room."

"You mean what was the point in beating a confession out of me? Oh, circumstantial evidence wasn't going to do it. They had orders."

"More than circumstantial, though, wasn't it? The paper said you were known to them, had been busted before."

"Sure, they knew me. They had me before on a possession charge they tried to turn into trafficking. They knew I was a runaway from Sarnia. They knew my parents disowned me. And yes, they knew I rented my ass out when I had to. In other words, no one would care if they put me away for some serious time. But none of that would have been admissible in a trial."

"They wanted a confession."

"Oh yeah. They wanted it done. They were men of their word. They told me if I pleaded to a lesser charge of criminal negligence, I'd be out in two years, max. If I refused, well … there was a very good chance they'd find a way to get my fingerprints on the needle they found by her body and book me for rape because the girl was violated."

"She was raped?"

"That didn't make it in the papers, did it? Damn straight she was raped. Had bruises on her face and arms. At least that was what they told me. I had no reason to doubt two cops holding my head underwater."

"That's what they told you, but you hadn't seen the body."

"I couldn't have. I was at a speakeasy two blocks away until five. I had witnesses."

"And I mean … you were not really into girls, were you?"

"Wasn't quite that simple. I wasn't out back then. That didn't happen for another ten years. I was such a small town kid then. Like so many of us."

"So many like Annelie Danziger."

"She used to come in to the Hi Fi. I knew she was underage but I just let it go. Can you imagine? Want to try that today?"

"She came in alone?"

"Not always. Sometimes she came in with this other chick. A little taller. Real cool and elegant. Looked like that Redgrave in Blow Up. I can never remember those sister's names."

"They'd come for bands?"

"Exactly. Groupies in the making, but I could tell they were just a little too shy, a little too sensible to actually do anything about it. So I talked to them, tried to be charming."

"I remember your trial, Nicky. I remember they had a couple witnesses testify that you were dealing out of your room, that they'd seen Annelie there before."

Nicky sighed, readjusted himself on his stool and crossed his legs. "Yeah. The cops had no shortage of assholes they could threaten. They would say what the cops needed to put me away. I wasn't a dealer. Look, it was a lot more innocent than that. I actually met a few real dealers in Kingston. They scared the hell out of me. Real businessmen have Glocks and pagers and friends in the Angels. If they aren't Angels themselves. Back then I just had some homegrown in a baggie and a little row of plastic pill jars along my windowsill that I doled out so the interesting people would come up to my room. Annelie Danziger was one of those people."

"Interesting in what way?"

"I liked her style. She had a boyfriend in a band by then named Tommy something, said she wanted to make movies. Had herself this movie camera she bought in Kensington. I remember how excited she was, showing it around. She had this idea she could project her movies behind some of the bands who played at the Hi Fi regularly. She wanted to cast me in one. For a drama queen like me, I mean I fell in love."

"She had written some scripts. Some poetry, a couple plays. And of course her diary. Drew and his friends got a hold of all this ..."

"I know. The kid told me. He said it would have proven my innocence. Whatever. That was a million years ago. I could care less."

"But you did the time."

"What doesn't kill you makes you stronger, right? I was fierce, man, coming out of there. Fierce and ruthless. Wish I had a bit more of that now again, believe me."

"Why do you think you were set up?"

Nicky let out a low cackle, rolling his eyes. "Seriously? I mean you're here because you're writing about that Wolseley asshole, aren't you? That little shit had old Toronto in his corner. They weren't going to let Kent Wolseley get charged, especially with the state of her. The bruises, the tranqs and heroin in her bloodstream, the needle."

"Old Toronto. Who do you mean?"

"All you had to do was look at Kent Wolseley and you knew he had the fucking keys to Daddy's car. The night she died, that wasn't the first time he'd been at the Hi Fi. He'd come a few times before with Annelie and a bunch of kids from the suburbs, all dressed in the clothes they bought a few hours before from a place like this. Gel in their hair, fake IDs."

Guthrie smiled, averting his gaze. "I know. I was one of them."

Nicky smirked as he took a deep drag. "Yeah, well ... there you go."

"But why do you say old Toronto?"

"Look, you think the cops would have ever cared enough about this case if they weren't given orders to have me put away? Girl gets raped and ODs in a room over the Hi Fi. Big fucking deal. They had nothing to cover up. I mean they told me as much."

"What do you mean?"

"I remember everything about that long ride to Cherry Beach. Because that is when I really grew up. I had fucked off out of Sarnia at seventeen, lived on the street, fended for myself, thought I knew how the world worked. Even when the cops had taken me downtown for selling a dime bag to a couple of kids out front of Maple Leaf Gardens … it was like I'd chosen this fucking pathetic teenage trapeze act, but somewhere down there, there was a net, right?"

Guthrie just nodded. It was hard to tell, given the lighting behind the counter, but it looked as if Nicky Poole's eyes were beginning to well up.

"But then to realize the net isn't there … as these two cops who'd picked me up were driving under the Gardiner, one looks back at me in the cruiser and says, 'How'd a little piece of shit like you manage to piss off Bill Platt?' And I'm just, 'Bill Platt? Who's Bill Platt?' And that just got both those fucking Nazis to laughing. Worst laughing I ever heard. I can still hear it."

"That's the Bill Platt of Platt Park?"

"Forest Hill. He'd been some MP for like a hundred years around there. Now I didn't know this Kent asshole at all. I only knew he was Annelie's boyfriend, the one who got her knocked up even though she wanted to dump him. All the teenage trauma. But I could figure out, in the back of that cop car, that some people were going to make damn sure this Kent Wolseley was going to stay out of trouble."

"And you were the one …"

"I was the one. Signed Nicholas J. Poole on the cops' report. That's the last time I ever gave a cop that name. Last time I ever will. I saw what they got from Kent Wolseley, the alibi that had him at the Cameron later that night, back in his frat house at Western that Sunday afternoon, that it was some fucking rah rah football game that he had come down for in the first place. I mean I didn't have to read between any lines. It was there in black and white."

"But a rape charge?"

"They buried the rape charge. The girl was pregnant so Kent Wolseley claimed she had told him she was suicidal. Unstable. Couldn't go through with an abortion and couldn't handle having a kid. All bullshit."

"You think so?"

"I know so. I had her up in my room because she told me she needed to get away from him that night. Had no protection, her boyfriend was out of town playing a gig. Thing is though, the girl wouldn't smoke anything stronger than a cigarette. I lit up a joint and she just shook her head. Asked me to water down her rye and Diet Cokes. She said she told him she was having the kid and that's why he was there at the Hi Fi. Wouldn't leave her alone. She said she was scared to go home alone so that's when I gave her the key to my room."

"So scared she OD-ed?"

"I knew this girl. I think I'd seen her smoke a spliff maybe once or twice and even then you could tell she wasn't into it. No, somebody put the tranqs in her drink. And the H? That girl would have never touched the needle."

"How could you be sure? I mean, I knew her, at least a little before she went off to OCA. The heroin was around. Suddenly everybody I knew at least tried it."

"So you were around. I probably would have seen you in the Hi Fi."

"Among about fifty boys from the suburbs, dressed in black, looking miserable at the back of the room. Annelie was out of my league by then."

"But you're convinced Annelie Danziger wouldn't have touched it, that somebody must have—"

"Not the kid I knew."

Guthrie nodded, reached for a cigarette of his own. This would be the fourth of the day but there was too much to think about right now. "Thank you for all this, Nicky."

"You didn't write much down."

"No. I guess I have to process a lot of this."

"Process. That's a good word. Is that like decide how much you can make up?" Nicky Poole rose from his chair, stretching out his lower back with a wince.

"Listen, I understand you want to remain anonymous. But if I emailed you some questions, identified you only as, say, someone who had been around the Hi Fi in those days, would that be all right with you?"

"It would be a lot better if you bought that old projector you were looking at."

Guthrie pulled out his wallet from his back pocket and handed over three twenties. Nicky Poole put his hands together as if in prayer and nodded. It was only after Guthrie got out of the store, lugging the projector, when he reached into his jacket and turned off the pocket recorder. As he was fumbling with the device and cursing himself he almost missed the white SUV pulling out from a spot a few doors from Diamonds In The Trash.

***

The receptionist at the front desk of the Torontonian's offices looked up from the page and smiled weakly.

"Did you have an appointment?"

"Actually, no. I'm just dropping in."

"Um. Let me check with someone. Mr. Clarke doesn't seem to be here anymore." She rose from her desk and wandered off, murmuring to herself.

Guthrie could feel a heaviness sink through his chest and shoulders. He began to scroll through the emails on his Blackberry. Nope, not one from Stephen. Then he just stared down at the penciled line through Stephen's name in the receptionist's purple binder and realized there was no reason to wait for her return. He turned and walked out of the glass doors, careful that the sound they made in closing was nothing more than the faintest click.

28.

I COULDN'T TELL David of course. I just wiped his tears away. I didn't want him to hurt. But it would be a lie to live as his wife, pretend this was his child. So I'm alone, and now my family will cast me out.

This life inside me has now put an end to living in truth. But what kind of choice do I have? My mother's decided how this must be done not me. So I lie to everyone, not just David.

I can't help but feel that Annelie's work came to us for a greater reason. At first I just believed it was all about creative inspiration or something. And then, when your mom realized she had given us those final few letters, I could even understand why she regretted it and wanted to take them back.

But it is too late. There is nothing more powerful, nothing more full of poetry to me than the way Annelie wrote about her night on the lake. The full moon, the petals of the black iris falling away.

I've never been more certain about anything. I am so sorry.

The phone rings again as Ojal reads. Who else could it be? Don't get up. Just let it ring. Just let Jagdeep get used to you out of his life. He's probably parked across the street again, his headlights glowing with his pathetic need, his boy-man's persistence. Well, sorry, this takes precedence now. One drama at a time, thank you very much.

So Bella did not disappoint. These last letters were a revelation. And yet when Ojal had asked her whose child she believed Sydney was carrying she just shook her head, then said please-don't-ask-me, and that it would make no difference now. She had promised Sydney she'd never reveal it, she said, and someone else's fate depended on it remaining secret.

That could only mean Drew Trask's fate. Well, that could hardly matter now, could it?

And yet there was no answer, radio silence from Bella as Ojal has sent her text after text. "Run tomorrow morning?" "Run tomorrow morning?" No . . . it was clear she had decided to run on her own now, run from all of this.

***

The funeral for Drew Trask would not be held in Newton. Ojal had called his mother Shereen, fully expecting her to hang up or worse, to calmly tell her how the police had failed her. But no, the woman just sounded weary and medicated in her blank responses. There would be a short, intimate service at the Elder Funeral Home off Davenport Road, near Drew's last place of residence. His companion Derek Reiner had been kind enough to make the arrangements. No public wake afterwards but those coming to the service could sign a book of condolences with any last thoughts or prayers for her boy, Andrew. If Ojal had any reservations about going, they dissolved with the way Shereen Trask said her son's full name.

As Ojal made her way into the city, the clouds loomed heavily and bruised over the highway. First snow of the year coming, the radio said. Perfect weather for grief and mourning. Shereen Trask and the few who would make it to the Elder Funeral Home would have at least one day when fate wasn't at odds with Drew.

Because it was true that nothing seemed to find alignment in Drew's story. It was hard to see him as an innocent wrongly accused and martyred for his difference. He was too reckless, guarded and unrepentant about his days when he disappeared, the tattooed iris on his wrist being the only sign that he was affected in any way by Sydney Brewin's death. He didn't want any forgiveness or understanding from people in Newton. He maintained his innocence with a brittle, defensive edge to the tone of his voice. He was happy to turn his back on all of the people he once knew in town and at least play-act being an adult here in the city. Everything—the rich older boyfriend, the job, the plan to somehow continue with his education—seemed built on sand, components of some life of normalcy with no foundations, no sense they would ever really come together to form a whole.

As Ojal entered the funeral home, she followed the Trask Family sign and the line of shiny silver poles with a red velvet rope threaded through them. Seemed a little tacky, like a premiere for a movie that would quickly close. She came to the small room where she could view the body. The door whined open and there she discovered the "everyone" Shereen Trask had told her was more like simply the core contingent of the loyal, the concerned and the caring throughout the course of the boy's life: a couple of teachers in boxy suits, his therapist who looked like a goth astrologer in her satin, beaded dress, Reverend Norris Arbic—must have been Drew's pastor once he left the Catholic church, and a whole pew of well muscled and salon tanned men that could pass for an ageing boy band. And then there was Bella Lang and her mother, sitting with Guthrie, interestingly enough; the boyfriend Derek Reiner, pudgier than Ojal had imagined, with a dirty blonde goatee and flushed cheeks, his hand clasped in Shereen Trask's where it rested limply in her lap. Just barely beside them was a tall handsome man, with high cheekbones and swept back silver hair, sitting up too straight in the last pew. Had to be Drew's father. Ojal figured she hadn't made a noise as she took a seat, yet who else but Guthrie would look back and give her a quick smile and a nod.

She read in the program she had taken at the door that there would be a ten-minute eulogy delivered by Doctor Marco Wagenhauser, Minister of the Thornley Road United Church. She was expecting some old ghost with foggy glasses, but the gentleman who came in through a side door in a banker's suit and lilac coloured tie looked sleek and barely middle-aged, a Swiss accountant who had been asked to fill in one day and never returned to his office.

"We are here today to remember the young man who was still in so many ways a boy, who seemed as much ashamed of his innocence as he was his difference, no matter how much love, support and affection that you here in this room tried so hard to give him every day of his life. We have come here not to try to make sense of his death, because there is no sense to be made of the circumstances of his passing, but to celebrate the brief time this soul with such light within was with us."

There was a soft, Spanish lilt to Wagenhauser's recitation. Shereen Trask's shoulders began to shake and her thick black hair shimmered under the potted light directly above her. She sunk further down in the pew when the minister awkwardly enunciated "innocence." Derek Reiner put his arm around her. Ojal watched his stubby hand move in circles across her back. Drew's father only bowed his head lower, looking like the loneliest man in the room.

After perhaps a minute more of the eulogy Guthrie glanced back at Ojal once again and discreetly motioned with a nod that he was heading for the door. When she came out to him he had already lit up his cigarette and pulled up the lapels of his suit jacket. "It was good of you to come, Staff Inspector. I mean it. Showed a lot of class."

"Glad I've earned your approval once again. You doing a story on this one too?"

"I'd like to, but Bruce Gallant doesn't see this as a piece with sufficient local interest. I'm serious. That's what he wrote to me."

"Bruce Gallant's a dickwad."

"Listen to you, the townie."

"I thought you were covering the election campaign."

"Not for Gallant, no. And it looks like not for anyone."

"Thought it was going to be a big magazine piece?"

"Yeah, well . . . what do they say in politics? Events, dear girl . . ." He shrugged, flicked his cigarette butt into a flower bed, barren save for a thorny cluster of stalks long clipped of roses. "I think the future of Kent Wolseley's political career might turn out to be the least interesting thing about the story, if it ever does get written."

"Is that something you want to share or . . ."

"I don't know. I guess I'm just more interested in whether you've found out anything more about the death we're here for right now. Or should I say, murder?"

"Even if I was still working on this with 52 division, you think I'd be able to talk about it with you?"

Guthrie nodded, stared down at the smudges of his footprints in the snow. "You spoken to Bella in there?"

"Not for a while."

"You should. You really should. She's transferring to Seton Secondary for her last semester. Sooner if she can manage it."

"We were running together in the mornings for a while."

"Yeah, well … the girl's doing a lot of running on her own right now. In fear of kids like David Goring."

She reached over, gently clasped the sleeve of Guthrie's suit jacket and lowered her voice as if she feared them being overheard. "Patience, Ian. That's all I ask, okay? This has to be done right."

"If it's going to be done at all."

"I've got no stake in this."

"Oh I think you do. You've already written the story in your head."

"Haven't you?"

"Fifty-two has got a couple of videos from nearby security cameras that have those out walking Drew's street at that time."

"Except it was the back alley where the assailant came from. Nothing else? You sure about that?"

"I've already given you too much."

"That's funny. I always walk away from our conversations with the feeling that you've been very precise with the portion of truth you've allowed me."

"Moments like this must feel like a kind of victory for you. Look, it might be hard for you to believe but I want to help you too. It's me who reached out to 52 on this. You don't think I'd love to give you something that you could take to Bruce Gallant and say here, there's a bigger story to all this?"

"You don't have to do me any favours."

"I have gone over all this about your Annelie Danziger, okay? Talented girl. Lovely, the way Sydney and Bella and Drew kept her memory alive. Lovely and morbid, in that way only kids in drama class can be."

"Look, a couple weeks ago, I was the first one to tell you all of that really didn't matter."

"I can't pore over the facts of some thirty year old case, no matter how sad and important to you ... and Bella's mother there."

"It's not out of sentimentality, Ojal. You should talk to Tanis. I think you'll realize —"

"I've got a case right in front of me. The facts at hand. And I don't have a margin for error because we both know these fuckers will ruin my career if I go after a cop's son like Goring's and don't nail this one."

"I'm sorry this has become about your career."

"Really, Ian? Or are you just angry that you don't have one anymore. I can't help you with whatever revenge plot is in your head. I don't even know who your enemies are. Kent Wolseley? The brass that fought your dad's claim, made his last years hell? Or is it just as simple as Bruce Gallant and the little coupon flyer you write for? I don't know your enemies. But I know mine."

***

Detective Danny Fortune was the only one downtown who drank tea. Just like his mother made it: weak with too much milk and sugar. Irish chai, Ojal called it. He liked that, he said. It is what he would call his first racehorse once he'd gotten back into the black. There were two mugs steaming at his desk by the time she arrived. She never had the heart to tell him she drank her tea any differently.

"Hey ... my little sister ..."

As they embraced she could smell a new cologne on him, something rich and too feminine. It had to be a new girlfriend. Danny's wardrobe changes—the popsicle coloured Italian shirts, the two hundred dollar jeans that fell off the back of a truck—were the only indications of his romantic life after his divorce, one presumably carried out through barroom flirtations out in the Beaches. He looked squeezed like a sausage into this new alcohol-free version of himself.

"So who is she?"

"Aah you don't want to know. Early days, anyway. Try my McChai there and tell me if it's how you take it."

"It's always how I take it."

"They keeping you busy there down on the farm?"

"They're trying."

There was a row of vitamin bottles by his computer screen, like little pillars, so precisely aligned in a row. Danny's obsessive-compulsiveness.

"Part of the job. I'm down here for a funeral. The one I asked you about, the kid from Newton who just died from his knife injury. Marty said it looked like it might be some homeless kids from the nearby park they got on a security video. I want to see if they might not possibly ID as some kids from Newton instead, given some photos I have."

"'S'all I've been doing as well around here for a while. Looking at security footage. Different case though."

Ojal squinted to take in the grainy image on his screen. It looked to be shot from a second or third story, security camera footage, all blurry greys, a streetlight with a ghostly aura.

"Ah. This. Place on Queen went up in flames."

"Restaurant?"

"Nope. One of them vintage places. Diamonds in ash, that's what the Sun wrote. Something just went pop on the main floor. Check this flare." Danny clicked his mouse to freeze the frame. A circle of a grainy white flash was suddenly visible through the storefront window. "See that? It's too big for an electrical."

"Arson? Guy torching his place for insurance?"

"Bad idea when you live upstairs. Guy didn't make it out. Look at this. Shot from some kid's phone in the morning."

There on YouTube, in the lurid colours of an autumn dawn, was a blackened staircase, flames still licking at its bottom steps. It was all that remained of the second floor of Diamonds In The Trash. The staircase looked like it was floating in air from the camera's angle, and then it hobbled and collapsed with one gust of wind that sounded like a muffled breath.

"So you're on this yourself?"

"Nah. Me and Richie, if he can get out of the courthouse for five fucking minutes."

"Listen, I might need a hand with this case."

"You're killing me. Look at this desk."

"Danny, I've got nowhere else I can go. I'm getting nothing from Canning and nobody upstairs has responded to my emails. For four days now."

"What do you want me to do? I know as much as you. Look, it was probably a fag hunt. We always get 'em when the weather gets warmer. Christ, when I started, it would be one a week."

"I need to know this hasn't gone completely fucking cold. Can you do a little digging and see if anyone's actually still on this?" She blew on the rim of her mug.

"I can dig but don't expect much. Their best lead's the footage of the park life behind that place. That and a sole print in the alley."

"They had a sole print?"

"I'm not saying ... I'm just saying I wouldn't expect much."

"But you'll try."

Danny Fortune clasped his hands in his lap and sighed. He nodded at the clip, still paused, on his computer screen, that weird ancient light and the collapse of the staircase.

"I love you, Danny."

"I know."

She put the mug down on the corner of his desk and rose from her chair. "And I love your McChai. I miss it."

It was when she was idling at the first stop light on Front that she glanced at her device and saw the flashing red light. Her first thought was that Danny already had something as soon as he called Canning. But no—looked like a Newton number.

Hey, it's me. Listen, I know what you said, but if we can just sit down and talk this through. You know what I'm in the middle of and what will happen to this campaign if I tell her everything right now. If we can just talk ... doesn't have to be at your place. I'll meet you anywhere. You can tell the goras we were just talking gurdwara stuff if anybody asks. And maybe that's all you really want to talk to me about anyway and that's fine. Just tell me we can meet. Call me, okay?

She tossed the phone as if it had scorched her fingers. It bounced off the passenger seat and clattered on the floor. Men like Jagdeep Minhas made you appreciate a Danny Fortune, even though he was probably no different in his younger days.

She turned and accelerated up the feeder lane onto the Gardiner, promising herself she would not respond to that message tonight. And probably not ever.

29.

GUTHRIE AND TANIS sat in his car, waiting for Bella to finish saying her condolences to Drew's father. Once the service had ended, Shereen Trask had hurried away in a taxi with Derek Reiner, leaving Drew's father standing by a stone pillar on the porch. Aside from the long grey hair tied in a braid and his funeral suit he had the prairie weathered look of some ranch hand from another age. "Somebody's got to talk to him, that's just cruel," Bella murmured, as she glided away from Tanis.

And then, as if he was summoned by Drew's guardian angel, came Norris Arbic from around the pillar to offer his consolation. The two men looked like a couple of old hippie musicians who might have been in the same band. It was the beards, the fluid solemnity of their gestures.

"Tanis, I understand why you've never told her about you looking at her emails. You know there's never been any judgment here."

"How could there be? You don't have a daughter."

He could sense the edge in Tanis's voice and the distance that had suddenly opened up between them. Yet he couldn't retract it now.

"I'm just thinking this has all gone a bit further than imagined. She's too tough to show she's scared. I think she probably needs to know."

"Or maybe it's simply that you need to know if she has any new secrets. That way you can write your story."

"Tanis, I don't give a damn about the story. You know that's not what this is about. The girl's being bullied. Stalked."

"Really, Ian? I wasn't aware. Perhaps I should read her emails."

"I'm worried about your daughter. And yeah, I'm also worried about you. Am I not supposed to say I care about you both? I don't know the rules here."

Tanis raised her hand to her hair, tucked a few long dark strands behind her ear, staring into her lap. She had only become so much more attractive to him since they had begun to sleep together again. She had opened up about her past, and he realized he had misread her as cynical and detached about what all this could mean between them. In their being together now both the present and past seemed subtly transformed. Tanis was no longer simply the girl who had been Annelie's best friend, the one so in a hurry to grow up, the one who would eventually take that familiar path from the one bedroom apartment off Queen Street back to the suburbs, with boxes of black clothes packed off to Goodwill. No, Tanis had whole chapters in her life never spoken of when she returned, with husband and daughter, to settle down in Newton. She had lived in Vancouver before she had married, had a long relationship with an actor who slept around on her, then a cokehead who was a chef at once-famous restaurants in Toronto, each flameout a premonition of the man's descent into addiction and bankruptcy. Then, this marriage to her first love, the man who was like a mentor, this too had frayed from his infidelity until it tore irrevocably.. This was all new to him, both comforting and unnerving. As she slowly blinked and reached to clasp his hand, he felt sudden, intense gratitude, less from her than from fate itself, the way it twisted and made this happen.

"I gambled here, with Bella. Gambled that I could invade her privacy and control everything that might happen to her. This happens with a kid, Ian. Nobody prepares you for this kind of fear. So I was wrong, if that makes you feel any better. Or feel that you're right. Because you are."

"I don't care about being right."

"I know. I am going to tell her. Just let us all get back home."

They turned to look where Bella might have gone and there she was, already leaning against Tanis' car in the parking lot, arms folded, listening and nodding to a young man in jeans and hockey jacket, her gaze fixed on the ground before him. The young man looked to be offering more than his condolences; he no longer had his hands meekly stuffed in his front pockets but was gesturing to her to show he was speaking from the heart. Bella would not look him in the eye but her gentle nod indicated she was accepting what he was saying. Then the young man turned from her and yes, it was David Goring.

She wouldn't speak about it in the car ride back to Newton, just gazed out the window at some distant point on the horizon

Bella had little interest in speaking with anyone when they returned. When the Thai food came she emerged to barely fill her plate—the rice, red curry and salad could not touch each other, little islands of food on a sea of white porcelain—and then she padded back down the hall into her room. As she opened the door there was a muffled squall of death metal coming from her laptop and then the sharp click of the lock.

After they had finished eating Tanis opened another bottle of Riesling and brought it out to Guthrie on the balcony. She took the cigarette from his fingers, brought it to her lips and in that moment she was all he ever wanted. This was the way life inevitably had to work, it seemed; everything else had to go to hell for a glimpse of something like love to offer him sustenance.

"Nicky Poole. Remember I said I met with Nicky Poole?"

"Diamonds in the trash."

"The fucking guy's line's gone dead. I'm getting bounce-backs from the email address he gave me. Perfect. Just fucking perfect. What I managed to get on tape is barely audible. Nothing I can use."

"Does it matter though? I mean, it sounds like this story on Kent's not going to happen."

"It has to happen. I'll make it happen."

"It didn't sound like your friend Stephen Clarke was too encouraging about that."

Stephen. On the day they finally met again it was for coffee in the PATH. He looked shrunken and defeated, his hands gnarled as if he had been twining rope rather than allegedly recovering quietly from his operation and subsequent dismissal from the Torontonian. Stephen had met with his financial advisor that morning, discussing the state of his retirement. All Stephen would say, with a clipped formality, was that the prospect of him not having to work anymore was less promising than he imagined. Michael Rainford at Broch-Leonard, he had suggested Stephen hang out his own shingle as an editor. There were lots of first time authors out there willing to pay well for a good editor. One had to muddle through, it was ever thus, Ian. His hand shook as he wrote down a few names and phone numbers on a napkin, friends of Stephen's that Guthrie should speak with to try to get his story on Kent placed somewhere. Yet they both knew it was little more than a bit of theatre, and Ian quickly folded the napkin and stuffed it in his pocket. He watched Stephen walk off for his train at Union Station, realizing he would most likely never see him again.

"Stephen was a good man. One of the best."

"You make it sound like he's dead."

"Didn't mean to. Put it down to my pessimism here. But I've got to see this out, get it all down in a first draft at least."

As they spoke they could see Bella emerge from the hallway.

"Come, Ian. Let's talk to her."

As they re-entered from the balcony Bella did not look away from the television. There was some sort of idol competition on, with three poor souls dressed as a producer's conception of a pop star—hair coiffed into an approximation of stage fright, pirate clothes.

"Hey."

"Hey. How you doing. You all right?"

"I'm tired, I guess. I just want this day over."

"Bella, you know when I first started looking into Sydney's death for the Monitor, the cops told me they were going through her email accounts, pretty much every message she ever sent."

"They told me the same thing. It was the cop who was there today. Call-me-Ojal. We went for a couple of runs together."

"I'm going to try to write on Drew. Nobody wants me to at the Monitor. And I don't really think the cops want me to either."

"And this concerns me because?"

"Bel, listen to him. A little respect."

"Yes, mother."

"It's okay. It is a little ridiculous."

"So what do you want from me, Ian Guthrie?"

"Look, your mom, me ... the first person we ever knew who died ... like knew as a friend ... was Annelie Danziger. And the first thing that cop said to me after Sydney's death was 'Guthrie, you grew up here, what was the deal with—'"

"Are we doing this? Now?" Bella looked to Tanis, wide eyed. "The deal is my mother and your obvious girlfriend or whoever took a great interest in my homework. Isn't that right, Mom? Not all my homework, mind you, because really, my calculus is a disaster and I was told architects had to know math but neither my dad nor her have been any help at all, really."

"Bella."

"This is fucked up. Mom, I know you've been looking at my emails. I'm pretty sure you spoke to that cop too. Why else would she have gone to me. It's okay. I probably would have too, given all that happened."

Tanis leaned back in her chair, unfolded her arms. She had been holding them tightly to her chest and now they hung lifelessly at her sides. She flashed a brief glance at Guthrie—a kind of "what now?" and then just stared into the carpet as she summoned up a response.

"You know it was only because I was worried sick about all this."

"It's fine, okay? Look, Ian Guthrie, I kind of like you. I mean, the jury's out but Mom, you could have done a lot worse. Like that guy who sold cars."

"I'm not sure that's supposed to be your business."

"All of this started when Syd and me and Drew, we were in the drama elective. Syd, before that class started, she was like the straightest, most boring chick. At least she looked that way. But then a certain something happened at that fucking Trinity Baptist Church. She left it, didn't want to see her boyfriend neither. About a month later in drama class Drew and her they did this exercise together, created characters and it was like boom. Total connection. They're out having a smoke. I ask Drew for one. Me and Syd, we started talking and like boom again. Big boom."

"For you too."

"Uh huh. But there was no way I was going to show it. Which I guess just made her more intrigued. And confused. So fucking confused."

"But for you?"

"I'm so over that opera. And I didn't want to lead her into anything. I mean you've got to understand, she'd been dating David Goring for like a year at least."

"And Goring . . ."

"You saw him there, right? At the funeral."

"What did he say to you?"

"I kind of couldn't believe it. He apologized . . . for everything he and his friends had done . . . how they were to me and Drew after Syd had told him it was over between them. The bullying, the fucking bleacher girls . . ."

Tanis moved towards her to take Bella in an embrace but she could tell, by Bella's folded arms, her daughter wasn't quite there yet.

"Well that's good. That's very good. He should apologize."

"I guess I believe him. I mean I realize ... I mean, they were awful, all right. Far worse to Drew than me. But murder? No."

"Then who?"

Bella looked down at her shoes and shook her head. "I promised, okay? Promised Syd."

Tanis leaned forward again. She put her hands on the hassock in front of her, gripped its cushion as if she had her hands on the neck of Sydney Brewin's murderer.

"Honey, think about this. Sydney would have wanted you to protect yourself. If this person murdered Drew because of what he knew, don't you think he'd come for you?"

"Mom, really ... like you can stop it? I'm out of that fucking school in January, I can handle it 'til then. And I can still talk to that cop."

"Ojal?"

"Pardon?"

"Staff Inspector Dhillon." Guthrie muttered, suddenly a bit too conscious of Tanis's eyes on him.

"That's her. Don't worry, Mom. She said she's on this and I trust her."

"Thanks for telling me. Bella, I've got no reason to doubt you. Tell me, did you ever watch Annelie Danziger's movies?"

"Of course. Her own pregnancy ... that's what this movie she wrote was about. Black Iris. 'Dark seed, dark sorrows, dark petals falling.' That's from the script. I mean, to be honest, I thought it was kind of lame, but Syd was all over it. And Drew, he just liked anything that required cool clothes, right?"

"You think he gave her the drugs that night?"

"Of course! He had the oxys. Still I really don't believe she wanted to go through with it—just like Annelie didn't up at that lake.

She just wanted to show David Goring and her mother she wasn't fit to have any kid. Then she fucked up. She just went too far."

"Then why did Drew walk away?"

"He was going to get help. He told me and I believe him. Drew didn't drive. He couldn't have taken her back to a hospital. He headed out and then he heard the car crash into the lake. Then he knew how bad it looked. That's when he took off."

"So, no suicide pact or anything."

"I heard about that version going around. I just laughed. Hell no. You know, her parents, Goring's parents, nobody was going to let her abort that baby. They weren't going to let it be her decision. She was just . . . she'd rather hurt herself. It was like, I'll show you what a fuck-up I am. Instead of saying who the real father of that child was, to make clear she had her reasons. That fucking mother of hers, Karen Brewin, she knew, but . . ."

"But what?" Guthrie said.

"She'd rather protect the evil fucker who raped her daughter. That's the truth."

"How could anybody have that kind of power . . ."

"He confessed he sinned out of weakness . . . the same way he sinned with fucking Karen Brewin herself. And that crazy woman . . . she forgave him, turned her back on her own daughter. Protected herself, her fake marriage and wanted to force her daughter into a fake marriage with David Goring."

Tanis rose from her chair and moved to the window. She just seemed to be staring at the frost pattern on the window until she finally turned to face Bella.

"Have you told your new cop friend any of this?"

"I told her some."

"You saying nothing about this man . . . protecting him because you're sworn to the secret . . . you're protecting a murderer now, as far as I'm concerned."

"Your mother's right, Bella."

"Well why don't you tell her then, Mr. Guthrie? I think you've got an idea who I'm talking about."

Bella rose from the couch with the remote in her hand. She pointed it at the screen and clicked off the flickering images. "I'm tired." She trilled a good night, stole a quick glance at Tanis, and then she headed back down the hall to her room.

Guthrie knew enough with Tanis now to realize there was nothing he could say that was better than silence. All that was necessary was just a brief touch of her hand. She held it tightly and then she let him wrap her in his arms.

***

He woke up with a start and checked his watch. It was just past two in the morning. He gently kissed Tanis on the forehead and stole out in the dark, silent but for the click of the door behind him.

When he got back home he glimpsed the projector, still on the dining room table where he left it upon his return from Nicky Poole's store. He drew the curtain, took out the brown tin canister labeled BLACK IRIS in Dymo tape and threaded the little film through the machine.

There, flickering in the murky half-light on the curtain was Annelie, with peroxided hair and shiny black dress, running through a two-lane underpass. Cut to her walking through the old Evergreen cemetery in town, dropping the petals of a flower each step she took. She'd spliced a sequence in reverse: a petal floating up from the grass and back in place on the flower.

Guthrie was watching intently, yet there was another sequence he was imagining now. It was of a loud argument at first, a young Kent railing against how resigned Annelie was to her fate. Had she no idea how having this child could ruin his life, the bright political future that lay before him? It didn't matter if she asked nothing of him for the child, and that they were over. She throws open the door in the ugly little room, demands he get out. He refuses and slams it shut. A young Annelie would cut to the petals falling here, then cut back to her weeping alone in a stranger's room, broken and violated. Cut once more to her fixing up, the plastic needle piercing the vein in her arm. Close-up on her eyelids fluttering, her falling asleep … the sleep she'd never wake from. Did she want to die? Who would ever know? But she wanted to sleep and forget her sorrow.

The last frames ribboned through the projector and there was just a white square of light on the curtain. It couldn't burn through the images of a stubborn remembering now. Guthrie flicked the projector off and cupped his face in his hands, wishing he could erase what he knew.

30.

OJAL HAD TO meet him face-to-face. It had implications beyond the two of them, should he actually win this by-election. And sure, it was only right that this played out at the gurdwara, where she had stood up, so naïve, so unaware of how she was being manipulated, and actually endorsed this man.

With snow clouds heavy in the sky, the steel dome over the Darbar Sahib looked grey and dingy, the flag quaintly vivid at its top. And the parking lot, no doubt because of the kids Jag had working the phones and knocking on the doors, was more than full with cars parked on the soft shoulder of the side road. Maybe he even had the Leader of his party here, the two of them sitting together, so close and brotherly, so poised and ready for the photo op. She could have told him what every cop knows; somebody always talks, it's just a question of when. She turned and graced the few stares with a quick, smug grin as she breezed through the glass doors, lightly draped her chooni on her head and shoulders, and then slipped off her shoes.

The singers had apparently just arrived from Rajasthan. The three of them sat cross-legged on the altar in simple white linen salwar kameez, looking grave and frail as they began the next hymn. They all had the same doleful eyes, like sons of one guru with different mothers. As they sang they did not look up to take in the row after row of those who had come today.

Ojal ventured out from the back of the room, smiling and nodding at the few heads that turned, those she recognized. She was performing the pantomime of the late arrival, one who simply couldn't find a place in the back rows but had to take hers with the luminaries near the altar.

And there was Jagdeep in the second row. He was sitting in between two heavyset white women, one who looked like she hadn't quite anticipated sitting cross-legged in the tight leggings of her kameez. To her left was the Leader of this party, as Ojal expected. As she approached, Jagdeep looked up from the floor. He understood her expression immediately. He murmured a quick apology to the younger of the two women beside him and then rose to follow Ojal out of the gurdwara.

Ojal's footsteps quickened as she led him through the parking lot to her car. She could hear the clicking of the heels of his ridiculously expensive shoes on the pavement.

"I've got two minutes."

"It's not about how much time you've got. It's how much time I'll give you."

"You know how hard it was for me to get the Leader here this weekend? Like do you have any idea what an embarrassment this is right now?"

They had made it to the second aisle when she had to turn to him.

"Prabhjot Kular."

"What about him?"

"You know what about him. You know what he did with those advance ballots."

"Prabhjot has nothing to do with me or my campaign. I don't know who you've been talking to."

"You're so fucking vain, Jagdeep. You don't think you have enemies too?"

"Tell me who it is you've been talking to. They're full of shit."

"You know, I actually don't care how you lied to me. How you're lying to me right now. It's how you'd be happy to keep lying to everybody else for the next four years."

"You don't know what you're talking about."

"I can't believe how I once trusted you."

"You've never trusted me."

"Are you trying to tell me you were ever going to tell your wife?"

There. She had done it, gone to where she promised herself she wouldn't. A couple of cars passed on the side road in the distance.

"No one in that gurdwara is going to have any respect for you as soon as you open your mouth. You destroy a man's marriage. You try to destroy his political career."

"You destroy yourself, Jagdeep! God, I'm just happy I'm not collateral damage. Like everybody else around you." As she turned she was suddenly aware of her outstretched arm, how melodramatic she was being. "I got nothing more to say to you."

"You're out of your depth, Ojal."

"Then that's me drowning in the shallow end."

He had turned and begun to walk back to the doors. He looked thicker around the shoulders and thighs. For a moment she thought of his naked body lying beside her, how he had slept on his back so at peace with himself and what they had just done that night. To a marriage and family. *It's been coming for some time. She knows it's over.* No, in his mind the end of his marriage was really never going to happen, and if his wife actually did find out about any of this, he probably just assumed he'd manage it. Enough people had told him he could get past anything on charm. He was really just a mama's boy, one who would become chubby and trivial in middle age, full of the vanity that belied his mediocrity.

As she got back into her car, she picked up her mobile device. Yes, it was really a teenage girl's gesture now, this erasing of all his emails and text messages, trashing his V-card. Still it felt good. Cleansing.

31.

IT WAS THE view of the lake from the ninth floor that Gudrun Danziger loved the most about her home—her last, she was sure. She had drawn the curtains to reveal to Guthrie just what she and her husband Rudi had seen when the real estate agent gave them that first tour of the rooms. The lake looked like a slab of black marble. She stretched out her liver-splotched hand as she spoke of the different colours the water took on with each season. There was a turquoise stone the size of a scarab beetle on her ring finger. "Rudi always wished we lived by the sea. As soon as he saw that view, he said he was ready to buy. What could I say? This is perfect for my painting."

Down there along that path, just by the parking lot, that is where Rudi collapsed. That was three years ago now.

"People used to say that mit Annelie she must have been most like me. With her painting and writing. The photographs and little films. Not the case. She was Rudi's girl."

"In what way?"

"You know she was headstrong. That was not me when I was young. I wish it was! I would have started painting much earlier."

"These are yours?"

"All three, yes. My dune series from a week I spent in Picton. But that one over there, the abstract . . . that is hers. You see with the gradations of colour in her palette, she was very analytical. We both thought she was going to be an engineer like her father."

"And then she started writing."

"It was the stories, really. They were like the fairytales I read to her before bed when she was a little girl. But they were so perfectly formed. You read them and it was like opening up a watchcase and seeing all the little parts work together so precisely. Rudi and I, we couldn't imagine where that came from with her."

"I remember she read one in English class. It was sly and sophisticated. We were thirteen? Nobody was thinking that way, never mind writing."

"You have children?"

"I don't, no."

"Maybe you didn't want them. Sorry if that is forward. I never know the boundaries."

"Not at all, it's fine. Really."

"You can never really imagine where their talents lie, you know?"

"Do you ever try to imagine the person she would be today?"

Gudrun turned and stared out at the lake. Her white, spiky hair was cropped so close, she looked like a little bird.

"You know, I can't think that way. You knew her well, yes?"

"Not as well as I would have liked. I suppose I had a crush on her. A lot of guys did."

"You knew this Kent."

"He was a friend."

She turned and sat on the corner of the sectional couch that smelled of new leather.

"A good friend?"

"I don't know if I would say that."

"Before she saw that boy, she was in Neufchatel for the summer. We thought that might be good for her. And she met a French boy there. Didier. I think he broke her heart."

"I remember her spending a summer in Europe."

"She would have never have seen this Kent if it weren't for that."

"You didn't like him?"

"He came to our house and he was full of himself. Talked about his plans for universitat. Dressed like a young banker because Rudi and I would approve. But I was watching Annelie ... and watching the way he looked at her. It was all wrong. It was so new to her, the attention from boys. Rudi and I, we didn't raise her to care about such things. And the other girls, were actually quite cruel to her."

"She was a threat."

"She was too innocent. No confidence in what her heart really needed. I blame myself. I never tried to talk of such matters with her. I was just happy when she broke it off with this Kent. She moved to Toronto, got a new boyfriend, more like her ... artistic. And then ... that Kent he just wouldn't leave it alone. If they were together again and that's how she had gotten pregnant ... all I regret is that I never asked her if he forced her."

Gudrun shook her head, staring out into the break in the clouds. In the light by the window it looked as if her dark brown eyes had welled up with tears. Then Gudrun slowly blinked and looked away.

"Did she tell you she was expecting?"

"She told us both, yes. You know we grew up in a small village. Rudi, he lived through the war. He saw things I didn't see. His faith ... he didn't talk about it but it meant so much to him. Annelie and him, they were so close also. He didn't take it well."

"He wouldn't allow her to see a doctor and get an abortion."

"We argued so much over this. You know, in so many ways, we ran away from small thinking. Moved to Bern as soon as we could. Away from all the katholische ...I knew girls who disappeared for months until they had their child and gave them up. I knew one who died because there was a woman who would do the operation in her house for a few francs. Terrible stories ..."

"But Rudi ..."

"He would not sway. You know, for many years, when he worked at the plant for such little pay ... him, an engineer back home

... it was like this country broke his heart. Broke his heart but for what he hoped for Annelie. This is why he gave her such encouragement with her paintings, her writing, her little movies. But when he found out she was pregnant, it was like all that he hoped for collapsed. He was broken. I know she saw it in him. She could not forgive herself."

Guthrie cleared his throat, gazed about the room. There was a low machine hum in the condo that layered over the silence like a soft coat of snow. "You think she might have become self-destructive?"

Gudrun shook her head, sniffed as if she had just tasted something gone off and bitter. "Absolutely no. You see we still had this trust when she went to art school. Rudi and I, we didn't mind this ... this bohemianism she was finding, mit the different clothes, the hair. And I liked her new boyfriend. I knew she was a good girl, she always told me the truth. This is why I did not believe about the drugs. She would have never done that, not mit her pregnancy."

"Even though she was going to go it on her own."

"She would have not gone it on her own. She had us and that boyfriend, the musician ... he would have understood over time. She had love and support. She did not need this Kent."

"And yet ..."

"Let me tell you this, the wrong person went to prison. I know this. I know it in my heart. This Nicholas Poole, he was nothing to her. I don't believe any of it. The drugs, the way she died. This Kent was there that night in Toronto and something very bad happened. I know this. Nothing about his story of him going home early felt true, and yet the police just heard what they wanted to hear. They wanted to put Nicholas Poole in prison. And nobody cared. They just hushed it all up, swept Annelie's death away."

"Did you try telling anyone this? Did you talk to a lawyer?"

"Rudi. He met with two lawyers Kent Wolseley's father employed. Big, fat men in suits too small. I called them Humpty and Dumpty. Rudi never told me what they agreed about. He just went to

Toronto one Wednesday afternoon to a steak restaurant called Barberians. Isn't that the perfect name? And when he came back at night, he just said, 'Gudrun, there is no point. Let's talk no more about this investigation.' Naturally I argued but there was no use. Then about six years ago, when I had my first round of chemo, that is when he told me how much money Humpty and Dumpty paid him to drop the investigation."

"You don't have any paperwork on this agreement. Anything signed?"

She shook her hand and stared out at the lake. "I trusted Rudi with it. He handled all that. Maybe I should have but ... it was all too painful."

"They knew there was more to this, or else they would have never have paid your husband."

Gudrun recrossed her legs. They looked as slender as a little girl's in these grey leggings. "Do you know something? I have it all when it comes to my baby. I've saved everything. Her writings, her paintings, her films. Your story will have readers."

"Yes. She's impossible to forget."

"You want to see them too? I'll show you, if you like."

"That would be very helpful."

"Come."

She rose from the couch and led Guthrie down a dimly lit hallway that had a faint smell of mothballs. She fetched a small key from the top of a jewelry box in her room. The key fit the last door on the left. As it clicked open, she let out a girlish little laugh. It was so discordant that for the first time Guthrie entertained the possibility that Gudrun Danziger might not be entirely all right.

She turned on the light and Guthrie felt his heart begin to thump, The room was like a shrine. Paintings and pen drawings, many of the latter dashed off on the lined pages of Hilroy notebooks, were all framed and lovingly hung on almost every inch of the walls. A bedspread of a garish alpine scene , was under six carefully placed stacks of journals and notebooks and photo albums. There was a print of a Georgia O'Keefe painting on the wall, one of a black iris. Gudrun murmured that it was Annelie's favourite. And there, with the accordion door half-open, was a closet full of girl's clothes, hung and wrapped in dry cleaner's plastic.

"You've saved everything."

Gudrun bit her lip and nodded as she closed her eyes in solemn affirmation. "It's all here."

She reached for Guthrie's elbow and pulled him close. It seemed as if she was about to kiss him until she whispered "I've got the last things she wore. Here …"

She opened a drawer in a dresser and there were the jeans, the underwear, the singlet, the blouse, laid out like holy relics on white linen. "I took these home from the hospital that morning. Always they will be mit me. Always my daughter."

Guthrie gently pulled himself away from Gudrun as he watched her hand caress the clothes. The faint tremble, the outsized turquoise stone on her finger, the sickly sweet, rotting smell on her breath when she whispered.

He forced a smile and nodded in reverence. "Yes. You have her here forever."

32.

THE MORNINGS WERE pitch dark now, and even when Ojal was in the final mile heading for home, the streetlights were still aglow and the lights on in each house near the pond revealed little scenes that unfolded in slow motion: the mother of the house preparing coffee in a kitchen, the father with thick-fingered finesse, knotting his tie.

Yet today, things seemed just a little less slow motion, the traffic busier on the streets as Ojal made her way to the pond. A line of flattened Win With Wolseley signs along the traffic island separating four lanes was all it took to remind her: "E-day." Such a relief it was all over. If he was elected, he'd be up in Ottawa most of the time and if he wasn't, he'd go back into his private life, with its carefully compartmentalized hypocrisies and delusions.

This morning also seemed of quieter significance simply because young Bella invited herself out for a few miles around the pond once more. It had been at least a couple of weeks since they had run together, before Drew Trask's funeral. And now, Bella wanted to talk.

Ojal slowed to a walk by the pond's edge to stretch and wait. She pulled back the cuff of her mitten to check her watch. But she could hear no footfalls, make out no hooded figure under the glow of the farthest streetlight in the distance. She waited for what seemed another five minutes and finally checked her BlackBerry, but there were no messages. An outsized pickup truck, all shiny chrome bumpers and wheel rims passed, the bass of its stereo thumping to a song Ojal could recall emanating from a boom box in the weight room when she was at university all those years ago. Tattooed football boys on steroids.

Then she made out the graceful bounce of Bella's at the top of that rolling hill. Odd, she was coming from the wrong direction. Maybe she had made a detour with all that construction around those condos.. She was certainly moving faster than usual, by the tension of her shoulders, the movement at her hips.

"Hey … sorry …"

"I was worried something happened."

"Got tied up but all good. Should we go?"

"Wanted to say that it was good, you showing up at Drew's funeral. Didn't expect that."

"I wanted to speak to his parents but I got pulled away with work stuff." Gradually, they started to slow and find their rhythm. Ojal could feel her breathing slow, the words come out easier. "How you doing with all that?"

"Funny, you ask." Bella slowed even more as they took in the lightening sky together. When both of them were walking, she turned to Ojal. "Want to tell you about what I know about Sydney's pregnancy, okay?"

"Of course it's okay."

"Want to tell you she had a good reason for everything she did. And that I don't think you should be trying to pin anything on David Goring with Drew's death. There was somebody else who might want him dead for what he might say."

"That means you might be in danger too."

"Uh huh. But here's the problem, right? I can't prove none of it."

Ojal turned and embraced her. Bella collapsed in tears in her arms. "Well that's my job, isn't it? Come. Let's just walk a while."

33.

IT WAS A door-shut morning for Bruce Gallant. When Peggy Vaughan arrived at seven-forty he was already in with his tea and a rock-hard breakfast cookie his wife made him take to work. Bruce would be brooding and angry until four in the afternoon because it was one of the few days he had to write something Toronto would read: the editorial on the by-election. He hated writing more than a few lines for the paper, bridled at the idea of perpetrating this façade that the Monitor was still a legitimate newspaper. "Potemkin's Post," Ian Guthrie had called it in one editorial meeting, and despite how adversarial their relationship had become, Gallant couldn't help but smile and give him a nod. What made it all worse was that Bruce and everyone in the office would be working late until the election results came in. Three deluxe banquet squares from Pizza Stop, with Bruce all grumpy about having to use his credit card too. Ian Guthrie walked in.

"It's good to see you, Ian. You're up early. You just dropping by?"

"Kind of. I was hoping to talk to Bruce. Is he in yet?"

Peggy turned to look at Bruce Gallant's door, made a face and turned back Guthrie with a pained look.

"He is, but do you really want to go in there? I think he's writing."

"I should. Sorry, Peggy."

She rose from her desk and walked over to Gallant's office with soft, mincing steps, as if any creak in the floorboards would only make the editor-in-chief irritated by her interruption.

Maybe it was how cowed Peggy seemed that caused Guthrie to come around the other side of the reception desk, unbidden. Here she was, four years away from retirement, walking on eggshells with this man. "Guthrie? What do you want?"

"I want you to be civil to everyone in here. It's going to be a long day and I guarantee you nobody's getting paid enough for your bullshit. Morning, Bruce."

Gallant leaned back in his chair and slowly made a steeple of his fingers. Waiting.

"Bruce, I know what you said about me writing anything on this election, but I've got something here … an audio clip from one of Kent Wolseley's old girlfriends … it's important … It casts a light on Kent's character and raises troubling questions. Toronto can't object about us running it now. It's E-day. It won't affect the vote."

"Guthrie, don't start."

"It doesn't have to be my byline. I can give this clip to Kerry-Anne, she can write it."

"That's not going to make much difference for Kerry-Anne."

"What are you talking about?"

"I've let her go. And not just Kerry-Anne. I got the word last night in a conference call. Powers, Morin, twenty percent of the operating budget here. I had to fight to keep Peggie on, for Christ sakes. The whole chain's tanking apparently. Everybody has to make sacrifices now … That's how they put it."

"Sacrifices."

Gallant swiveled and rolled forward in his ridiculous chair. There was a brick red sheen to his cheeks. He'd cut himself shaving just under his jaw and it looked like it could start bleeding again. "I can't keep you on, Ian. Not even as a freelancer."

"How hard did you fight that one, Bruce?"

"This may surprise you, but more than you think."

"Uh huh."

"Look, I really don't give a damn what you think, anyway. It's not as if it makes any difference now. For either of us."

"You too?"

"I'm done. End of December. That's the way to do it, start the new year on the right foot. I hate this business, anyway. This show's over."

"Bruce. Come on. Don't be silly."

"Look, don't think I went down just for you. I've got other irons in the fire. I'm going to be teaching down at Sinclair College in January."

Bruce carried on with his performance of detachment, gazing at his screen, avoiding all eye contact with Guthrie, waiting for him to shut the door behind him on his way out.

"Is Kerry-Anne here?"

"She's out covering the campaigns today. I wanted her to have something she could take to another paper, something that shows what she can do."

"She's going to be a good journalist."

"You think?"

"If she gets the chance, yeah."

"Whatever a real chance means. And what about you, Ian? You still working on that magazine piece?"

"I'm not."

"What happened?"

"Same kind of thing that happened here. Though I don't think Stephen Clarke chose to leave."

"He's gone?"

"The magazine wanted a new direction."

"That's a shame. End of an era, Ian."

"Apparently."

"Did you ever make any headway on that Sydney Brewin story?"

"Not really. I thought there might have been a connection to a girl from town here who died a long time ago, a girl I went to high school with. Annelie Danziger. Sydney and her friends, seemed to have a bit of an obsession about her, for whatever reason."

"Didn't hang together?"

"Not really."

"Shame. I would have run it. I did like the stuff you did, Ian. You never came to me and demanded a column, pulled the prima donna shit. And you could have after the Veterans Affairs piece on that Lacey guy. I respected that."

"Respected that I never asked you for anything?"

"Respected that you cared about the story more than your own opinions."

"Well thanks, Bruce."

"What are you going to do now? I mean, Lord knows, we were hardly paying you anyway, but …"

"I don't know. Maybe drive a cab. The skill set's pretty limited here."

"So are the opportunities in this town. You should move back into the city. Guy like you … it's got to be more your speed anyway."

"I've got the house, my Dad's settlement. It's not a lot but I can't sell now. It's all the retirement I have."

"I could keep my eyes open at Sinclair. They may need a good reporter to teach the kids what it's all about."

"Thanks, Bruce, but really, just think of yourself right now."

Gallant finally turned away from his computer screen and smiled at Guthrie. He was suddenly older, wiser. He had seemed such a poor actor when he tried to come off as wise in this job. Now it seemed as if it had finally come to him.

"I'm happy to be yesterday's guy. I couldn't really form any strong opinions about the present tense. I mean, who the fuck cares what I tweet about a blog post? And that's what they need, somebody who thinks that crap matters."

"They don't know what they need, Bruce. Everybody's flying blind."

"Come by before I'm out of here." Gallant kicked the bottom drawer of his desk—the drawer where he kept the J and B. "We can have a drink."

"I will, Bruce."

"And hey, if it's any consolation, it looks like your old buddy's going down anyway. The dipper's probably going to win."

"Really?"

"Anything you've got on Wolseley, it wouldn't have mattered."

As he returned to his car, the little red light on his BlackBerry was flashing. Quaint, how the pulsing rhythm could almost seem urgent. It was from Tanis. Bella had been at the police station. Could he come over? She didn't want to do this day alone.

So this was new, this realization that he was actually needed, possibly a part of Tanis's life now. And maybe even Bella's. Whatever was going on, he actually wanted to be there, to have a role. *I don't want to do this day alone.* Well, I suppose I don't either. He could already imagine Tanis opening the door for him, feel the wordless embrace. It was all he wanted.

34.

THE PUNJAB BANQUET hall was where Kent's "victory celebration" was supposed to be, but someone with Kent—Pincott or Senator MacDougall probably—had changed the venue over the last three days of the campaign to the Rotary hall, which had half the capacity. The risk of even one news camera panning a half-filled room of Newton's senior citizens, with a scattering of the young and too formally dressed and the last few members of the Newton Chamber of Commerce still committed to the Win With Wolseley team, well that was the worst case scenario, Kerry-Anne said. Yet to leave the biggest banquet hall in town suddenly empty so close to the election was also shrewd and vindictive in that petty way that marked most of Kent's campaign; they just knew Jagdeep Minhas would not suddenly pull out of the old Croatian Hunt Club at the eleventh hour to claim the space. Except he did. The word was he got the Punjab Banquet Hall for free.

Kerry-Anne would be up at the Punjab as the results came in—Gallant had managed it with the brass to keep her on until the end of the campaign. There was word that a couple of news stations from the city were sending out reporters and camera trucks but that was yet to be confirmed. As for the defeated, Gallant had mused about going to the Rotary Hall and filing something with Kent's concession speech. He liked to mix with the duffers, talk about the new work done on the Indian Hill course. But it was certain that Kent's team would be sending out a press release as soon as enough polls were counted, might as well go with that, what the hell.

"What the hell exactly."

"Weird, eh? I talked to Kent's wife, though. Virginia ..."

"Veronica."

"Right, Veronica two names. Anyway, she predicts it's going to be a lot closer than people think."

"Of course she does."

"No … I mean, sure, she has to, but beyond the spin she said the last day of polling they did, they were seeing an up-tick. As soon as old Newton …"

"That's old white Newton."

"Whatever. You know what I mean. She says as soon as it started to look like Jagdeep Minhas might actually take this, the uncommitteds switched back."

"You think it's going to be enough?"

"Myself?"

"Yeah. What do you think?"

"I don't think it's going to be enough, Ian. I think Minhas has got this. I mean, I'm writing the Wolseley victory story too, just in case, but really. It's not the Minhas victory but the way the Wolseley campaign fell apart, that's my angle."

Guthrie nodded, but he was thinking over how hard it was to put down to just one factor, how it all unraveled. Perhaps no one ever really trusted that Kent returned for his hometown constituents, that his commitment to Newton was real. It could have been his arrogance and ruthlessness when he had gone personal early on with the other candidates, looking into the debt they were carrying, what they spent their money on. That may have embedded in the minds of even the most conservative of voters in town the sense that Kent was incapable of rising to higher ideals, speaking to the best rather than the worst instincts in them. There was also, as murky and difficult as it was to glimpse a clear angle on, something about Kent's persona itself, all that he embodied as kind of a retro version of the prom king who went on to fulfill everyone's expectations. There was too much inherent detachment, you might call it unacknowledged irony, for even the younger voters to believe Kent could manage this façade for four years in office.

When Guthrie arrived at the Rotary Hall, the eight o'clock news update on the Argyle County radio was reporting that Kent was actually winning with more than a quarter of the polls in. That voice had to be Ken Fogel. Guy was doing the Saturday morning ag report when Guthrie was a kid. Surely he was over seventy now, his teeth and gums clicked on the air like his dentures were slipping. In the parking lot Guthrie could make out the muffled, heavy bass line of Springsteen's "Dancing In The Dark," two or three white haired stragglers dressed in immigrant overcoats passing under a streetlight and heading into the hall. They were walking slowly, as if they were already mulling the defeat over, carrying it with them with an old, churchgoing dignity.

"Ian, I thought that was you."

Ojal had emerged from the library parking lot, her small pearl earrings catching the light.

"I figured you'd be at the Punjab."

"Ah, no."

"Okay. This morning, when you and Tanis brought Bella in, I wanted to speak with you but you know, all that took a while."

"That's okay. I figured you were a little busy."

She tugged at his elbow, directing him to keep walking past the hall. It put him off balance, but in the confusing way that told him he was still vulnerable to possibilities that should have been extinguished from his thoughts of her.

"It's about Jagdeep. Or should I say it's about Jagdeep's campaign and a guy, Prabhjot Kular. He's been working for Elections Canada, doing the advance polls. Ian, I think I've got a story for you here."

"What are you talking about?"

"In the gurdwara elections last year Prabjhot was working for the Young Khalsa slate. They won, and virtually everyone responsible for that victory worked for Minhas on his campaign."

"What are you telling me?"

"Spoiled ballots. Missing ballots. No one at Elections Canada ever checked this guy out."

"I think all they would ask about are federal party affiliations when they hire somebody. Why would they care about that kind of thing?"

"That's the mistake all you journalists have made as well. You never watched the ball. The real politics, what decides everything, it all happens at the gurdwara with the community. If someone like Jagdeep knows how to play that, well …"

"Someone like Jagdeep. What do you mean?"

In the way her pace slowed, the way she kept her eyes on the sidewalk, averting his gaze, Guthrie knew she was betraying more than a friend right now.

"I didn't want to talk about any of this. I just figured someone at your paper would have been on it."

"I'm not at the Monitor anymore, Ojal. I've just come tonight for Kent."

"Are you okay?"

"It's fine, it's fine. It was inevitable. Should have happened a long time ago."

"What are you going to do?"

"I don't know. Maybe move back to the city. That's probably where I should be. When I came out here to look after my dad in his last days, it was never supposed to be a permanent move. I just got too comfortable, I guess. Nobody put any expectations on me. But this is a different kind of place than the town I grew up in, and not all for the better."

"I know what you mean. I think about getting back to the city myself."

"No, this is where you should be. They need you out here."

"Sure. But I don't need it, believe me."

"It'll get easier. I've got something for you too."

"What are you talking about?"

"I wanted to speak with Kent first but what the hell. Gudrun Danziger, Annelie's mother. Remember the girl Sydney and Bella and . . ."

"Of course. Of course I remember."

"Well. Pay her a visit. She's got the clothes that her daughter Annelie was found in. Has them preserved in her little shrine of the not-so-holy virgin. You can get a DNA sample."

"You think?"

"I think you might have at least one case solved."

"You mean Annelie Danziger?"

"It's taken twenty-seven years to find the right guy who raped Annelie. If she did want to kill herself, it was probably out of her own sense of desolation because of what was done to her. Done to her by Kent Wolseley."

They had walked all the way to the next intersection. The drops of rain had turned to clusters of snowflakes that dissolved on the collar of Ojal's long, black woolen coat.

"Ian, you should have been a cop like your dad. You've got it in your bones."

Guthrie tried to smile as he turned back towards the Rotary Hall. "Don't joke about that."

"I'm serious."

"There's a pay bar, apparently. Proceeds going to charity. Can I buy you one of those horrible cooler drinkies you seem to like?"

"That would be very nice, actually."

"I expect they'll have enough polls reporting in within the hour to call this one way or another. Something tells me it's not going to be a long night."

***

The hall smelled of pine sol and spilled beer. The Chamber of Commerce guys, thickset men in golf sweaters of pastel shades, had clustered around the few pub tables, with Dean Vickers, the riding president and his small, scowling wife orbiting around, looking for genial ways into the conversation. They were speaking in low voices, barely audible to those near them, given the squall of eighties pop hits coming from the speaker cabinets on stage. They seemed restive, uncomfortable with the atmosphere in the room. Empty bottles of beer stood abandoned on tables like the last hopes of victory.

"Guthrie, mind if we wait on that drink?"

"Not at all. Think I know what you mean. I'll grab you later after Kent's speech."

As Guthrie drifted into the crowd, looking for someone, anyone who could give him some word on the polls and of Kent's whereabouts, Ojal hung back and scanned the crowd for allies she could find. There were still quite a few uncles from the Chinna slate at the gurdwara, claiming two banquet tables near the back with their Win With Wolseley signs. Two teenage girls were seated by the fire exit with a bicycle pump, inflating some thunder sticks. One smiled and revealed her braces to Ojal. Narinder Deol, an old man with eyes the same milky brown of Ojal's grandfather, gave her a jaunty wave as she approached.

Over by the speakers in a pressed blue linen blouse, fiercely clinging to the arm of her yawning husband, was Karen Brewin. She had a tight smile for everyone passing, pumping her fist with a glare that was just a bit too spirited, too forced. How do you come to understand Karen Brewin if all that Bella had said was true? What strange drama of sin and corruption and her complicity with evil for some higher good, some unshakeable belief in a church and the charlatan—and murderer—who ran it, animated this woman? She was more mysterious than Norris Arbic really, who was a straightforward case of a narcissist-psychopath who suddenly found the license to do his worst. No matter how this ongoing investigation went, Ojal already knew no interview could get under that mask of a smile, that willed serenity of Karen Brewin's faith in some higher power.

Ojal turned from her and then, just as she passed the entrance to the hall once more she glimpsed a thatch of greying, reddish blonde hair that she recognized immediately. She watched it bob through the shoulders, turbans and campaign signs.

"Yo, look at you! Hoped I'd see you here. You clean up well, Dhillon."

"Danny, what are you doing here?"

"Just checking out what's been keeping my favourite cop so busy out here." Danny Fortune was taking in every angle of the room with his pasted on smile. "Jeez, doesn't look like much is happening yet. Come outside with me while I have a smoke?"

She trailed behind him, following the sway of his shoulders, reading the tension in his quick pace until he had found a spot to light up on the porch of the hall.

" Remember, when you came in to 52, I was watching this security camera footage?"

"Trying to recall."

"It was that shop that went up like a pack of matches out in the east end."

"Vaguely. I was a little scattered after that funeral."

"Well, I got some other footage from the old folks home across the street from the store. I started looking into any cars that parked nearby, what time they pulled in and drove out again. Usual stuff, right?" Danny squinted through his smoke as he inhaled, then blew out two rings, watching them evaporate in the night air. "This is the thing. There was a white SUV that parked and then pulled away right around the time that shop went up. I checked the plates and it's this guy Shane Valgardson. He was a staffer in the mayor's office but when I called they said he was on unpaid leave. Working for the Kent Wolseley campaign out here. How do you like that?"

"Shane Valgardson."

"You ever heard of him? Thing is, the guy's got a record. Assault. Impaired charges. Possession for the purpose of trafficking. All when he was living out in Calgary. I'm going to bring him in for a conversation but I thought I'd take a look at him first, see how he operates. I checked the parking lot and sure enough, that white fucking SUV's out back here."

"I'll find out what I can."

"Nah, don't trouble yourself. Seriously. This is the stuff I like."

"Danny ... that stabbing I asked you about ..."

"The Trask kid."

"Exactly. Was there anything ..."

Danny exhaled one last plume of white smoke as he flicked his half-smoked cigarette into the weeds by the porch. "You were right about the homeless kids. That amounted to nothing." He reached into his trouser pocket and pulled out a piece of white paper. As he unfolded it Ojal could make out a sole print in mud, photographed in monochrome. "Got a couple of clips from security videos too. Nothing too clear but it's a start. We got a beard—either blonde or grey." He smiled for her. "What, you think I'd let you down?"

***

The local cable news channel was now flickering on the large screen on the stage. It was blurry and muffled, as if the signal was coming in from a distant country. There in front of what looked to be the same graphic template from the last election was Frank Owendyke, who left the Monitor under circumstances never spoken of, not even by Peggy Vaughan, a couple of years before Guthrie had returned to town. Frank looked like an ageing weatherman on screen, hairsprayed and wan, his navy blazer shining in places under the glare of the studio lights. He was trying to summon up some charm with a crooked grin. Watching him, Guthrie's decision about heading back to the city was already becoming easier.

If the numbers on that graphic were correct, Kent had lost his lead now and the spread between Minhas and him was only increasing. Guthrie moved through the crowd to get closer to the stage and recognized Tyler, the chubby kid who had been driving Kent around. Tyler looked even more baby-faced as he stared up at the screen. His lips formed a small "o" as he cradled a beer to his chest.

"It's Tyler, isn't it? Just wondering if you know how many polls they've reported there."

"That's close to half. And once you get past thirty-eight, that's the brown part of town." Tyler shook his head and looked away. "I gotta get a job."

"You know where Kent might be?"

"They set him up in an RV out back. He should have been working the room by now but I guess they're still waiting for the hall to fill up."

"Good luck with that, eh?"

"I guess."

As Guthrie made his way to the doors even the thundersticks a few young Conservatives were looking they were wilting. There was that faintly metallic smell of a Newton winter in the air, carried in by all the heavy coats.

***

"That's him. I can tell from the photo on his driver's license."

Standing off by himself in a chocolate coloured suit, Shane Valgardson had his hands stuffed into his front pockets and he was slowly shifting his weight from foot to foot, staring up at the numbers changing on the screen. With his stubbly haircut and the slope of his shoulders he looked like most of the guys working under Ojal. Except for those eyes that set him apart. They were like a husky dog's.

"He looks a little nervous."

"Probably the coke. That's what they found on him with his last arrest. Half a gram."

"When was that?"

"Couple years back. I talked to an old buddy who's with the RCMP out in Calgary now. He says this guy gets lawyered up big time, hard to make anything stick."

"He's got money?"

"His dad, apparently. A fucking Sheik out there from way back. Keeps skin in the game with the politics out there. He called in favours to get Shane some honest work."

"Or into trouble. Torching a junk shop?"

"Still trying to figure it out myself. The guy who died, this Nicky Poole, he had a record but no charges for years. One of my neighbourhood guys, an old junkie, I showed him a picture of Poole and he says he seen him in the methadone clinic down there on King about a half year ago but guys like Poole, even if they do relapse, they don't get into any trouble on the business side. He'da been eaten alive."

"You should go up and introduce yourself, Danny."

"Naw. Not ready to poke a stick at him yet. Can you ask around about him out here though? See if he's been mixing with the locals."

"Of course. Danny, I miss you."

He smiled. Those teeth that looked like they had never been fixed from his hockey days.

***

As Guthrie approached the RV out back, he could see Veronica standing up and pulling on her coat, silhouetted by the beige translucent blind. It was too quiet and dimly lit back here. Guthrie held back from approaching, sensing, in Veronica's prim outline, the way her hand was briskly pulling up the collar of her coat, that an encounter of some seriousness had just occurred. The silhouette disappeared and then Veronica emerged a breath later, looking queenly, shaking out her last thoughts from her hair.

"Oh hello, Mr. Guthrie."

"Veronica. Nice to see you again. I was just hoping to get a minute or two with Kent. Not a work thing."

"Be my guest." She parted an imaginary curtain as she walked past Guthrie, making it clear with the theatricality that any solicitousness on her part should not be taken as genuine. "He's all alone, he's just getting ready to come into the hall."

"Thanks."

Of course he's all alone. They've already discarded him, a failed prospect. Whatever attempt at a speech Kent was fussing over now was not worth anyone's attention.

Guthrie knocked on the door of the RV and Kent, far merrier sounding than imagined, sang a come-in. He was at the kitchenette table in his shirtsleeves, Tiffany cufflinks, a bottle of Four Roses and an empty tumbler in front of him. He spun what looked like a nickel on the table. As it slowed Guthrie realized it was Kent's wedding ring. Kent stopped it with an outstretched finger before it wobbled.

"There he is. Last friend standing. Come here. We hug! I'm done with that uptight white man bullshit."

And so Kent rose from the table and they embraced, and the smell of bourbon was strong on the candidate.

"Kent. I hope I didn't interrupt anything with Veronica."

"Nothing that reality hadn't interrupted a while ago anyway. How are you, Guthrie? I heard about what happened at the Torontonian, the fuckers killing your story."

"Which set of fuckers might that be? I mean there are a few."

"Too true, my friend. You going to have a drink with me?"

"Don't you have to go back in there?"

"Of course I do. I said I'd do this damn speech off the cuff. That's not going to happen without some lubrication, I'm afraid."

"And they're okay with that?"

"Who gives a fuck what they're okay with? Tonight Veronica left me. She's walking away."

"Kent, holy . . . That's brutal. I'm sorry." Guthrie made a move closer to Kent but he sensed it was ill advised. Kent had pulled a pack of Belmont Milds out of his suit trousers. Had he become a smoker over the years? The answer seemed, as with everything else about him, maybe true.

"It is what it is." As he lit up he squinted through the smoke, raising a finger at Guthrie and wagging it. "You bastard, you knew from the very beginning, didn't you? Don't let the bitches get too fucking comfortable."

"Me? I think we can safely say I did not have a clue about women."

"You could have fucked Danny Graham's mom like I did. That old bitch was depraved. She would have given you an education. Wonder what the hell ever happened to her?"

"She's somebody's grandmother now."

"Jesus, eh?"

"Kent, this is kind of a lower priority, now that this happened with Veronica, but I just came back here to say I'm sorry it all didn't work out. I'm sorry I didn't get to write that piece."

"Ah, that piece, yeah." He sat down at the kitchenette once more, exhaled a stream of smoke. He was awkward with the cigarette clasped daintily between his fingers, like a teenager. "You, were very busy on me, weren't you?"

"What do you mean?"

"You know what I mean. They gave you a list. I told them right from the beginning you were going to work around them, that you were too good a reporter. Too much of a little shit disturber."

"What else could I do? Kent, you were like a hologram. They made sure I wasn't going to get any real time with you."

"Pincott. She's another cunt. Give her this, though. She's good at what she does. Being a cunt."

"It was your mother who really helped me, got me out of the box they wanted to keep me in."

"Okay, then. So she's the one. For the life of me, I couldn't figure out who got you in front of Lainie."

"Lainie Dunsmore."

"You know she's crazy, right? Fucking out of her mind. Bitch used to ask me to tie her up. Those marks on her neck. She got off on the choking. She demanded it."

Guthrie bowed his head, looked down at his clasped hands. "She never told me about any marks on her neck."

"No? Well. That was her favourite story for a while there back in those days. I said I wouldn't marry her, Ian. She fucking begged me and I told her it was just never going to happen. I mean, would you? She was nuts. Once I told her we were done, that's when she pulled that stunt with the cops."

"She didn't tell me about any police either."

"Well, you should have talked to some cops up there in Ottawa who remember her. I bet you they could tell you other stories about her too."

"Kent, listen to me. It goes much further than that. Nicky Poole. Gudrun Danziger. I mean, these people are still around."

The names quieted Kent. He raised one eyebrow as he nodded, arms stretched out on the table as if he was waiting for his hands to be cuffed.

"Look, I don't know what story you've got in your head ..." He raised the cigarette to his lips, squinted through the smoke. "In politics it's always about Daddy."

"I'm sorry?"

"I didn't kill Annelie Danziger, Ian. Was I angry? Yes. Did we fuck? Yes. Did I hit her? Probably. She was pregnant with my kid but she was fucking some Queen Street lowlife. Or hoping to. There was no way she was going to tell me the truth. And she would not be swayed. She was going to have the kid. That's why I lost it on her."

"You knew about her OD-ing . . ."

"I swear to you I had nothing to do with that but no one was going to believe me. Next morning, when I found out she never left that room I was scared. I called Dan."

"Dan?"

"Dan Valgardson. Don't tell me you don't know who Dan is."

"Just by name."

"I owe everything to Dan. I worked for him my first job on the Hill. He saw something in me that nobody else . . ."

"Not even Bob?"

"Bob's a bad haircut with a couple of party tricks. Bob's a fucking piano player."

"Thank God we never had kids, eh? I can imagine what they'd call us."

"Fuck you, Ian."

The look in Kent's eyes was of undistilled contempt. It was the first authentic moment of connection Guthrie felt with him in . . . well . . . decades.

"I'm sorry."

"You're not sorry. You wanted to fuck Annelie Danziger back then but you were a nothing. And you stayed a nothing."

"While you have risen to great heights, I know."

"I had this. I fucking told them they should have paid attention to the brown vote. I knew what Minhas was about but they wouldn't listen." He shook his head and poured himself another drink from the bottle of bourbon.

"Kent, Gudrun's got the clothes Annelie was wearing that night. The clothes her daughter was wearing when you beat her and raped her. Like you probably raped her when she got pregnant. Out of your own jealousy."

Kent lifted the tumbler to his lips and swallowed. He closed his eyes. When he opened them again all he could do was grin at Guthrie.

"You know Nicky Poole's dead, right?"

Guthrie just grinned. He wasn't really sure why. Perhaps it was just the most plausible way of preserving any moral authority. For the moment, anyway.

"I guess the question would be—how do you know?"

"Because I read the city newspapers, I guess. Not that it would occur to a journalist like yourself."

"They say how?"

"Does it matter? You talked to Nicky Poole. But Nicky Poole knew shit about what happened. Nobody knows but me and Annelie, God rest her soul. There was no rape ever, far as I was concerned. Did we argue? Yes. Was I rough with her? Prob'ly. But no one could make me feel that angry. No one ever since anyway. I guess that was love." He stabbed the cigarette into the bottom of a Styrofoam cup. There was the soft fizzing sound of it burning a black hole as it went out. "When I left her she was as alive as you or me. I did not have a clue about any heroin. In the morning, I went over to her apartment. I just wanted it to be okay again, wanted us to make up. I mean I was sorry, sorrier than I'd ever been in my life ... now or since. Her roommate said she hadn't come home. When I got to the Hi Fi, they were taking her out in a stretcher from Nicky Poole's room and he was in the back of a cruiser."

"And you just fucked off."

"Damned right I fucked off. That's when I called Dan and told him the trouble I was in. He was pissed but you know what? He fucking believed me, like nobody else would have. Least of all the cops."

"So he fixed it."

"He made some calls. He was tight with Bill Platt. Platt got it done, really. Ian, all of this, my schooling, everything good that has happened to me since, I owe it to those two men. You think I'm ever going to forget that? They made me."

In the canned air of the RV, with all the windows shut, they could faintly hear the music from the Rotary Hall. *Because you're mine . . . I walk the line.* The song brought back a memory to Guthrie, like a sun-bleached Polaroid, of the Newton Police Association summer picnic up at Kelso Lake. The bright yellow mustard on the hot dogs. Smell of chlorine from the Olympic pool on his skin. The years within him.

"Kent, I'm sorry about all this."

"Don't be sorry. You think anything we're talking about is going to matter? You think, what, that I'm guilty of something? I'll tell you what I'm sorry about." He rose from the table now, picked up the cufflinks and began to fumble with them. The wedding ring, a simple platinum band, he was going to leave behind as he made his way back into the hall. "I'm sorry about how things have gone for you, my friend."

"I don't need your pity."

"No. I wasn't offering any. I had something more concrete in mind."

"What are you talking about?"

"You know, what we're going to need—and by we, I mean my party—what we're going to need if we're going to win again are some people who can actually do comms. Not twenty-five year olds who can't keep a thought in their head for more than five minutes. I mean some corporate memory about how the media really works."

"Except it doesn't really work anymore."

"Maybe so. All the more reason to come over to the dark side."

"That's the first time I've heard that said without intended irony."

"Really. I imagine it's just the first time you've heard it, period."

"What are you telling me, Kent?"

"I'm telling you that if you were able to keep your mouth shut about all we've just spoken about, I could get you in with a Minister up in Ottawa as a D-Comm. I don't know what your particular situation is, whether you're planning on retiring on the chump change you're earning but ..."

"And you could set this up."

"You think my career is over because I didn't win this by-election? This is nothing but a speed bump, Ian. They need me. And they could use you too. What would you have to lose?"

"That's a serious question?"

"More serious than you take all that leftie bullshit you once believed in by now. Am I right?"

"Living in truth is not leftie bullshit to me."

"Living in truth. What the hell does that mean? You don't think I'm telling you the truth? How the hell do you know? You haven't known me for twenty-five fucking years. Who the hell are you to judge me?"

Kent leaned in closely. His gaze was flat, as if rays of sunlight would bounce right off his eyes without him squinting. He spoke in a calm, measured tone, yet Guthrie felt a threat of violence from him, one he hadn't felt since they were boys.

"I'm not judging you, Kent. It's not my place."

"You're right about that. About something, at last." He turned from Guthrie and pulled a royal blue necktie from his other pocket. He began to put it on, looking at his shadowy reflection in the blinded window. "I'm just suggesting you think about my offer. I'm going in there to see where we are. You're welcome to see yourself out."

"I was just leaving."

"Try to stay for my speech. I think you'll like it."

"I just might."

"We're good, then. So let's talk about this, once this is over. See you in the movies."

Kent bounded off the metal stairs of the RV and marched, with his big, powerful stride, around the back of the hall. He was the leading actor who had his lines down, eager to get back on the stage. And why not, there was probably never going to be a repeat performance for him.

As Guthrie walked back alone through the parking lot he figured this was the best place to reach into his pocket and pull out the little tape recorder. Yes, still rolling. Got it all.

He could finally relax and have his second cigarette of the day. He sat on the bumper of his car, took in the view of the hall. The cold night air felt like it was cleansing the confusion of memories and responses he felt with Kent. It looked like someone had tried to scrub off old graffiti on the side of the building but to little effect. He recalled the first night he had come out here during the campaign, the surprise of the camera trucks, the reporters milling around the entrance, through the banter and the rumours, of Kent's candidacy as a story. The doors were shut on the hall now, the little tin circle that umbrella-ed the single light bulb, painted fern green and flecked with rust, cast a small halo of light over the wrought iron door handles. Guthrie could hear some tired whoops and a desultory round of applause as he approached. Kent was slowly making his way around the crowd, no doubt, shaking hands, embracing the faithful.

Still, as soon as Guthrie entered and saw the numbers on the screen, it seemed it was finally time for Kent to concede. And yet it had been far closer than imagined, close enough that they had been ready to send Tyler back out to the RV and get Kent to rewrite his speech, the boy said. There were finally enough polls reported to give the win to Minhas, even as the gap between them went back and forth between two and three digit numbers. Just two minutes ago though, as Kent was poised backstage, Frank Owendyke's frown on the big screen said it all.

Veronica accompanied Kent to podium. She held his hand tightly, brushed his cheek with her hand as she kissed him then stepped back and let him stand under the spotlight alone. It was a harsh, shadowless light..

"Friends, as I stand up here, to let you all know that the race we have run together has not brought us to the tape first, I look out at you all and suddenly winning or losing seems to me the most irrelevant part of any message I'm compelled to deliver ... "

The room had gone quiet. Kent was speaking like the candidate they had hoped he would have been from the beginning. He looked born for this, with a preacher's sense of cadence and modulation, a world-weariness transmuted into a dignified, wise man's gravitas. Veronica looked on from over by the wings and there were tears in her eyes. Perhaps there was a promise of forgiveness and reconciliation in that smile. Hard to know. Indeed it was difficult to tell what this moment would come to mean, given what lay ahead for Kent.

The big doors to the hall opened with a low, metallic croak, a blast of winter wind that Guthrie could feel leaning up against the back wall. He could hear the slow, heavy steps of one who knows he has arrived late and does not want to call attention to himself. The figure emerged from the entrance, filing past two young conservatives in their campaign t-shirts. He was a tall man, powerfully built. Clusters of snowflakes were melting on his bushy grey eyebrows. In profile it looked like the marble bust of some Roman senator had come to life. His eyes took in Guthrie just for a moment as he surveyed the room, those eyes of a husky dog.

Someone was coming through the crowd just behind Guthrie, a heavyset man in a chocolate coloured suit. In the way Shane Valgardson moved, a kind of slumped, waddling, little boy march, he seemed reduced to some state of humility that made you want to look away. He held out his arms for an embrace. The tall man in the elegant topcoat just put a hand on his shoulder to gently calm him, move him aside.

Dan Valgardson looked up at Kent on the stage and slowly nodded. And Kent, pausing but for a moment in this, the speech of his life, slowly nodded back.

35.

AFTER GUTHRIE HAD taken the cube truck to Goodwill the day before, there really was not much left to move, not much to call his own from this house. He had a two-day rental and the strategy for what he would get rid of had been simple: be ruthless. Whatever remained would go today as he and Bella moved him in to the condo while Tanis was at work. So, ruthlessness in action meant the sectional couch, the two old club chairs, the arm of one pock marked with the old man's cigarette burns, the coffee table he remembered hiding under as a child, the collection of clothbound classics from Readers Digest his mother ordered away for in the mail, the Royal Doulton figurines kept in a tall corner cabinet (okay, the cabinet too) and the black leather recliner he'd bought for his first apartment were all gone now, never to be seen again. Guthrie walked into the living room with his first coffee in his hand and took in the emptiness.

He heard Bella in the next room, going through the LPs, stacking, in that fourth milk crate, the few that he had in rotation before this move began.

"These have got to be worth a bit of money now."

He wasn't sure whether she was actually addressing him or not. She hadn't raised her voice. Bella never did, it seemed, probably because it could be interpreted as enthusiasm.

"You think?"

"You've got the original pressing of Parallel lines here. Lodger . . ."

"I figured your mom might still want to listen to those."

"Or me, more like. She doesn't listen to anything anymore."

Guthrie shuffled into the next room.

"She will if you put them on."

"She'll have to. Suck it up, I've got an ally now."

He grinned and was tempted to respond, but Bella's eyes were solely on the album covers as she riffled through them.

"That's a Japanese pressing, that one. I got that at Sam's on Yonge Street. My last twenty in my wallet, too. I had just lost ten bucks playing chess with this crazy old Russian guy out on the corner. Had to miss *Apocalypse Now* that night and I didn't see it for another decade."

"Stop talking like an old person."

"I am an old person."

"Apparently."

"That's old people music in your hands."

"Yeah, but it doesn't sound like it. Know what I mean?"

"True enough."

"So it's just these four crates and the turntable?"

"Yup. Let's ease your mother into this."

"You really were ruthless."

Guthrie smirked as he turned from her and began to put the last books on the shelf into one of the liquor store boxes .

"They give you guys Vonnegut to read in high school?"

"What's a Vonnegut?" Bella played the pause, waiting for the predictable reaction: Guthrie's tired sigh. "Of course, Mr. Crankypants."

Bella was probably not wrong about his curmudgeonly state of mind. He had spent close to a month in a funk of quiet pessimism after the election, telling no one what he was spending his mornings writing. He'd summon up his best self for the three or four nights of the week he would be with Tanis, strolling downtown in the afternoon to shop for what he would make her and Bella for dinner, stretching out the time he spent browsing for wine in the liquor store. Nothing said unemployment like twenty minutes in a Vintages section, deliberating on a fifteen-dollar bottle of Shiraz, wondering how long this tap dance on credit would last. He told himself he was preparing for the worst case scenario—the house selling far below asking, the prospect of getting his cab driver's license and then meeting Gallant for coffee, as contrite as possible, to ask him about any courses he might be able to teach at the local college. Journalism for dinosaurs, or something.

Then there was the call from this Sharon Griffin, the Monitor's new editor. She had heard about how he had helped Kerry-Anne break the Elections Canada story that had gotten national coverage. No matter how ambitious Kerry-Anne was, she had grace beyond her years for mentioning him. Sharon Griffin said there was a gaping hole that only a seasoned professional could fill for local stories now that Gallant was gone too. It had to be someone who knew the cops, who had a long memory here in town. For once in his life he was the right guy at the right time.

As he took the box of books out to the truck he was replaying his lunch with Sharon Griffin in his head. Maybe he shouldn't have chosen the Lido, with its "fine Chinese and Chinese-Canadian dining." He could tell Sharon Griffin was uncomfortable as soon as she came in. With the dim lights and the red curtains, it still looked like the one restaurant in town where a murder had occurred. Two sips into her gin and (flat) tonic with the bloody lemon slice rather than a lime, she asked the question that sealed his fate: "So you worked with Stephen Clarke as well?"

From that point on he was too nervous, too effusive. He probably could have argued for more money and the column if he had kept calm and seemed more enigmatic and serious. Maybe it was her saying she had practiced law before she got on to the Toronto paper as a summer student five years before, the way she'd pulled her white-blonde hair back tightly and looked like some Scandinavian plutocrat in her power suit, but he found himself playing the role that didn't quite fit—the prodigal son Stephen Clarke never had—for the woman who was probably the daughter Stephen had always wanted. And yet despite how he was she called just three days later and said the opening for the columnist was his.

As he eased the books down on the lip of the bumper he heard Bella clump down the stairs of the back porch. He took one of the crates from her embrace and he caught her looking at him with the vulnerability of a little girl, not a young woman. Then she quickly looked away. It was in these moments that he knew his intuition was right: the script that both of them had been handed by the decision for him to move in would require him to play the father and her the daughter, no matter how they both tried to perform it differently with each other.

She was breathing heavily as she finally slid one crate along the rusted metal floor of the cube. "Wow. Time to stop smoking."

"I'd do it now so you don't end up an idiot like me, agonizing over three a day."

"You try, I try."

"You might have a deal."

"You remember why you started?"

"Same as you, probably. The most interesting people smoked."

"Like Annelie Danziger?"

"That's right. They had all the stories. All the drama. I imagine it's still the same, eh?"

"I guess. I've had enough drama for a while though, thank you very much."

He thought of Kent, the oddness of him smoking on election night. Guthrie was trying to forget the last image he had of him: walking out of the Rotary Hall and into the darkness of the winter night with Dan Valgardson beside him.

Guthrie just wanted to remember Kent when their friendship was real; the tennis sweater that smelled of a middle-aged man's cologne, the gawky, long limbed amble that he transformed into the swagger of the young leading man, planning some horrible empire in his head. Kent had no stories back then, no way of telling that drew you in. The real stories were all in his future, all to be kept secret for fear of what he couldn't bear to reveal. Why does someone become a public figure? Maybe it's the temptation to validate that fiction they've created. If the world believes it, somehow they can believe it too.

"What are you thinking of with this new high school thing?"

"It'll be fine. I mean, I'm just going to get through it, know what I mean? I don't know what the hell I want to do, if that's what you're getting at."

She reached for the screen door before he could open it for her, and then she slipped through ahead of him. No stilted niceties, please.

"I wasn't thinking . . ."

"Good. I don't really want to have that conversation, thank you very much."

"It's not that. It's . . . your mother had one favour she asked of me today."

"Her just one thing deal. Good to know I'm not the only one who gets that."

"It's the Monitor. With this ongoing investigation into Drew's death."

"You can call it murder. I do."

"I'm going to be covering it. I can't take a pass. It's not the kind of job I have now."

Bella nodded. Her hands were busy, moving just a bit too fast as she wrapped a bundle of knives and forks with Scotch tape then stuffed them in a bed of crumpled newspapers in a box. "That's it? That's what you had to tell me?"

"It means I'm going to have to write about you. About the bullying, about Sydney. Let me tell you, I hate the idea just as much as your mother."

She turned to look at him with Tanis's quizzical smile..

"You going to, like, interview me?"

"Probably."

"Why can't I just say what your politician friend said on the news about his own trouble?"

"Which was?"

"I can't comment while this case is before the court. Could I get away with that?"

"It's worth a try."

Guthrie felt a twinge of guilt about his grin. And yet it seemed a natural response now, a concession of the ultimate futility of truly knowing who Kent was. All the words he had put down over the last few weeks about their history, the notes from his interviews here in town, in Calgary and Ottawa, the episodes from this campaign ... he had come as close as he could to writing Kent out of his system. And yet he still hadn't gotten close to what was at the centre of Kent or how guilty he was in the assault of Lainie Dunsmore or the death of Annelie Danziger. Perhaps the DNA test and the review of the post mortem from twenty-seven years ago, all that had remained confidential as a part of this investigation, would clear it up once and for all. But that seemed doubtful. Kent was, to use a favourite phrase of Stephen Clarke's, "an unsolved mystery to himself." Perhaps he was only truly authentic when he was up on that Rotary Hall stage, just a blank canvas where all the ideals, the fears and the resentments of all those in the room could be projected and given voice. In those brief moments he could be whole. No wonder it was all he lived for.

But he would write the story. And Guthrie knew at last, it was the only one he was meant to file. With or without Stephen, it would find its readers. Call it faith, but he just knew this to be true.

"Should we do a sweep?"

"A sweep?"

"When Mom and I left our old house, we did a final scan of each room. There's always something you forget."

Guthrie just stood with his hands on his hips. His gaze was fixed on the living room window, on some still point just past the front yard. He knew what was left behind. In the basement now was the projector he got from Nicky Poole's store. He couldn't take it with him, couldn't drop it off yesterday, and now he couldn't leave it at the curb for the town garbage truck to pick up. A problem that couldn't be solved.

"You know what? I think we're good. It's not necessary."

"Suit yourself." Bella shrugged and walked into the hall with him following close behind. She reached into the pocket of her coat and then handed him the house keys. "You can't look back then."

"Deal."

He turned the lock until it clicked then closed his eyes. Nothing had to be said now.

36.

OJAL RELENTED AND agreed to the meeting, but on the condition that if it took place anywhere, it would be over at the Hampton where she used to meet Guthrie. She gave them a half hour at lunch, no more, and probably less.

She was waiting for them at exactly twelve fifty-nine. She should have learned by now that these political people were always late. It told you they were always busier than you.

She had finished half of her drink and read the menu twice when she glimpsed some movement in the parking lot. She parted the curtain and yes, that smoky grey Buick Regal with the rental sticker had to be them. She looked away, took a deep breath, then parted it again to watch Senator MacDougall and one of his beefy pals cross the lot, squinting through a blast of Arctic wind as the snow swirled. It was not too late; she could bolt now and say she was called away by an emergency.

MacDougall entered first, flapping the chill out of his overcoat with his hands dug deeply in his pockets. He nodded with the smallest of grins for Ojal. The suit with him followed and gave her a big smile. Out of the two of them, she instantly trusted MacDougall's friend less than the Senator himself. She had complied with their request for a meeting and real trust mattered little in whatever transaction was on offer.

"Good to see you, Ms. Dhillon."

"Senator."

"Sorry we couldn't get here sooner. Tractor-trailer on the 401 spilled." He turned to his sidekick as if he blamed him. "Every time I come down here, there's always something on that bloody highway."

"That's the way," his friend said, his coat already off, as he tugged to loosen his tie.

"Ojal this is Davey Belanger, my colleague from the party headquarters up in Ottawa."

"Mr. Belanger."

"Heard a lot about you, Ms. Dhillon."

"Hope it's all good."

"Of course it's all good," the Senator croaked. "Wouldn't be here otherwise, would we?"

Ojal smiled as she crossed her legs. She was sure she was turning red. It was the same kind of embarrassment she felt the last time she was hit on.

"So what's going on with this challenge to the by-election, gentlemen? You know what the judge is going to say yet?"

Of course they knew. Even she knew, for God's sakes. But there was no point with the niceties, just get this over with.

"Should work out for us." MacDougall was scanning the page on the menu, "It's confirmed there were irregularities. Came down to twenty-six frigging votes in the end. Twenty-six."

"And so what does that mean?"

"Means the PM's going to call another in eight weeks, Ms. Dhillon." Belanger was asserting himself, determined not to play the beta to MacDougall's alpha. "We've been doing a bit of polling. It's looking better than we thought."

"So Kent Wolseley's going to get another shot at this."

"Kent has got a few things to work out right now." The Senator tried out a smile then seemed to think better of it. "Until his involvement with this old Danziger case is cleared up, never mind the death of this Nicholas Poole . . ." He shook his head, as if the turn in the conversation brought back old suffering. "We believe he'll be cleared of these allegations but for the time being he's got a full plate."

"This is why we've come to speak with you, Ojal, if I can call you Ojal. Gordon tells me you were a part of the town hall on crime during the campaign. Everyone was impressed. Very impressed, indeed, actually."

"And everyone would be?"

"Everyone back in Ottawa. The Prime Minister himself, Ojal."

"This town is growing and changing. The party needs someone who can reflect and represent the direction it's heading. Someone who speaks to Newton's future rather than its past."

"Gentlemen. I'm flattered but I've lived here all of ten months."

"We realize that. We don't believe that will be a factor. We heard you spoke at the Gurdwara. A lot of people were very impressed."

"I'm not a talker, gentlemen. That's why I'm a cop."

"And we respect that. Ojal, if I may, I know we've just met but I can tell the quality of leadership you bring to your job. Less talk, more action. It's about serving the people. That's the highest calling. Well this is no different. I'd argue you'd see it as a natural progression."

"Davey and the whole team back in Ottawa would give you the kind of support few candidates in the country could ever hope for. We know you could win this. If I were you, I'd be asking myself what do I have to lose."

"Hah! You're kidding, right?" Ojal knew her laugh was not quite convincing. They were looking into her eyes and she could only look away. She realized she had begun to shred the paper napkin at her fingers, tearing off little strips and rolling them in her fingers.

"I'd also be asking myself what I would have to gain, and Ojal, as a Senator, one who's been around for a while, let me tell you, you'd have a lot to gain indeed. When I first saw you at that Rotary Hall, I could see it. You're a natural."

As he went on, Ojal realized why they had sent MacDougall. He treated this conversation as a seduction, spoke in this lower register as if he was baring his soul, offering his heart. Out of all the tactics they could employ, this was where she should have been most invulnerable.

And yet here she was, tearing her defence to shreds at her fingertips.

"You two are very good at this."

"If we're good, you could be better."

"Just exactly what does better mean?"

And for the first time in a very long while, the Senator was not quite sure what that answer might be.

—The End—

Acknowledgements:

I have a few people to thank for all their work and support with this novel: Marilyn Biderman – for her wisdom and counsel; Dinah Forbes – for all she did to get this book where it is; Susan Delacourt – for her big-sister-ness in all things; and of course AS, who continues to believe. This is a work which could have never been written without my source of inspiration and community – the tribe in Ottawa who claimed me as one of their own so many years ago now.

Author Bio

Black Irises is John Delacourt's second novel. His first, *Ocular Proof,* was published in 2014. His short fiction has appeared in numerous publications in North America, including the New Quarterly and Black Heart magazine. He is also the author and co-creator of more than ten plays, two of which made Toronto's NOW magazine's "Best of" lists in the late nineties.

He studied at the Humber School for Writers after graduating with an MA in English Literature at the University of Toronto. Aside from writing fiction, he has also written for television and has reviewed books for the Ottawa Citizen and the Ottawa Review of Books.

CPSIA information can be obtained at www.ICGtesting.com
Printed in the USA
LVOW10s1153100916

503986LV00002B/2/P